An Ambush of Years

Time Alleys Book 1

J.A. Enfield

WAYZGOOSE PRESS

Edited by Dorothy Zemach

Cover art by Morgen Witt

ISBN 978-1-961953-22-2

Printed in the United States of America

CONTENTS

For Magda, who worried about these kids.

CHAPTER 1

A SONG OF COLORS

Mick's shady spot was far enough from the family picnic that people didn't try to drag him into their conversations but near enough that he could relax inside the safe sounds of his cousins yelling during soccer and his aunts and uncles having opinions about everything. Head propped on a foam football, he watched the clouds make and dissolve patterns against the blue sky. Between his bent knees, Lake Michigan shimmered blue and green to the horizon like a second sky. It looked like the air felt—heavy and alive. He'd played enough soccer for the day and eaten enough barbecue for a week, and the only thing left for him was to float in and out of daydreams while the grass tickled his neck. He loved his family, but they could be a lot sometimes, and half the time he needed to look after his baby sister Emilia. So it was nice to get a little time to himsel—

"Hey, Mick."

Sigh.

Mick swiveled his eyes to see who it was. Tía Verónica. That was okay. She treated him like his brain worked.

"Hi, Tía."

She sat down next to him, also staring out at the lake. "Wanted to be alone, huh?"

Mick shrugged.

"Too bad. I don't get to see you as much now that you're with Dan."

Mick shrugged again, which seemed fair. Uncle Dan was basically a shrug in cargo shorts. Mick had moved from Tía Verónica's to Uncle Dan's a couple months earlier because she'd had to start taking longer hours at the hospital and Mick's dad supposedly had been getting back to the U.S. soon. But his dad's assignment kept getting extended, so Mick, Emilia, and Uncle Dan were stuck with one another for who knew how long. On their weekly video chats, Mick's dad kept saying, "The assignment took a new direction, and they want me to stay on, but it shouldn't be much longer." But his dad had been saying it wouldn't be much longer for so long that Mick could recite the line along with him. His dad had gotten mad on the last call because Mick had done just that.

"Dan's okay," Tía Verónica said.

Mick shrugged yet again.

She laughed. "I said 'okay,' not 'magnificent.'"

Mick smiled a little. "Is Emilia all right over there?" he asked.

"Last I saw, she was in Julieta's lap, hugging Swaggy Bear and smiling like crazy. She had those big eyes."

Mick smiled. When Emilia was happy or just interested, her

eyes would pop open and stay open. It was like she didn't blink. And her teddy bear definitely made her happy. Tía Julieta was always bragging about how she'd made it the old-fashioned way —natural fibers, natural filling, all of her usual crunchy stuff. She'd even stitched "J" into one ear and "E" into the other. Mick thought if he'd made a bear with a lopsided head, too-close eyes, and barf-orange fur, he maybe wouldn't have signed it. But Tía Julieta signed everything, from her paintings to the custom detailing she did on her wheelchair. Tía Verónica liked to say that if Tía Julieta ever robbed a bank, she would sign the vault before making her getaway.

"Your friend is named Aiden, right?" Tía Verónica asked.

"Sure." Although Aiden wasn't his friend anymore, not really. He hadn't seen Aiden for months. Aiden hadn't even come to the picnic. Mick didn't hate Aiden or anything. They'd just lost touch because, after Mick's mom died, Mick had needed to change schools—first when he went to live with Tía Julieta and then when he went to live with Tía Verónica. And now that he was living with Uncle Dan, he'd have to change schools again for fifth grade in the fall.

"His dad was gossiping with Gabriela about the assistant principal at your old school," Tía Verónica said. "Your mom would've been all over that. Your mom pretended she didn't like family picnics, but she did. Dorotea was nosy, and the whole point of picnics is to get into everybody's business." She sighed. "I still expect I'll see her by the barbecue, you know? Asking people whether they really like their jobs or if they ever finished retiling their bathrooms."

"Me too," Mick said. That was another reason he liked Tía Verónica. She talked about his mom. His mom had died a few months after Emilia was born, and a lot of people didn't talk about her anymore, including his dad. Of course, his dad had left home right after Emilia was born and right before his mom had gotten sick, but still. When Mick complained that nobody talked about his mom anymore, Tía Verónica said people probably didn't want to make him sad. But what made him sad was that they acted like they'd forgotten her.

Like she was reading his mind, Tía Verónica said, "We do miss her, you know. All of us. Including your dad, even if he is being a pain in the butt."

Mick laughed a little.

"I think he's a little lost without her," she said.

"Then he shouldn't have left."

"Maybe not. But it gets messy with adults sometimes. And I don't really understand what happened between them, so I'm not going to shoot my mouth off."

Mick didn't understand what had happened either. His dad hadn't been there to explain, and his mom had refused to talk about it. And then she'd gotten sick, so Mick had stopped asking. It was so frustrating not to have answers. Mick's parents were both reporters, and they'd taught him to get answers. His mom had always said, "Find people who give you honest answers and belly laughs." She'd loved to laugh. His dad had too, until he'd moved out. Now when Mick saw his dad on their Sunday calls, his dad no longer laughed or gave honest answers, not about important stuff, anyway.

Mick sighed.

"Still want to be alone?" Tía Verónica asked.

"It's okay," Mick said. "I just don't feel like talking."

Tía Verónica sat silently next to him and looked at Lake

Michigan while he stared through slitted eyelids at the bright clouds drifting slowly across the bottomless sky.

After a while, she patted Mick on the shoulder and stood back up. "Hang in there, kiddo," she said.

"I'll try," he said.

"Best any of us can do."

Later that night, after Uncle Dan had finished watching cop shows and Mick had tried and failed to sleep a few times, Mick sat with his legs pulled to his chest in the big, ratty chair under the window, staring around the little bedroom he shared with Emilia.

It was dark inside and out, except for a sleepy streetlight smothered by thick August leaves and thick August air before being split by the bars outside the window and then filtered by the thin curtain. The room was a grab bag of grays, and it was hard to tell where Emilia ended and her blanket began.

It was quiet inside and out too, except for the old building's squeaks and thunks and the occasional shushing sound of a car gliding past the first-floor apartment. The yelling that poured out of the bar up the street every night at closing time had gone silent, and the man upstairs was taking the night off from stomping back and forth while arguing with his furniture. The room was warm but not so warm that the ancient air conditioner in the other window had to clunk and wheeze against the Chicago summer. Sometimes Emilia gurgled and giggled in her sleep, one of Mick's favorite sounds. Sometimes Uncle Dan, from the next room, snorted especially loudly in his sleep, not one of Mick's favorite sounds.

But Mick knew those sounds—what they were, where they came from. In the pauses between those sounds, he realized that he was hearing something new. Probably. There was a murmur right at the border of hearing and imagination, a hum or a whisper. He closed his eyes and listened, trying to figure out where it was coming from. It disappeared under a series of snores from Uncle Dan and then again under the growl of a bad muffler.

But then it was back, louder. Even when the wind picked up, shaking the trees, he could hear it. It seemed to be a song, except there was no singing and he had no idea what the instruments were. Well, maybe "song" wasn't exactly right. It was a humming that somehow wasn't a sound, exactly. But it *felt* like a sound, something that vibrated under his skin like rhythm and sang in his skull like melody. It made him want to follow, like the melody was going somewhere he needed to see. Like a band was marching down a nearby street, leading people on an adventure, and he should put on his shoes and follow it before he missed out.

But the song wasn't coming from outside. It was somehow coming from inside the room, where there was nothing except the drab shadows of sleeping furniture. Then Mick realized the shadows were getting fainter. The room was getting brighter, almost shimmering. At first he thought the wind was brushing aside the tree branches to expose the streetlight, but the shadows weren't moving right for that. And, he realized, the shimmer was coming from inside the room. It was a bluish light, like somebody had turned on a tablet beneath a sheet.

Except his tablet was turned off.

The bluish light kept getting brighter, and now Mick could see where it was coming from: between Emilia's crib and the bed that Mick had abandoned when he couldn't fall asleep. It was hard to tell because the light had gotten brighter so gradu-ally, but Mick thought the light might actually have slid *through* the outside wall. It did seem to be moving, just a little. Moving and growing. It was shimmering now, a mix of blues swirling like juices in a blender. And the song was louder, too. It was paired somehow with the light—the music changed when the light changed. Or maybe the other way around.

The room got bright enough and loud enough that Mick braced himself for Emilia to wake up crying. She was usually a quiet, cheerful kid, but too much light woke her up cranky and loud.

But Emilia just giggled happily from inside a dream, moving her hand a little as if reaching for Swaggy Bear, which was out of reach near the foot of the crib.

The shimmer had gotten big enough that Emilia was now inside it. It was beautiful, and it didn't seem to bother her. But he was pretty sure that you weren't supposed to just leave babies inside mysterious lights that wandered in off the street. He should move her. But moving her probably would wake her up. And then she'd cry, and Uncle Dan would yell, "Some of us need to work in the morning."

Besides, a shimmer that glorious couldn't be dangerous, especially not with such a beautiful song playing inside it. Well, not *inside*—through? The shimmer was round, like a globe, only way bigger. Inside, it was a shifting, swirling, flickering bundle of blues encircled by stainless steel rings. It looked like the planets he discovered when piloting imaginary starships, like a ball made out of joy plasma that he could bounce off the floor and grab again on the rebound, grab and hold tight and forget about starships because it would soar into the heavens under its own power, with him dangling weightlessly beneath it, the solar wind in his hair, the constellations between his toes, and the song that wasn't a song pulsing through his quivering bones.

The scratchy blanket slid off Mick as he stood to stare at the shimmer. It was almost within reach.

Mick had the uncanny feeling it was staring at him.

He took a step, half raising his arm. The shimmer spun a little, parts of it turning smooth and still and dark like a pupil. From top to bottom, its different colors became the same dark blue just for a moment. Then, from bottom to top, it started to shimmer again.

Had it just *winked* at him?

He felt an almost overwhelming urge to finish raising his hand and touch the shimmer. Or leap into it. It was so beautiful.

But a little part of his brain thought of the fishing lures his mom had taught him to use when they went camping. Beautiful songs made out of humming colors that suckered fish out of the water and into somebody's frying pan.

He made himself lower his hand and step slowly around the shimmer, edging closer to his sleeping sister. He got his feet set and rehearsed the next steps in his mind: lean over a bit to get his shoulders past the top of the crib, plunge his hands down, and then lift her out. Maybe he wouldn't even wake her up.

He took a few deep breaths and reached into the shimmer. But his hands weren't moving toward Emilia because they weren't moving at all. He strained to reach Emilia only to realize there was no crib, no Emilia.

He realized that he was inside the shimmer and its song.

Inside a strange world that didn't allow things to happen— no reaching, no moving. As if the air were crystal.

Only his mind was moving. *I told you so*, it said. *Fishing lure.*

And then there was movement without sound. The air

became a hundred quiet hurricanes, each whirling and hurling a different part of him in a different direction. His silent screams and sick stomach spread out around him, across the whole world, across every world, until in all directions the distant air was nothing but stars, and then nothing but darkness.

Chapter 2

All the Worlds in the Hurricane

Mick thought he might be dying. Or dead.

But he was pretty sure you were supposed to go into a light when you died, and there was no light. The world was dark and nowhere in particular, and so was he. When he wiggled his fingers, he could see what he thought might be movement more or less where he thought his fingers should be, little shadow puppets without a light to cast shadows or a wall to cast them on. There wasn't any floor, either. He seemed to be floating. He was pretty sure he was spinning slowly as he went, long, lazy cartwheels, but he couldn't have said why he thought so. He didn't know where up and down were, or if there even was an up or a down. And every time he felt like he might have an idea, things shifted somehow. He might be spinning in the opposite direction. Or he'd feel like he'd gotten shorter or taller, and the hint of his hand would wave at him from closer or farther away than the end of his arm. Sometimes he had to pat himself to be sure that he was still there. Wherever "there" was.

As he floated, he started developing weird notions. That he was being tugged slowly along by an unseen hook attached to his spine, like the glowing sphere really had been a fishing lure. That he was trapped between two sides of a piece of paper. That he was floating through other people's dreams. That he was watching himself go by in the other direction, floating next to his mom. That he'd grown a third kneecap.

He was trying to pat his legs to check about the extra kneecap when all of sudden he was very sure that he only had two kneecaps, which were at once very cold and fiery with pain. And now he knew which way was down because he'd fallen very thoroughly down and bashed his knees into a ground that very definitely existed.

More specifically, when he opened his eyes, he noticed he'd fallen knees-first onto a thick tree root dusted with snow. He craned his neck back and found himself far below the shaggy branches of a great pine tree laddering endlessly upward. The scent of vanilla filled his nostrils. He breathed in as deeply as he could, savoring the scent while the agony in his knees slowly turned from frozen knives and hot pokers into a round, calm throbbing that hardly made him want to cry at all.

A rustle behind him turned out to be a huge buck standing nearby. Not so close he could touch it, but not much farther. The buck had fierce, flaring nostrils, outrageous antlers, and a faintly orange coat with complicated undertones that almost shimmered in the cold sun.

No, not almost—they were shimmering. And getting brighter. And then there was the shimmer-song, alive under his skin and in his mind, calling him. Without thinking, he leaned forward a little. And then he was inside the shimmering.

It happened again. The locked silence. The hurricanes. The

floating, the spinning, the shadow puppet hands in a dark, formless world. The singing that wasn't singing. The fish lure tugging his spine, a dim glimpse of himself and his mother fading into the distance. The sensations weren't quite as forceful, but they were still overwhelming, still confusing.

And then again the blinding pain, this time in his arm, which he'd thrown out to break his fall onto a rutted dirt road that blended into barren brown grass and dull green cactuses stretching in all directions to the pale blue horizon. This time there was no buck, only a distant cloud of dust that might have been from someone or something moving slowly toward him. And then there was a shimmer, pale blue like the sky and flecked with white like desert bones, and the shimmer-song, filling him with humming and longing.

Again came the locked silence, the hurricanes, the spin-floating, the tug at his spine. Again and again.

He learned to stay crouched at all times, hands dangling at the ready. That way he landed on soft and ready feet, able to balance himself, except the handful of times he landed in water. Each time the sensations were a little weaker, the transitions a little quicker.

Sometimes it was hot, sometimes cold. Rainy or dry. High noon, darkest night, and all shades in between. Mostly it was just him and some rocks or some trees. Occasionally there were people, usually in strange clothes and strange cars. Or no cars— horses and wagons. More often there were animals. Mostly dogs and cats, but also other things. More deer. Fish. An angry bear. A turtle on a leash. A rabbit in a garden so scared by his unexpected appearance that it looked ready to burst into tears. Mick knew the feeling.

At first, he couldn't get his brain working fast enough to

speak to the people he saw. A couple people managed to speak to him, but he couldn't understand them. He'd just be scraping some words together to ask for help when the almost-song would get loud and the people would disappear into a shimmer. Soon, it didn't matter how fast his brain worked. By the time his lips were moving, the shimmer would come and everything would disappear before turning into something totally different.

Eventually, the floating and the landing came so close and felt so similar that he couldn't always tell which was which. He was soaked to the skin from the water landings and his terror sweat, and he was sick to his stomach from the vague spinning in the gray nowhere and from the lurching landings in the unknown somewhere. His body ached and burned from his early bad landings, and his legs trembled from spending so much time in a crouch. Sometimes, the shimmer and the song seemed to be fading away, and he almost wanted to let them go because if they went, he might be able to rest. But he felt compelled to follow. The shimmer and the song were still beautiful, of course. But, even more, he had a terrible feeling that, as bad as all this was, it would be worse to let go. The shimmer and the song had gotten him into it, and he felt sure they were the only things that might get him out.

So, although he was tired from being constantly on guard and constantly confused, he kept going. Legs bent against the drop, he stumbled toward the humming light, eventually more by habit than by choice, sometimes lifting his foot in one world and setting it down in the next.

As things moved faster and faster, he felt like he'd been going for weeks. He wanted to sleep. He wanted to stop. He wanted to go home and listen to Uncle Dan snore.

He started to think that if he wasn't dead already, being dead might be a step up. He wouldn't even demand a light to go into. A dry mattress and a pillow would be fine.

While he thought that last bit, a dozen worlds flickered by, and then a dozen more. Worlds shot by in slivers of a blink, and Mick knew in his gut he was doomed to suffer forever.

And then it stopped.

CHAPTER 3

AN UNFORESEEN YEAR

Mick landed in a tired crouch, and the world stayed in place. He sighed with relief and took a deep breath.

The deep breath was a mistake. Something smelled like when his old dog Scootie had rolled in rancid poop at the park. He tried to move away from the stink, but his legs vetoed the idea. He settled gingerly on his rear end instead.

From somewhere behind him, he heard a clatter, maybe a board falling onto a sidewalk. He realized that he was now lying face down, with his cheek on cold, lumpy gray stones. Meaning, of course, that he had passed out at some point. He had no idea how long he'd been out.

There was still a painfully bright light coming from behind him. It got brighter, flickering faster in various colors for a little while longer before exploding into white light and then disappearing entirely, except for the floaters that lingered before his eyes.

Wherever he was, the stones were chilly and slick with rain.

He was pretty sure he could hear horses clopping. Which was weird because you only got horses on Michigan Avenue, tourist carriages or horse cops on patrol.

He lay there until he heard footsteps coming close before stopping. With heroic effort, he managed to get to his knees and found himself confronted by heavy black shoes and dark gray skirts and pant legs that looked like lifetimes of itching. He didn't look up further. Looking all the way up might make everything real.

Based on his limited view, he and whoever had all the legs seemed to be in an alley paved with uneven gray stones. There were walls or buildings made out of bigger stones of more or less the same color.

From above, a voice said a few sentences that could have been English. He was pretty sure he'd heard "blues" and "eight" in there somewhere.

"Perhaps a Seven?" asked a higher-pitched voice. The accent was like the first voice's. Like one of the old Doctor Who episodes his mom had made him watch.

"Let the poor dropper have his Eight, Dolly," said a third voice. It also had an accent, though maybe a different one.

One of the pairs of legs bent inside a wool skirt. Mick found himself looking into the long, straight face of a girl with long, straight hair. Beneath a weird standalone hood—a "bonnet," Mick thought it was called—her hair was light brown, her face pale. Her expression was neutral, but her eyes were kind, although they were an electric blue that reminded him unnervingly of the shimmer.

"Alison?" the third voice asked.

"A moment, Leech." The pale girl held up a hand, her face thoughtful. She stared at Mick a little while longer. "Hmm." She pulled a notebook from an inner pocket and jotted a couple quick notes before standing.

Mick's eyes followed her as she stood, sending a spike of pain into his neck. Apparently he'd hurt it along the way.

The pale girl, Alison, turned out to be taller than the other two, about a half a head taller than the one named Dolly. Dolly had long, midnight black hair that was mostly tucked under her bonnet, though here and there a strand shot out as if she'd poked a pinky in a light socket. Atop a heavy, square forehead, the one named Leech had a pile of dark brown curls that appeared to be slowly digesting a floppy red cap. Leech was taller than Dolly but shorter than Alison.

Dolly and Leech were just as pale as Alison, and they had the same bright eyes. Dolly's were a yellowish brown, a color Mick remembered seeing in a summer moon just above the horizon. Leech's were the color of a green glass bottle lit from within.

They were probably in an alley, Mick decided. To either side, there were gray walls, and beyond them steep roofs a few stories off the ground.

The clopping of unseen horses and clamor of voices was replaced by a nearby clangor of church bells. Then the bells fell silent, before, almost as an echo, another set of bells started in the distance.

"Why are there horses?" Mick asked. "And what are your names? Mine's—"

"No," Alison said sternly. "Do not tell us your name."

That was rude. Or weird. Mick thought about getting up and walking away. But even thinking about walking made his legs hurt.

"I shall ask you a few questions," Alison said. "Kindly answer them, and we'll put you in dry clothes near an excellent fire.

17

And there will be biscuits. Again, do *not* tell me your name or where you come from."

"Speaking of fire and biscuits and not standing in a mucky alleyway…" Leech said.

"We must follow the steps, Leech," Alison said. She rattled off a sing-song list and then stared at Mick expectantly.

Mick hadn't understood a word. "Huh?"

"You were somewhere else," Leech said, "some nasty things happened, and now you're here."

Mick nodded, though "nasty things" was much too mild.

"We wish to know what you saw immediately before the nasty things happened,'" Dolly explained. "Possibly something you stepped into?"

"What were the choices again?" Mick asked.

"Whirlpool, glow-orb, fairy path, or horse kick," Alison repeated.

"Is a 'glow-orb' like a big ball with a bunch of different Christmas lights inside it going on and off super-fast?"

"Glow-orb," Alison said, jotting a note. "Color?"

"Blue. Lots of blues."

"Was there an occlusive event?" Alison asked.

"Did the glow-orb stop flickering and turn darker?" Leech translated.

Mick remembered it winking at him just before he'd reached for Emilia. "Yeah."

Alison jotted a note "Do you have your letters?" she asked.

"Like, letters with stamps?" Mick asked.

"Can you write?" she clarified.

"Duh."

Alison tore a sheet of paper from the notebook, and one of her hands disappeared into her coat and reemerged with a stubby pencil and a thin rectangle about the same size as the paper. She squatted slightly to hand everything to Mick.

The rectangle turned out to be a thin piece of dark, smooth wood. The paper was thick and slightly rough at the edges.

Alison said she was going to ask him some questions and reminded him not to write his name or his family's names. Or where he came from. That still seemed like the exact opposite of what you were supposed to do when you found a lost kid in an alley, but Mick didn't argue.

She then gave him more instructions before asking, "Understood?"

"No," he said.

"What was unclear?" she asked.

"Why I have to take a pop quiz from a girl who sounds like my first-grade teacher. Where I am. Why everything smells like a bucket of sweaty dog poop."

Leech and Dolly laughed, though Dolly quickly stopped.

Alison took a slow, deep breath. "This place has an unfortunate odor because it is a large city filled with dirty trades and no true sewer system. And you should endeavor to answer the few, brief questions that I ask you because, if you do, we shall take you indoors to warm fires and hearty food."

Mick wasn't sure he wanted to go anywhere with these Comicon-looking kids. On the other hand, he was cold, alone, and hungry. "Will it smell better than here?"

Alison smiled slightly. "It will."

"Then okay."

Alison let loose a river of questions about the shimmer and what had happened after he stepped into it. It dragged on forever, but at least he was on solid ground the whole time, in a world where his arms stayed the right length. He was almost out of paper when the questions stopped.

"Very good," she said, taking his answers from him. "You will be able to pick your own name eventually. Until then, we shall call you Mr. Stone. Every dropper, including you, who has not yet chosen a name is Mr. or Miss Stone."

"Why can't I just use my own name?" Mick asked.

"That will be explained soon enough," Alison said.

They helped him stand and then looked over his clothes, which had been sandpapered to rags by the endless sequence of worlds and soaked from his falls into lakes and oceans and whatever else. Having lost their elastic, his socks flapped damply at his heels.

Alison and Dolly turned their backs to give Mick some privacy while he tugged off the fragments of clothing that didn't fall off by themselves. Leech handed Mick dry clothes from a bag and shoved Mick's scraps into the bag. After a long, tiring struggle with underwear that had more fasteners than Ikea furniture, Mick found himself in a heavy, itchy suit like the one Leech was wearing. It was too big, and it looked and felt like he was going to a funeral, maybe his own.

They started walking down the alley, but Mick's legs trembled dangerously. He had to lean on Alison, who turned out to be a lot taller than he was.

"Don't worry," she told him. "We shall hail a cab."

After staggering for a bit, Mick could finally see the source of the clopping. It was the street ahead, which was full of horses. And carriages.

"Where are we?" Mick asked.

"London," Leech said. "The center of the world. Proving again that the world is an unwiped arse."

Mick stared. It was all carriages, no cars. But London had cars. He'd seen it on TV. The cabs were black instead of yellow, and everybody drove on the wrong side of the road, and sometimes they just went around and around in circles like a surly carousel.

"Now ask the big question," Leech said.

Mick almost asked Leech what he meant. But then he understood. "*When* are we?"

"Tuesday, the eighth of March, year of our Lord eighteen hundred and fifty-three," Leech said.

Mick didn't faint, but that wasn't really a good thing. It just meant that when his legs gave out, he was able to watch himself fall.

CHAPTER 4

THE FORSYTH INSTITUTE

After being helped to his feet, Mick was nudged into the back of a long, black horse-drawn carriage that looked like a hearse. So at least it matched his borrowed funeral suit.

Inside, there were two lightly padded benches facing one another. Dazed, he sat shoulder to shoulder with Leech, staring blankly at Alison and Dolly on the opposite bench. There were windows along the side, dusty and sooty but clear enough to see through.

Outside, it was London.

Outside, it was 1853.

Mick's right shoulder and cheek pressed against the dry leather padding of the carriage's side, while his tall, rigid collar tried to saw through his neck whenever they hit a bump. Which was pretty much all the time. London roads seemed to be made out of bumps, holes, and drivers screaming at everyone.

The bit of his brain that still worked could accept that it was

London out there. Above was a sky like a damp rag, all smoke and dirty clouds. Tall buildings with steep roofs crowded upon one another, some of them proud and frilly with curved stones, others slack or tilting like gingerbread houses too long after Christmas. Below were brown, spit-water creeks flowing along sunken gray roads of uneven stone that jarred the carriage unpredictably.

Cobblestones, he thought, pleased to remember what the uneven road stones were called. *Yup,* his last functioning bit of brain said sarcastically, *"cobblestones." You've solved all your problems.*

A series of strange stenches muscled through the carriage's drafty windows. So did unfamiliar sounds—the endless clopping of hooves and rattling of carriage wheels, whinnying horses, bellowing drivers, the staticky hum of rain on the carriage's roof. All very London-ish, he assumed.

Anyway, it definitely wasn't Chicago, so it might as well be London.

But *1853?*

His abuelo was always warning him that he'd get old way faster than he expected because time sped up when you were a grown-up. Well, it looked like it worked the other way too. You got younger a lot faster when you were a kid. One day, you're ten and three quarters, and the next day it's 171 years earlier, and you're so young that you'll have to get old and die and then hang around as a ghost for a few decades before you can even be born.

"Where are we going?" he asked.

"To see the Vicar," Alison said. "He runs the Institute."

"What's that?" Mick asked.

"It's what the Vicar runs," Leech said.

"Leech," Alison said sharply. She looked at Mick. "Leech mocks me because I sensibly hold my tongue where I might be overheard. Leech, on the other hand, wags his tongue like a dog on a hot day."

Maybe so, but as London thudded and lurched and stunk, Mick noticed that Leech wasn't wagging his tongue about the Institute. Neither was Dolly. Maybe they were afraid of Alison. Maybe they were all afraid of something else.

The smells got better, and trees started to soften the stern stone and brick faces of the buildings. The horses' clopping stopped, as did the carriage. The driver appeared at the doors, opening them away from one another and helping the girls step down. Leech slid out next. Mick's legs worked well enough to carry him down with only minor stumbling.

Accepting a few coins from Alison, the driver tugged the soft brim of his cap before climbing nimbly back to his seat. He flicked the reins at the horses, and the big beasts shrugged forward, jolting the carriage to life.

Mick looked around. They were in front of what looked like a park that had been thrown in prison—an island of trees, grass, and flowers behind a high, wrought iron fence. The buildings near the park were gray stone or red brick, trimmed with gray and white stone. The street was wide and tree-lined, and across the street from the park, a tall stone building covered a small block. The building also looked like it had been jailed for serious crimes—set back a couple yards from the street and fronted by a fence of long metal bars tipped like spears. The bars ran in sections between heavy stone pillars set a few yards apart.

Alison strode across the street. Mick sighed and hobbled

behind her, Leech and Dolly walking on either side of him and waving their arms at a carriage that threatened to run them down.

In front of the huge building, Alison walked between the pillars supporting an open iron gate. One of the pillars bore a metal plaque turned green with age: "The Forsyth Institute—Boys' School." She nimbly skipped up a few steps to stand before a large, heavy wooden door. She pressed firmly on the doorbell, twice, and matching muffled rings came from inside the building. By that time, Mick and the other kids had caught up and were waiting at the base of the short stone stairway.

"Boys' School?" Mick asked, looking at Alison and Dolly.

"It's after hours, so the door to the Girls' School is locked," Dolly explained.

"It does so lower the tone having girls traipse through our sacred hallways," Leech said. "But the Vicar is charitable to a fault."

Dolly leaned across Mick to swat Leech in the shoulder.

Soon, the big front door swung open with uncanny silence, and a man in a fussy suit stepped into view. He was very blond, with flecks of gray in his enormous sideburns, and his shoes shone like they had their own spotlights. His eyes had a bit of the same glow as Alison's, Dolly's, and Leech's, but otherwise he looked exactly like a butler in the old-timey television shows Mick's dad liked.

Shows about old-timey England, Mick realized. Where he now *was*.

The butler nodded at Alison, who nodded back. She and Dolly stepped inside, and Mick leaned on Leech as they went up the steps.

Mick stood with the kids in a narrow, dim hallway while the butler closed the heavy door and slid various bolts into place.

"Thank you, Mr. James," Alison said. "Mr. Stone will be sharing Leech's room in Tory Six. He'll need linens and the rest, if you please."

Mr. James nodded slightly and strode off down a hallway, eventually turning out of sight.

After a few steps in the same direction as Mr. James, everyone stopped. Alison knocked at the door frame of an open door.

"Come," said a woman's voice.

Alison stepped inside, tugging Mick's coat so that he'd join her. Leech and Dolly stayed outside. Mick found himself in a good-sized office dominated by a big desk piled with papers, many of them held in place with clips, spikes, or heavy paperweights. The room was brightly lit, mostly by big windows that faced the street and the park beyond, but also by a smaller window with an excellent view of the gate and the door that they'd just come through. Behind the desk was a glow-eyed, mocha-skinned woman with her hair pulled back into a frizzy ponytail. She was probably college age, though her grim gray dress made her look like an old-fashioned lawyer or accountant. She was trying, without apparent success, to stifle a series of yawns.

"Miss Mitchell?" Alison said in a friendly but surprised tone. "You're warden of the day?"

"Of this day, as it turns out. Mr. Fescue having taken ill, you see," the woman replied, covering another yawn. "This is our dropper? Welcome," she told Mick with a friendly smile. "'Dropper' means 'temporal new arrival,' by the way. Newly 'dropped' from the future, you see."

Mick nodded back hesitantly.

Alison and Miss Mitchell talked for a couple of minutes, more gobbledygook about glow orbs and apertures. Mick looked around the room. There was a large map of London on the wall and a bunch of cubbies of various sizes holding everything from books to coins to a small wheel of cheese to something that looked like wigs of different colors.

"Your rasher, if you please," Miss Mitchell said.

Alison handed Miss Mitchell a skinny slip of paper. "My notes?" she asked.

"Miss North says you're to bring them—and your team and our dropper here—to the solarium. I'm sure in your case it's unnecessary to ask, but I do hope you properly ciphered your notes?"

"Of course," Alison said, sounding faintly offended.

"Of course," Miss Mitchell said with a smile. "Miss North and the Vicar await you in the solarium, so please proceed without delay. A pleasure making your acquaintance, young sir."

Alison nodded her thanks and led Mick from the room. Struggling on weary legs, he followed her down a low-ceilinged corridor so dim he could barely see his own feet.

After a couple turns, he stepped into a room so bright he had to squint. It was bright partly because most of its surfaces were white—not just the marble floors but also the smooth, mostly bare walls. But mostly it was bright because the sun had come out, and Mick knew the sun had come out because the roof was made out of glass.

It was surprising to see something so airy and gleaming in that gray and gloomy world, where it felt like the sun itself wouldn't be born for another century. There were patterns of some kind etched in the glass roof, which created little rainbows across the surface. It was really quite beautiful.

"Do keep up," Alison called to him.

Mick lowered his gaze. Alison, Leech, and Dolly were already on the far side of the room, waiting at the bottom of a set of stairs that switchbacked up the wall. They led him up long flights of white marble pain that ended with him leaning against a railing on the top floor, his legs trembling.

Alison made him stand up straight and looked at him critically. She bent down to try straightening his collar, his lapels, his hair. Her expression indicated that she'd failed on all counts.

"He's meeting the Vicar, not courting him," Leech said.

Alison smiled faintly and stopped fussing. She led them down a couple corridors until they reached a heavy door. She pulled a delicate bronze chain. Mick heard nothing, but he assumed she had rung a bell because soon a tall, sharp-featured woman opened the door partway. She was a lot older than Alison, but a lot younger than Mick's dad. The woman had a bit more color to her face than Alison but still looked like his dad's family in February.

The woman hardly glanced at the other three kids but gave Mick a careful review.

"Miss North, this is, ah, Mr. Stone," Alison said.

"Of the Cobble Stones," Leech said. "Latterly known to appear barefoot and gormless in dingy alleyways in dingy parts of this dingy city. Due to a scandalous lack of planning on Mr. Stone's part, we had to give him the suit we were supposed to deliver to the Society for Chronal Fancy."

"Thank you, Mr. Charles," Miss North said crisply.

Miss North stepped aside, letting them enter a room that felt like a smaller version of the grand lobby below, including skylights and bare white walls. But there were some differences. The floor was some sort of blond wood rather than marble. The walls were straight, not curved, and the long outer wall was more than half window. The sun had disappeared again, and the view consisted mostly of cloud, fog, and smoke, plus a few nearby slivers of roof.

Not far from the wall of windows, a tall, thin man in a wool suit jacket stood at a large table. He was running a fingertip over the tabletop. From the doorway, the gesture looked idle, but when Mick followed the others toward the man, he realized the tabletop was a huge map under glass and the man was following lines on the map. It looked like a bigger, fancier version of the London map Mick had seen downstairs.

"Vicar," Miss North said, "Miss March and her team have returned with the dropper."

The Vicar turned around. He had wavy chestnut hair flecked with gray on the sides and a neat beard darker than his hair. He was probably a little older than Mick's dad, although it was hard to tell once people got that old.

"Ah, greetings," he said, smiling with large, slightly yellow teeth. His smile looked real enough, though his thoughts seemed to be somewhere else. "It's a pleasure to make your acquaintance. Please," he said, gesturing to the far end of the room, where a sofa and a few stuffed chairs were clustered around a coffee table.

Miss North strode ahead, quickly crossing the distance.

Mick looked at Alison, who nodded and followed Miss North and the Vicar. Mick did the same.

The Vicar settled into the sofa at one end. Miss North took a seat at the opposite end.

"Pray be seated, children," the Vicar said. "Especially you," he told Mick. "You must be sorely fatigued."

Mick collapsed into the nearest stuffed chair. Leech plopped down on the sofa between the Vicar and Miss North, grabbing a couple of cookies from the table in front of him and inhaling them. Alison sat primly at the front edge of one of the stuffed chairs. Dolly moved to another empty chair and started to gather her skirts as if to sit, but then seemed to change her mind at the last moment. She ended up standing there, resting a hand on one of the chair's high arms, which reached her ribs.

The Vicar looked at Mick and pointed to the cookies. "Biscuit?" he asked, his big teeth again arrayed in a friendly smile.

"If you insist," Leech said, his hand blurring to and from the cookies. As soon as he'd shoveled them into his mouth, he tried again, just as fast. But Miss North caught his hand and returned it to his lap.

Mick, who was starving, took a few cookies. Alison took one, as did Dolly, after some coaxing from the Vicar. The Vicar poured tea for everyone and served it in white cups so thin that Mick could see the shadow of his fingers through his cup. There was too much milk and sugar, but the tea was hot and soothing. Mick had a second cup while the Vicar formally introduced himself and Miss North. He was Vicar John Clayton, and Miss North's first name was Clara, pronounced "Clah-rah." The Vicar was director of the Forsyth Institute and headmaster of the Boys' School, and Miss North was headmistress of the Girls' School.

Once the Vicar reluctantly accepted that nobody could force down more tea, he said, "I believe Miss March has a report for us regarding your arrival."

"Miss March" turned out to be Alison. Speaking mostly

from memory, she told a long story about "luminous phenomena" and "unheard noises disturbing to dogs and cats." The weirdness apparently had started about a half hour before Mick had appeared.

"Only a half hour for an Eight?" Miss North asked.

"Dolly thought it might be a Seven," Leech said. "She needs to review her *Broome's*, I'm afraid."

Dolly stuck her tongue out at him and then clapped her hand over her mouth, embarrassed.

Alison went on for a while longer and then answered questions from the Vicar and Miss North. The adults seemed deeply interested in stuff like the exact size of the shimmer and whether its colors had spun in the same direction. But they showed no interest in what seemed like the key point to Mick— that he'd *traveled back in time*.

Alison concluded her report and passed the answers that Mick had written to the Vicar. Miss North ejected Leech from the sofa so that he couldn't read them over the Vicar's shoulder. After reading them carefully, the Vicar passed the answers to Miss North, who read them while the whole room remained silent. Miss North tucked them into a book and let Leech sit back down.

"A commendably thorough and precise report, Miss March, particularly for one whose duties do not typically include greeting alleys," the Vicar said.

"Yes, competently done," Miss North added.

Alison blushed but kept her features composed. "Thank you."

"Miss March, Mr. Charles, Miss Tee, I believe you have duties elsewhere," the Vicar said.

The other kids nodded and stood up. Miss North stood too,

swatting Leech's hand before it could reach the cookie plate. Leech patted Mick's shoulder on his way past.

Miss North led the other kids to the exit, waited for them to leave, and closed the door behind them with a thud that echoed heavily through the room.

CHAPTER 5

EVERY ONE AN ALLEY RAT

Miss North walked briskly back, resuming her seat on the sofa. The Vicar also sat back down. He had taken advantage of Miss North's absence to light a fire in the fireplace near the sofa. The light outside was fading, and the room had grown chill, so Mick was glad when the fire began to radiate heat.

Mick's million questions must have shown on his face.

"Truly, we shall do our best to answer your questions before our chat concludes," the Vicar said. "But first, Miss North and I must tell you a few important things. Understood?"

Mick nodded.

"Good lad," the Vicar said. "Miss North?"

Miss North looked Mick deep in the eyes. Like Alison, Leech, and Dolly, she also had strangely bright eyes, as did the Vicar. Hers were gray, and his were green. They weren't murder droid eyes, but they were bright.

Miss North began. "Now, you've not told anyone your true name, correct?"

Mick nodded.

"Good," she said. "'Stone' is a name we give to all new droppers. It is only temporary. You will choose another, with first and last names that are easy to say and easy to forget for a Londoner in 1853. Do not use any of your real names, your mother's maiden name, or other names of people close to you. That protects them—and you."

Mick nodded, though he wasn't sure he wanted to give up his name.

"Miss March doubtless told you to tell no one when you come from," Miss North said. "We owe a duty to the future. To protect it and the people in it by not speaking of it and thus changing it. Words or deeds that might change the future in some important way are called 'mortal anachronisms,' both because they are unforgivable and because they might cause unnecessary death, perhaps on a grand scale. Do you understand?"

Mick shook his head.

"Well, let us imagine for the moment that time is a place, and—"

"Is it?" Mick asked. If time was a place, he could find a way to get back home.

"No," she said. "I am merely offering a metaphor. If we could, however, put time on a map, your date of birth, and your late point—"

"That's the moment you left the future," the Vicar interjected.

Miss North continued, "Your date of birth and your late point are the most important spots on your personal map. If someone wished to harm you or your family, they would want to know the locations of those spots."

"It is unlikely that anyone actually wishes you or your family harm," the Vicar said from beside the fireplace, prodding the logs with a poker before pushing the fire screen back in place. "Still, one must be cautious. Time travel is a confusing and dangerous business."

"Okay," Mick said, though it wasn't.

The Vicar smiled at him a little sadly, as if reading Mick's mind. He then nodded to Miss North.

"Thus, we do not wish to know too much about your future," Miss North said. "Yet we do need to know enough to add to the research record. Please do not speak until I ask you a direct question. Understood?"

When Mick nodded, Miss North said, "Miss March thought you were American. Was she correct?"

Mick nodded.

Miss North wrote that in her notebook, squinting in the fading light.

The Vicar returned with a large glass vase from the mantel. He set it on the table in front of himself, removing the top of the vase. He struck a match on the side of a box, and Mick caught a faint smell of rotten eggs and medicine. When the vase began to glow, Mick realized it wasn't a vase but a lamp. The Vicar fiddled with a knob at the side until the flame was steady and bright.

Miss North positioned the lamp to light her notebook before continuing. "As to your late point, we wish only to be within a range of years."

A series of questions from both adults established that

Mick's late point was closer to 2020 than 2030. Mick got the sense they thought that was important.

During a lull when they weren't peppering him with questions, he got in one of his own. "How does time travel work?"

"We haven't any idea," the Vicar said cheerfully. "It's the most utter, impossible balderdash. It's deucèd inconvenient that it keeps happening."

The Vicar chortled at Mick's crestfallen expression.

"But... Alison's report," Mick said. "All the questions..."

"Oh, we are certainly *trying* to understand it," the Vicar said. "But when it comes to the phenomena of time travel, we are like butterfly collectors. We can tell you a great deal about the shape and color of their wings. But we cannot tell you how a caterpillar turns into a butterfly, or why different species of butterfly have wings of different colors and shapes. Even worse, we can't predict when time-travel will happen. Imagine a poor butterfly collector if caterpillars stopped becoming butterflies. Or if butterflies began to turn into caterpillars. Or if butterflies appeared from thin air, and then suddenly became camels, or caramels, or clouds."

"Quite," Miss North said. She looked at Mick. "Now, you must learn some fundamentals. First, you, as an alley rat, are exceedingly rare."

"We call those who travel in time 'alley rats,'" the Vicar explained. "That is because the methods of time-travel—such as the glow-orb that brought you here—are called 'time alleys.'"

Miss North continued, "Second, alley rats are always children, nearly all of them younger than twelve."

That checked out.

"Third, alley rats can travel only backward in time."

"Why?"

The Vicar shrugged apologetically. "It has been that way for many decades. And even when a few alley rats supposedly could travel forward, it was only by a day or two."

When the daylight had faded, the room had mostly disappeared, shrinking to the lamp-lit circle of sofa and chairs and faint, firelit flickers of furniture and shadow. Beyond the windows, 1853 London was a jumble of dark shapes at the bottom of a heavy sky in which a sliver of moon glinted like a single, bared fang.

"So I can't go home? Ever?" Mick asked. His stomach started to hurt, and he felt like he might start crying.

"I'm afraid not," the Vicar said.

Mick couldn't think about that. "Is Em— my sister okay back home? The shimmer didn't hurt her, did it?"

"It is unlikely she even noticed the glow-orb," Miss North said. "The principal difference, possibly the only difference, between alley rats and arrows—"

"'Arrows?'" Mick asked.

"People who go through time only in the normal manner," the Vicar said. "Straight ahead like arrows shot from a bow, you see."

Miss North resumed. "As I was saying, quite possibly the crucial difference between arrows and alley rats is that time alleys do not affect arrows."

So the shimmer hadn't hurt Emilia. That was a relief. Of course, it meant Emilia was still in the future, with only Uncle Dan to look after her. No, that wasn't true. There was Tía Verónica and Tía Julieta. And his dad. With Mick gone, his dad would have to come home, right?

After a moment, the Vicar said, "Regrettably, there is more bad news. Even could you somehow step into a time alley and travel forward, you still could not return home. Even in the children's tales in which alley rats can travel forward more than a few days, no one has ever claimed that alley rats could travel all the way forward to their late points. At the instant of one's birth, you see, there is a sort of unbreachable barrier."

Miss North stepped in. "There are a few known cases in which alley rats grew old enough to reach the hour of their birth in the normal way. The barrier stopped them all. Witnesses describe the rats simply bursting into flame. The 'birth flame,' it's called. Remorseless and fatal."

"Why does that happen?" Mick asked.

The Vicar frowned. "Perhaps it would be dangerous for a person to live twice in his or her lifetime. If a rat were to return to his future life, he might stop his future self, his young self, from ever becoming an alley rat. Even though he could only do so because he is an alley rat. Such a thing would make the impossible real. Perhaps the angels and devils will not accept it. Perhaps time herself forbids it."

Mick had seen enough time travel movies and read enough time travel books to understand what the Vicar meant. But the Vicar was leaving something out. "Couldn't I do that anyway?" he asked. "Here in the past? By, like, convincing my great-great-grandmother not to marry my great-great-grandfather?"

"Bright lad," the Vicar said. "You're quite right. That's precisely what Miss North meant by protecting the future. Talking about your future might actually change it. History, the great broad sweep of it, appears largely immune to that sort of change—"

"*Appears*," Miss North emphasized.

"But it is possible that individual lives might not be

immune," the Vicar said. "It is possible that loose words might somehow change our own future or our families' futures."

Mick stared at the lamp's steady flame. It seemed preposterous that the flame could hold so steady while time itself was flailing around, crazy and out of control.

Then his brain noticed something. "*Our* families' futures," the Vicar had said. That meant… "You're alley rats too?"

They both nodded.

Mick stared at their faces, which were bright in an otherwise dark room. They had fallen from the future as kids. They had gotten used to the past. Learned to dress in old-timey clothes. Learned to light lamps with matches and to study the impossible. Grown up and grown old, with no hope of ever going home.

As terrible and terrifying as that was, at least he wasn't alone.

CHAPTER 6

A BRAND-NEW PAST

As Mick struggled to absorb what he'd just learned, the Vicar rose from the couch and strode to the wall to pull a cord dangling from the ceiling.

Seconds later, a teenager in a plain, gray dress opened a door that had blended into the wall and shadows. Her curly hair was pulled back in a loose ponytail that fell from her soft white cap, and she wasn't vampire pale, which was a nice change of pace.

"Miss Weathers," the Vicar said to the teenager, "though our dropper friend here appears to have *weathered* the storms of time quite well, I should be grateful if you would examine him."

Rolling her eyes at the dad joke, Miss Weathers circled around the sofa and chairs, stopping in front of Mick. "If I may?" she asked, looking Mick in the eyes. She had the same weirdly bright eyes as the others. Hers were dark hazel, glowing slightly golden underneath. That underglow almost matched the hue of her face in the lamplight.

Calm but intent, she took Mick's pulse, checked his reflexes, and otherwise prodded and stared for a while.

"He seems well enough," she said. "Though Doctor will wish to examine him in the morning."

Collecting her skirts and the Vicar's thanks, she bustled off.

Miss North, the Vicar, and Mick sat quietly for a moment, enjoying the quiet and the fire. Soon, though, Miss North rose and lit her own lamp, telling Mick to follow. She walked briskly through a maze of mostly empty corridors, and Mick forced his tired legs to keep up.

"Here we are," Miss North said as she tugged open a large, solid door to reveal a large room where two big fireplaces yawned at each other like dragons dozing atop separate hoards. Near each fireplace was a bank of long tables, and there were other, smaller tables scattered about. Lamps glowed at intervals from the big tables and from a scattering of the smaller ones, illuminating kids confronting books and papers. Mostly, Mick could see only the tops or backs of their heads, but a few faces turned up as he and Miss North wove through the tables.

What sounded like a large clock chimed once from some dark corner, and soon Miss North and Mick passed through a door set in a deep archway. They continued down the bare stones of a narrow corridor, passing evenly spaced doors with small bronze numbers. Small lamps dangled from the walls, their dim glows overwhelmed by Miss North's lamp. She halted and raised the lamp to a glinting "5" and rapped the door several times with her knuckles.

There were scuttling sounds from the other side, followed by the door swinging inward and Leech's face appearing out of the gloom.

"Evening, Miss North."

"Good evening, Mr. Charles," Miss North said. After a moment, she added, "If we might?"

"Sorry, miss," Leech said, stepping out of the way.

The small room was dimly but adequately lit by a pair of candles near one of the two cots. There was laundry folded on the other cot, which Mick assumed was his. He obeyed his aching legs and sat down on the cot.

Miss North was standing just inside the doorway, Leech between the cots. "Mr. Stone should see Dr. Quinn tomorrow morning," Miss North told Leech, "and I shall consider the other details of his induction in the meantime. At present, he is in your charge, so his welfare is your responsibility, and his mistakes belong to you."

"Yes, miss," Leech said solemnly.

"However," she said, pointing her chin at the candles flickering behind Leech, "his candles do not belong to you. Kindly condescend to revise your lessons in the common room with the others. The Institute furnishes rather costly lamp oil for just that purpose."

"Yes, miss."

Miss North said goodbye, and Leech closed the door. He turned and stared hard at Mick, apparently thinking.

Mick looked around the room, which didn't take long. Beneath a plaster ceiling and above a stone floor bare except for a small square mat beside each cot, the whitewashed stone walls crowded in on each other. Nearly everything in the room came in pairs: two narrow cots against opposite walls, two unlit lamps hanging on the wall above the head of the cots, and two small dressers at the foot of each bed. The only thing without a twin was a squat cast-iron stove between the cots, its flue curving from the back and disappearing into the ceiling.

When Mick turned his gaze to Leech's face, Leech said, "So. I suppose I should start with some tory rules."

"'Tory'?"

"Short for 'dormitory.' We're in Tory Six, the Institute's finest. The first and most important rule is that lying is wicked and sinful and dreadful and you ought never do it. Unless it's to an adult or an arrow. Or it's amusing. But don't ever lie to a torymate."

Mick wasn't sure if the rest was a joke, but the last bit clearly wasn't.

Leech continued, "You've arrived with three weeks left in Epiphany term, so your schedule likely will not match the rest of ours for those weeks. But I can tell you the normal way of things. Our customary activities begin with condy."

"'Condy'?"

"Constitutional development. Also the head-to-toe sweat-sack we wear during constitutional development. You've one on the cot there."

Mick noticed that there were some clothes in the laundry pile beside him. "So it's exercise?"

"Correct. After condy, it's showers. Bring your instisuit there"—he pointed at the laundry pile—"with you to condy in your satchel. Don't lose it. Or any of your clothes. Lost clothes are severely punished."

"'Insta-suit'?" Mick asked.

"Instisuit," Leech said. "Institute suit. School uniform. After showers, we've breakfast. Then possibly matutinals, which are early tutorials."

"'Tutorials'?"

"Lessons with professors. Then, in the normal course, it's either regular tutorials or patrol. Then luncheon. Then patrol or tutorials, whichever you didn't do in the morning. Alison, Dolly, and I have afternoon patrol. Then dinner, which is what we call the evening meal."

Mick wondered what else you'd call it.

Leech continued, "After dinner, if you're unlucky, you might have a vespertine. That's an evening tutorial. Otherwise, it's revision if you've lessons. There are oil lamps in the common room for reading. The prefects have the oil. There are candles in the bedrooms. We each get one candle per day. A candle is good for an hour or two."

"And you were using mine?" Mick asked.

"Merely testing the wick," Leech said with an angelic expression. "We have this stove," he said, gesturing, "but generally we get coal or wood only December through February, so treat your blanket gently and learn to darn your socks."

Mick did notice that the room was chilly. Maybe all the wool everybody was wearing wasn't a terrible idea.

"The stink room is at the end of the corridor. That's the 'water closet,' if you're nobby, although we haven't actual WCs in the tories yet. The professors' and dons' wings do, however, and there are others scattered about the place. When you're in the tory and you must relieve yourself, use the stink room. You've a chamber pot under your cot, but that is for only the very direst of predicaments. Understood?"

"Okay," Mick said.

"That's another rule. No more 'okay.' Londoners of 1853 don't say 'okay,' and a good alley rat blends in. Use the words I use or, better, the words Alison uses. Imitate the masters' accents. You'll learn other accents as well, but that's for later."

Leech saw the confused expression on Mick's face. "Yes, my accent is different. But that's political, that is."

"Where are you from?"

"Another rule: don't ask that question. And don't tell anyone, not until you understand this world better."

"Sorry," Mick said.

"As you should be," Leech said sternly. "Ireland."

"What?"

"I'm from Ireland. I can sound like many kinds of Londoner, but I only pretend for the arrows. When I'm myself, so is my accent."

Mick thought this over. "But I sound American, right?"

"As American as whatever the American pie is," Leech said. "Ignorance pie? Bluster pie?"

Mick ignored the bait. "If I sound American, why can't I say I'm American?"

"Well, there's no real harm in saying you're American, if you truly say no more. But it's easy to say too much. Let's say you're from the state of Michigan. If you say so, is it a problem?"

"Yes," Mick said.

"Why?"

"Because you just told me not to say anything."

"And I am right about all things," Leech said. "Well done. Also, it's because—and I know this because I asked Alison—Michigan became a state in 1837. So it wouldn't be a problem to tell me now, in 1853, that you're from the state of Michigan. But it would be a problem if this were 1833, when Michigan was not a state. We call those 'connans.'"

"Like, the barbarian?"

"'Conn-an,' not 'coh-nan,'" Leech said. "Although Conan the Barbarian is a connan."

"Huh?"

"'Connan' means 'conspicuous anachronism.' Something that

is obviously in the wrong time. Like Conan the Barbarian, who hasn't been invented yet. Avoid connans as best you can."

Leech patted him on the shoulder and started the tour of the Institute in the stink room, which actually didn't stink much—a bit whiffy, but better than stadium bathrooms.

"I am going to explain this slowly," Leech said. "Listen with all possible attention. Their first time in the stink room, some new arrivals get confused and do something revolting. A gentleman makes a stink tidy and proper-like, and in Tory Six we are gentlemen to the bone, including the girls."

Candle-lamp held high, Leech pointed out the key features. Each of the three stalls was a solid, tall wooden box with no roof that reminded Mick of the old-fashioned confessionals at church. Each stall had a big copper funnel for number one. Afterward, you turned a spigot to fill a small pitcher with water, and then you poured the pitcher down the funnel.

Mick suddenly realized how badly he needed to pee and borrowed the lamp from Leech. Afterward, he felt lighter and more optimistic. He laughed a little at how much peeing had raised his spirits.

Leech explained how going number two worked in excruciating detail. It involved sawdust, leaves or pine needles, dirt, and very carefully putting a lidded bucket in a small elevator called a "dumbwaiter" that was used only for poop buckets. Empty, clean buckets came up one dumbwaiter, and full, dirty ones went down another.

"We call it 'the dumpwaiter,'" Leech said, "though that's probably a connan." He rubbed his hands. "Well, that's the tour, then," he said, heading for the exit. "You've seen everything that matters at the Institute."

Mick scurried after him. "Really?"

"Course not," Leech said as they exited. "But we should do the rest tomorrow, in sunlight. It's a large building and hard to understand in darkness. This evening, it's enough for you to meet the Sixers and eat dinner."

"Sixers?"

"Your torymates. Most of us should be around the tory at this hour, except the ones sleeping outside."

"Are they being punished?"

"What? Ah, no. 'Sleeping outside' means living somewhere else whilst you do something for the Institute. If it's interesting, we'll never hear the end of it. Snorer spent a month learning about steam engines and didn't shut up about it for a year."

"Does everybody get nicknames?" Mick asked.

"Many do."

"How did you get yours?"

Leech sighed. "I looked at the approved list of names in the *Practical* and said to myself, 'Leigh Charles, that's as bland an English name as any nation-thieving brigand ever named a bland English lad. There's even a Charles Street and a Charles Place nearby. I'll blend in like sand on a beach.' Two days later, Leigh Charles became Leech, and didn't it just stick to me like a leech. Ah, well. At least I'm not Piles. Or Bell-End." Leech thought for a second. "There's a thought. Pick a nickname you can endure, I'll start using it, and we'll pray it catches on."

Mick frowned. He liked being Mick Conway. Also, he liked electric lights and toilets that flushed. And his sister. Tía Verónica. Tía Julieta. Uncle Dan. His dad, sometimes. Suddenly, he had a hand against the wall to steady himself and was fighting tears.

He won the fight, mostly, though he had to wipe his eyes with the heavy sleeve of his borrowed coat. Leech was looking off in the distance, pretending he didn't notice. Mick appreciated that.

When Mick got his balance back, Leech resumed walking. They quickly reached the doorway to the big room where the kids were reading by lamplight.

The nearer fireplace was elevated, and a stone bench projected out from just beneath it. Leech hopped onto it and called out, "Friends, Romans, runty men, lend me your ears."

This earned Leech some cheerful jeers. He gestured to Mick to join him. Mick hesitated, but Leech gestured more forcefully, and Mick climbed up.

"This is the newest member of the glorious Six. He has dropped at our feet from the future this very day. He will sup with us this eve and every other."

There was a bit of cheering. Some of the kids went back to reading, and others came over to warm themselves at the fire and meet Mick. The first was a tall, broad-shouldered girl who introduced herself as Florence Dylan, the girls' prefect. The next was an even taller and somewhat narrower boy who introduced himself as Brian Braddock, the boys' prefect.

"The prefects are the tory's gentry," Leech told Mick. "Remember to bow."

There were a lot more kids after that. Most were his age or older, but plenty were younger, including some who couldn't have been older than six.

The introductions had mostly finished when the grandfather clock in the corner chimed dinnertime. By that point, Mick wasn't sure he remembered anybody's names. He wasn't sure he could have told most of them apart, either. They were all wearing the instisuit, which was much like the borrowed suit he was wearing, except his was a lighter gray and came with a loud orange and red tie. The girls got skirts and no ties. Most of the kids were pale, though some like Miss Dylan were as olive-skinned as Mick and a few were darker. Mick had never seen kids as pale as the palest Sixers. Pale or not, nearly all of them had oddly bright eyes, some much brighter than others.

After Leech stopped at the tory entryway to show Mick how to pull the bell for the night porter in an emergency, they joined in a migration to the dining hall. All the students at the Institute ate in the same dining hall, Leech explained, except the toddlers and sometimes the "dons," who were older students, except not really students, or something. Mick got the vague impression that they were time commandos who spoke ten languages.

The dining hall was on the ground floor, which was different from the first floor. Apparently in 1853, the first floor was on the second floor. The dining hall was packed with long tables packed in turn with students. Though not as tall as the Great Hall, the dining hall rose two or three stories. There seemed to be a mural of some sort on the ceiling, but most of the lamps were hanging from the wall or from scattered metal stands no taller than Mick could reach, and only a thin gauze of light fluttered up to the ceiling.

Leech steered Mick through the narrow aisles until reaching a table with some familiar-looking kids who were probably Sixers. Leech pointed out a couple of empty stools beside one another, and they settled in. Mick found himself sitting next to a tiny girl with mousy brown hair piled into a sort of pyramid built from braids. Like a meerkat with a brontosaurus egg, she held a huge baked potato in both hands, her nose buried in it as her jaw worked methodically.

After a few seconds, she extracted her face from the potato and turned to face Mick. She was wearing gold-rimmed glasses fogged over from the heat of the potato. "I'm Samantha Winchwood. You must excuse me. I am a most particular eater." She reinserted her face into the potato and gave no sign she heard Mick when he said hi.

The food was simple but delicious. In addition to the baked potatoes, there was roast chicken, some greens, and a dense brown bread. Mick wanted more but got enough to feel a little heavy and a lot better about life.

Mick looked around and realized he didn't see any grown-ups. He asked Leech about that. Leech pointed toward a curtained platform against a wall on one of the long sides of the hall. "Some of the faculty and dons eat there every night," he said.

Soon, they and the other kids carried their dishes to a sideboard near a rear door and returned to their tables. Some kids swapped seats so they could talk to new people. Leech explained that the Sixers always ate together, but every term they shared tables with a different tory. That term, it was the Threes.

Mick tried to listen while the other kids used words he'd never heard to discuss people he'd never met doing things he didn't understand, but soon the pleasant weight of dinner and the overwhelming weight of the day began to drag down his eyelids. Leech noticed and steered him back to their room. Mick fell into his cot, and the world disappeared.

CHAPTER 7

THE ANSWER THEY HAD

There was an ungodly clanging followed by a rude shaking.

The clanging turned out to be from an old-fashioned alarm clock in one of Leech's hands. The shaking came from Leech's other hand.

"I'm awake," Mick said.

The alarm went blessedly silent.

After a moment, Mick sat up, his feet dangling off the cot. The air was chilly, and the stone floor felt cold even though his feet weren't quite touching it yet. That explained the little mat.

The room was brighter than Mick had expected. Looking up, he realized that he'd missed something in the previous night's darkness. Although the walls crowded in on each other, the room actually had a high ceiling, and the top few feet of the wall containing the door consisted mostly of windows.

"All shipshape and Bristol fashion?" Leech asked.

"Does that mean am I okay? I'm okay."

Leech tsked, and Mick remembered he wasn't supposed to say "okay."

"Right, then," Leech said. "I've condy soon, but there's time enough for a tour."

Mick took another pee that made him feel way better about life. By the time he got back to the room, Leech had almost finished pulling on a grayish cotton outfit that looked like baggy long-johns—the condy.

Leech pulled on a pair of moccasins—"mocks"—and explained they were only for condy. Since Mick wasn't going to do condy, he should wear his "brogues," the heavy shoes they'd given him in the alley the day before.

Mick had fallen asleep in the clothes they'd given him, and Leech told him to keep them on for now.

Leech rolled up some complicated underwear and his instisuit and tucked everything into his satchel along with his brogues. He then showed Mick how to do the same. The instisuit Mick had been issued looked and felt a lot like the clothes he was already wearing—scratchy pants, scratchy shirt, scratchy jacket, scratchy socks, and a tie that would probably find a way to be scratchy too. At least there was no scratchy vest like the one he was wearing, and the instisuit jacket and pants were a little lighter.

"Right," Leech said cheerfully. "Our tour begins in our own room." He pointed up. "The windows open to the roof. There's a rope ladder behind the curtain. It's an escape route in case the time ghosts attack."

"Are there really time ghosts?"

"Probably not," Leech said. "Mind you, some of the Twos are insisting that there's been the ghost of a faceless nun floating about the place lately. But then, the Twos, well ..." Leech paused to shove some things in his satchel. "Now, when the weather is fair, going to the roof is a good way to get some fresh air. As fresh as you'll get in this city, anyhow. Mind, we mayn't go to the roof without a don or a professor, but that's one of those rules everybody ignores. But if you do break the rule, don't fall off the roof. If you fall off and dash your skull to pieces, the professors will know straight away you've been on the roof without permission."

Leech led Mick from the room. Mick had to admit that Leech had been right—things did look different in daylight. When they left the room, the sunlight wasn't particularly strong yet, but even so, things looked less gloomy. The corridor leading to their room had a series of thin, sooty skylights that let in just about enough light to see by. There were also several generous windows and skylights in the common room, where there were already a few older kids in instisuits staring intently at their books. Mick recognized some of them from the night before, but he couldn't remember any names.

"Grinds," Leech whispered as he and Mick walked toward the outer door. "When you're fifteen or sixteen, give or take, you sit the sorting exams. They determine what you study next. Whether you study next."

"How do they know how old kids are?" Mick whispered back. "We can't tell anybody our birthdays."

"And time travel confuses matters in any event," Leech pointed out. "The professors just make a good guess as to your age and set a new birthday."

Leech pulled open the common room door and ushered Mick through to another dim corridor lit by skylights. Leech looked at the grime coating the skylights and tutted. "The

Eights can't wash their own arses. Ambitious to trust them with skylights."

A few twists and turns took them out of the corridors and into the Great Hall. Leech stopped at the top of the stairway and leaned on the thick white marble railing. Mick joined him, standing tiptoe to see over the railing and down to the lobby floor several stories below.

"If you get lost," Leech said, "remember that Jimmy Gunner loved sunlight. He put windows or skylights wherever he could. The outside edge of the building has windows to the outside, and the inside ring has windows facing the Great Hall."

"Who's Jimmy Gunner?"

"James Gunn," Leech said. "Built this place. That's him down there." Leech pointed to one of the marble heads and chests stuck in niches in the wall.

At that distance, Mick couldn't really see the face. "He started the Institute?"

"He designed this building. But the school is older than this building, and has had different names across the centuries. Some people say it goes back to 1652, when Old Noll was still killing my many-great nan. Some say even earlier, back when it wasn't much more than a few books, some straw beds, and a pot of dodgy rabbit stew down south in farmland. But eventually your man there came along." Leech pointed down to a bust next to James Gunn's. "Edward Forsyth, Viscount of Summat, and second son of the Earl of Whatsis." Quoting something, Leech added, "He brought order and vision to an institution sorely in need of both."

Leech started moving again, still talking. "'Order and vision' means 'big piles of money.' He bought a building for the Institute near the Houses of Parliament, about a century ago. Then it all moved here in 1806. That's why he's also got a statue outside."

At the head of the stairs, Leech stopped and looked up at the large gold and silver clock in the wall not far below the glass ceiling. It was just after seven-thirty, meaning Leech had almost a half hour till condy. Without pausing too long in any one place, Leech continued the tour. As they descended, the dormitories, faculty offices, and classrooms on the upper floors partially gave way to larger meeting rooms on the lower floors, including the dining hall on the ground floor. Leech opened a door and took a few steps into a covered stone walkway that ran along a wall and connected to a large back yard in which tall trees rose above patches of grass, stone benches, and neat rows of various plants that Leech said were mostly herbs, fruits, and vegetables.

"Those," Leech said, pointing down the walkway at a separate, two-story building, "are the kitchens. And now I really must get to condy."

They went back inside, and Leech led Mick along a curving corridor, then through a gymnasium to the boy's dressing room. There, Leech stashed his satchel in an open cupboard, as a few other boys were also doing.

"Oi, Owl," Leech called to one of the boys.

Owl looked a lot like Leech, except that he had huge eyes. It was easy to see where he'd gotten his nickname.

"Aye?" he asked warily.

"Kindly inform Miss Mitchell that I am attending to my solemn mentor duties to our newest dropper and regrettably must arrive behind my time."

"That's all?" Owl asked.

Leech nodded.

"Acceptable," Owl said. Looking at Mick, he added, "Welcome to the Institute. Listen to Alison and also Dolly, if she speaks. But don't trust Leech." He walked away without another word.

Leech looked a little pleased.

"Who's Miss Mitchell?" Mick asked.

"She often leads our condy session. And she's a don, one of the best. Stay on her good side. Now, I must show you the shower. You cannot live in filth like an Eight."

Grabbing a coarse towel and washcloth from a nearby cabinet and tossing them to Mick, Leech led him through some doors into a shower room. Leech plucked a sliver of soap from a bowl hanging by the door and handed it to Mick.

At Leech's instruction, Mick hung his satchel and towel on a metal hook on the wall and fought his way out of his itchy clothes.

Mick shivered. The tile was cold underfoot, and the air was no better.

There was a complicated arrangement of copper pipes, including stalactite pipes that turned out to be weird shower heads. You pulled a chain to start the water. Leech explained that there was never enough hot water, and that sometimes there wasn't enough water at all, so Mick should have a light hand on the chain. "Don't drink any shower water, either. Most of it comes from cisterns, some of it is piped in, and this filthy city has touched all of it."

Once Mick showed he understood how everything worked, Leech scampered off.

Mick pulled the chain and regretted it immediately. Obviously, somebody had used up all the hot water. After rushing through a freezing shower, he toweled himself aggressively, mostly to warm himself with the friction.

Then he fought his way into the instisuit. There were Martian rovers less complicated than old-timey clothes, and wearing a rover would probably be more comfortable too. The clothes had too many pieces, and each piece itched, bunched, and bound. And the only mirrors in the locker room were no help. They were barely big enough to show whether you had lettuce in your teeth, and they were dull and foggy, like most of the mirrors in the Institute. Mick had been trying to figure out whether he had the same bright eyes as almost everybody else at the Institute. He seemed to, but the mirrors made it impossible to be sure.

Eventually, he had all his clothes on more or less right. He managed to find his way out of the locker room and back to the Great Hall, where he bumped into Alison.

"Leech forgot to show you to Dr. Quinn, I take it?" she asked.

Oh, right. He nodded.

Alison rolled her eyes and led Mick up a back stairway, along a couple corridors, and into a pleasantly sunlit room overlooking the Institute's huge courtyard. In the corner, a few toddlers were cheerfully throwing ragdolls at each other. Nearby, Miss Weathers, the teenager who had examined Mick the day before, was sitting in a rocking chair by the window, reading a hefty book.

"Miss Weathers," Alison said, "our dropper here is meant to see the doctor."

Miss Weathers closed her book and placed it on the small table beside her. "I'd best fetch her here. There's a student sleeping in the infirmary, you see."

Miss Weathers exited through a different door than the one Alison and Mick had used. A moment later, she reappeared, followed by a woman with long black hair streaked with gray whom Miss Weathers introduced as Dr. Quinn. The doctor looked like a plumper version of Mick's mom, which made him sad and reassured at the same time.

He was also reassured that his height and weight hadn't changed. He was still about four-seven and seventy-eight pounds (or, Miss Weathers informed him, five stone and eight pounds in 1853 units, which apparently had been invented by cave trolls). There wasn't any logical reason his height or weight should have changed, but there wasn't any logical reason he should have time-traveled either. After being measured, Mick sat on a tall stool while Dr. Quinn poked and prodded him while explaining to Miss Weathers what she was doing. Mick didn't understand most of it, but there was a lot of "normal" and "healthy," so he relaxed a bit.

Eventually, Dr. Quinn straightened up and took a couple steps back. "Good, good," she said. "You give all the signs of health."

That was what Mick's dad called a "lawyer phrase." So he asked, "But am I actually healthy?"

Dr. Quinn laughed merrily. "I believe so, yes. But the human body is mysterious even without time travel. And I very much regret to inform you," she leaned toward him and fake-whispered, "that you recently traveled through time."

Mick laughed despite himself.

"In this time and place," she said, "doctors hate to confess uncertainty. Hospitals in this time and place are too often places of unshakeable certainty and avoidable death. But doctors here already ignore me because I'm a woman and they confuse whiskers with wisdom, so I feel free to confess uncertainty as appropriate. Which it is in this instance. Very few doctors have ever studied how time travel affects the body, which means we know far less than one should like." She smiled at him. "Still, you do seem in splendid health."

"Nobody around here seems to know much about time travel," Mick noted.

"So imagine how ignorant the arrows are," Dr. Quinn said. "About time travel and everything else. At least Miss Weathers and I wash our hands before we tend to our patients, avoid feeding opium syrups to infants, and ensure that Mrs. Robbin and her cooks prepare meals that prevent rickets and scurvy. And those are some of the reasons why the students here are far healthier than children outside the walls. And are even, like you, notably taller."

Mick blinked. In 2024 Chicago, he was shorter than most kids his age. Being tall would be a nice change. Not that it was worth all the other changes, of course. But, under the circumstances, he needed to start looking pretty hard for silver linings.

CHAPTER 8

THE ROOM OF FUTURE PRESENT

Afler seeing the doctor, Mick left the nursery with Alison, who had to rush to a matutinal with Mr. Victor.

"I'm already tardy," she said, "and Mr. Victor can be most severe."

"Sorry," Mick said, trotting to keep up with her brisk pace up the stairs.

"It was important that Dr. Quinn examine you," Alison said. "It's Leech who should apologize."

"Still, thanks," Mick said. "Will I have classes someday?"

"Once Trinity term begins, you likely will have tutorials like the rest of us. Until then, I suspect the faculty will try to determine what you most need to learn."

Mick managed to get a few more questions answered as they walked around the edge of the Great Hall. Then Alison stopped in front of a doorway and said, "I must go in now. Luncheon is at noon. Till then, do as you please, except you mustn't set foot outside the Institute. Miss North would flay me alive, and Leech too."

She ducked into her classroom, which had windows facing the Great Hall. Through the windows, Mick could see the backs of a small group of kids under the scrutiny of a stiff-collared, stiff-faced professor, presumably Mr. Victor, who had broad shoulders and a solid waist. Mick recognized Owl's profile as the boy looked up and then scooted his books aside to allow Alison to slide quietly into the empty seat beside him.

Mr. Victor looked at Alison briefly before his expressionless stare turned outward to Mick. He tilted his head a fraction of an inch as he contemplated Mick. The professor's unblinking eyes were the same bright eyes so common at the Institute, and the rest of him was as pale and cold as a January sidewalk. He looked like a white walker wearing a human costume. No wonder Alison hadn't wanted to make him mad.

To escape Mr. Victor's gaze, Mick moved down the corridor. On his left was the airy expanse of the Great Hall. A balustrade of white marble with gray veins ringed it on all sides, except one, where the main stairway switchbacked all the way up. On his right were the classrooms, their windows facing the Great Hall. Occasionally, he rose to his tiptoes to look in. They were small rooms mostly, with only one teacher and a few students. Some of the students were kindergarteners. Some were teenagers. The classes mixed younger and older students more than he was used to.

He wondered what kind of teachers he'd get. A few teachers looked like college professors in black-and-white movies— flowing academic robes, bushy gray hair, gold-rimmed spectacles. One such professor, a short, gray-haired woman, was striding back and forth in front of a small chalkboard that she was filling with a terrifying blend of numbers, letters from different alphabets, and graphs that looked like a demon's nightmare journal. Some of the other teachers looked like kindly parents. But most of them were like Miss North and Mr. Victor—sharp. Their eyes were sharp. The creases in their clothes were sharp. Their gestures were sharp. If they were your babysitters, you'd floss without complaining and go to bed early.

By this time, he'd walked almost all the way around the Great Hall. He didn't want to keep going far enough to step back into Mr. Victor's line of sight. Besides, thinking of babysitters made him think of Emilia, and then his whole family, then his whole life back in the future. He started to ache with loneliness. This was the first time since he'd dropped in 1853 that he'd been alone and just thinking, and he could feel sadness trying to overwhelm him.

The corridors were almost empty, except for a few older students who ignored him by pretending to check their pocket watches. The Great Clock said he still had hours until lunch, and he didn't want to spend them alone.

Mick decided that the best thing to do would be to go back to Tory Six, but of course he got lost.

Trying to find something he recognized, he came to appreciate how many stairways the Institute had: iron spiral stairways, narrow stone stairways, rickety wooden stairways, and dusty forgotten stairways that led to locked doors with rusty hinges. None of them took him anywhere familiar.

For a while, his irritation at getting lost replaced his loneliness, but then the irritation and loneliness teamed up, and Mick was considering just sitting down in the dim hallway and waiting to starve to death. Then a short, roundish woman staggered around the corner, under attack by an enormous pile of books.

He watched her struggle for a few paces before his mom's voice came into his head and told him to make himself useful. He hustled over just in time to catch a toppling side-stack. He set it on the floor and lifted off some other books that looked like troublemakers. All the books were the same height and width—slightly bigger than grown-up paperback books—and bound in the same dull brown material, probably leather.

"Bless you," the woman said.

The stack had shrunk enough that Mick could see her face. She was youngish for a grown-up. She had a normal bright smile and the weirdly bright alley rat eyes—deep brown with yellow specks. As best as he could tell in the faint light, she looked less pale than most of the people at the Institute.

"I'm headed to that door there, to the library," she said, tilting her head. "If you could just..." she added, looking at the books Mick had set on the floor.

Mick stacked the books together and picked them up, struggling a little. The woman was stronger than she looked.

When they reached the door, the woman set down her stack of books with a grateful sigh and pulled from her robes a metal key the size of Mick's forearm. The door unlocked with loud clunks. After effortful arranging and rearranging of books, the woman managed to get everything inside and lock the door behind them.

"Rather inconvenient, so many locks, but such is the way of things when one must safeguard precious items," she said.

"I thought this was just the library," Mick said.

"I shall pretend I didn't hear that," she said, picking up the books and heading down the hallway. "Books can be valuable, and are often invaluable. Certain students and professors would pilfer this place like rabbits in a garden, I can tell you. Some scalawag tried to force that lock not a week ago."

Mick followed her into a large room that looked like an abandoned battleground where the combatants had used books as ammunition. There were three long tables in the center of the room covered in books, a few of which were arranged in neat stacks but most of which sprouted from jumbled mounds like mushrooms. Against the walls were a dozen or so smaller tables with similar stacks and mounds of books, and beyond those were shelves lining every inch of the walls and books filling every inch of the shelves.

The woman laughed at Mick's expression. She cleared a patch on one of the smaller tables with a few forceful shoves and then filled the clearing with the books she and Mick had been carrying.

"We're reorganizing, you see," she explained. "We finally managed to agree that we need a system for shelving the books more precise than 'that's where old Nathaniel Grimbsy himself put that book when he got drunk and forgot about it thirty years ago, and he was a fine librarian with scholarly eyebrows.'"

She tilted her head at Mick as if seeing him for the first time. "Newly dropped, I gather. I'm Miss Emmet. Have you chosen your new name yet?"

Mick shook his head.

"Good, good. Not a thing to rush into headlong, choosing a new name. Shouldn't one of the children be showing you the ropes?"

"They have class. At least until lunch," he said.

"But you don't? And there's nobody expecting you until luncheon?"

Feeling sad and alone again, Mick shook his head.

Miss Emmet patted him on the shoulder. "Well, then I shall dragoon you into service here. You can read, yes?"

Mick nodded.

"And the Vicar and Miss North have already given you the fundamental cautions? Instructed you to keep mum on your late point, and all the rest?"

"I think so."

She cocked her head to the side. "You *think* so? Miss North is a very definite person. Magnetic North, we called her, even when she was a girl. Because she always told people which way to go."

"She and the Vicar said a lot about protecting the future."

"Excellent. If you've heard the sermon already, we may safely turn to the task at hand. These," she said, gesturing at the books he had helped lug into the library, "are future journals destined for the Room of Future Present." She paused. "Have you started your future journal?"

Mick shook his head.

"Newly dropped, indeed. Well, for the first month or so you're here, you will go to the Scriptorium every day and tell your future journal everything you can remember about the future. After that, you'll do so less often. Eventually, you will finish your journal, and it will be locked in the Vault. And then many decades will pass, and you'll pass, and your late point will pass. And then the Institute will remove your journal from the Vault and review it. Provided the Institute endures that long, naturally."

"Why?" Mick asked.

Miss Emmet pursed her lips thoughtfully. "I suppose the main reason is to see if we alley rats are changing the future by dropping into the past. There are many theories and many quarrels about whether that is possible. On those rare occasions when we manage to learn something new about time travel, half the theories dissolve like sand castles at high tide. In contrast, the quarrels... well, a good alley rat academic quarrel is built from steel and diamonds and arrogance. Sturdier than Windsor Castle and Notre Dame put together."

Mick remembered watching on TV as Notre Dame's roof had turned into ashes during a huge fire and then had gotten rebuilt. He figured that was the sort of future event he wasn't supposed to mention.

"In any case," Miss Emmet said, "we do check the journals against reality to see if we can detect any changes."

"Are there changes?"

Miss Emmet grinned wryly. "Some say yes. Some say no. People's memories are often unreliable, especially if they've suffered loss and sorrow, like all alley rats. And, of course, children often do not understand the adult world. Besides, for all we know, the journals themselves change when the future changes. Perhaps the time fairies move the ink around in our journals and the memories around in our minds, and we're none the wiser."

Mick sighed. He needed to understand time travel so he could go back home, but it was starting to seem like if he ever did understand it, he'd be the first. He looked around a room full of books that might hold the answers he needed but might also be lies written by time fairies.

"Are these all journals?" he asked.

"Only the books that you and I carried in. And you, young man, are going to help me shelve those."

They spent the next little while sorting the journals into

chronological order. The oldest described 1747 and were very short because, she explained, they were stingier with paper back then. The most recent journals described 1852.

Once the journals were sorted, Miss Emmet placed them on a "trundle cart" and lit an oil lamp that she hung from a hook atop a thin brass pole at the front of the cart. She pushed the heavy cart through dim corridors before unlocking the door to a room covered in dust and crammed floor to ceiling with books on all the walls. In the middle were a few leather chairs next to small tables and a single, long table with a few wooden chairs.

"The Room of Future Present," Miss Emmet said. "It has a right case of the dismals. Still, I'm fond of it. Cozy chairs, quiet walls, and some rather delightful books scattered about."

Mick spent a while helping Miss Emmet shelve the journals, which were arranged first by year, then by author. The older books were a mix of colors and sizes. But eventually they became roughly the same size—about as big as a fancy paperback—and the same brownish color.

The year and the first four letters of the author's last name were stamped on the spine, so shelving them was easy enough once he got to the right shelf, but getting there was hard work. Some of the shelves were tall, and the little ladders that slid along the wall were hard to move. Still, Mick managed to shelve quite a few before they finished.

"Thank you," she said, when he returned to the trundle cart where she was standing. She checked her wristwatch. "Does your tory eat at noon?"

Mick nodded.

"You still have quite some time if you'd like to sit here. When I was a girl, I liked to come here and read the most recent journals." She looked at him carefully. "I was sad in those days. Most of us are, after we drop. I dropped in 1832, and at first it made me sadder to read about all the children who had dropped from 1831 into 1731 or somesuch year. They were so confused, and you could feel how much they missed their own time. But they were very useful books because they were written by other children who wanted to write down every-thing they could remember about 1831 and explain what it meant. I didn't know any more about 1832 than you know about 1853, and I needed to correct that if I wished to go outside. It can be dangerous on the outside, especially for"—she paused—"especially for those of us who are different to most of the people outside." She paused again and seemed to be thinking hard. "But then it turned out they were also cheerful books, in a way. Many of them, at least. After a while, they changed from 'Poor, poor me, I miss my home' to 'I hope they have game pie for Michaelmas dinner' and 'Tom Parsons has a fine leg, and I intend to dance with him at the next ball.'"

She obviously could tell he didn't understand. "They moved, you see, from missing the future to caring about the present. They had pleasant lives. Some of them, anyhow. As many as do now, I'd wager. When I was a girl, that was reassuring." She smiled. "Students aren't permitted to be here by themselves, but I found a kindly librarian who overlooked that rule. As have you."

It was nice of her. But he didn't want to sit alone in a gloomy room haunted by the ghosts of people who had died before they were born.

"The offer stands if you change your mind," she said, reading his face.

Mick helped Miss Emmet sort books until he had to go to

lunch. She showed him to a corridor that led to the main stair-case, and he found his way to the dining hall with time to spare.

He found an open seat near the middle of one of the tables the Sixers shared with the Threes. A few kids were pushing rickety carts bearing trays heaped with food. They plunked the trays at either end of the table, and the food worked slowly toward the middle. That explained why the middle seats had been empty.

At about the same time the food eventually reached the middle of the table, so did a girl who looked a year or two older than Mick and was probably a few inches taller. She was pale, with a thick mane of light brown hair decorated with so many ribbons it looked like a toddler had tried to gift wrap a cat. Mick said hi, but the girl delicately selected her food while avoiding eye contact.

Mick thought about throwing his mashed potatoes at her, but he didn't have any to spare. Besides, Miss Winchwood the Most Particular Eater had sat down beside him, and she was ignoring him too. So possibly the ribbon girl was the Second Most Particular Eater. Maybe in 1853 being particular was different from being rude.

Mick amused himself by looking up at the ceiling. In the daylight, he could see the mural covering most of it. There was a picture of a golden globe in the middle and four smaller globes at each corner of the ceiling. Gold lines of differing thickness connected dozens of spots on the small globes to a single spot at the center of the big globe. That spot was on an island that looked like a bunny hopping toward the mainland, just above the bunny's foot. Mick assumed the bunny was England and the spot was London.

Leech arrived, slapped Mick on the back, and sat next to

him. "Greetings," he said, filling his plate as best he could with the remaining scraps of food. "Miss Winchwood. Miss Paisley."

Miss Paisley, Mick assumed, was the ribbon girl.

Miss Winchwood showed no sign of hearing her name. Miss Paisley did, but it was a faint flicker, quickly suppressed.

"I do hope they haven't worn you down with all this chatter," Leech said to Mick.

Mick tried to smile at the joke but didn't quite make it.

"You oughtn't frown so," Leech told him. "Frowning, and Anglo-Saxon chauvinism, are Miss Paisley's domain. She's famed for her frowns here and at Demeter Farm," Leech said, casting a glance at Miss Paisley, who gave no sign of hearing him. "Now, Mr. Stone, have you decided upon a name?"

Mick shrugged. He'd been thinking about it. He liked being Mick Conway, and he really didn't want to be called anything else. Then again, they were already calling him "Mr. Stone."

"Well, think on it," Leech said before shoving the last bit of food in place and stepping up from the table. "Must dash. We've patrol in half an hour."

It would be nice to get outside. Mick almost asked if he could go along. But the answer was pretty obviously no. And he should probably try to learn more about the Institute first, so that he didn't get lost again.

He spent a couple hours wandering around the Institute. Then his tired legs started to complain, and the afternoon shadows stretched long and snoozy. He went to the room he shared with Leech, intending to brainstorm how to get back home but actually falling unaware into a well of sleep so deep and dark that he was disoriented when Leech woke him hours later. Leech dragged him to dinner, dragged him back from dinner, and shoved him at his cot.

CHAPTER 9

THE OMINOUS SHROUD

The next morning, Leech dangled his horrible alarm clock over Mick's head, moving it out of the way as Mick flailed at it groggily and turning it off only when Mick sat up.

In the early morning cold, the boys tugged on their condies and mocks—still stupid words, Mick thought—and shoved their instisuits and brogues into their satchels before going downstairs to ye olde gym class. The gym felt weird. The ceiling wasn't quite enough, and the wood floor didn't look right without basketball and volleyball lines. Still, it was airy and nicely lit by a high bank of windows, and there was even a little running track wrapped around the main court. A few people, who seemed too old to be students and too young to be teachers, were running at various speeds, including a young woman passing everybody with ease.

There were about a dozen kids clustered at one end of the court, mostly standing or sitting. After leading Mick to the cluster, Leech sat down and began stretching.

While Leech stretched, Mick looked around at the other kids. At first, Mick didn't recognize anybody other than Alison and Dolly, though a few kids might have been Sixers. Then he spotted the sulky ribbon-haired girl from the dining hall, Miss Paisley. Mick exchanged waves with Alison and Dolly and gave Miss Paisley a little wave, big enough to be polite but not big enough that it would be embarrassing if she didn't wave back. And she didn't.

The young woman who had been lapping the others cranked up to a full sprint for a couple laps, then glided for a couple more laps before trotting over to the group. Mick belatedly recognized her as the woman from the little room near the front door. She was sweating lightly but not breathing hard.

"Good morning, everyone," she said with a smile.

The other students, except for Mick and Miss Paisley, said, "Good morning, Miss Mitchell."

It was uncanny how they said it at exactly the same time.

Eyes down, Miss Paisley fidgeted with one of her ribbons.

"Good morning, Miss Paisley," Miss Mitchell said.

"Good morning," Miss Paisley said sullenly. Miss Mitchell stared calmly at her until she added, "Miss Mitchell."

Miss Mitchell turned her gaze to Mick. "Our new dropper. Good morning, young sir." She looked out at the class. "Right, you lot. Concentration and course. Perform satisfactorily, and there will be footie."

"Concentration" turned out to be something like the Pilates his mom had made him do sometimes, only with fancy flashcards with shapes and colors on them. While the kids held themselves in difficult or awkward positions, Miss Mitchell moved around the group, apparently at random, and held up a card, instructing individual students to say what it showed without moving their heads. After about ten minutes, Miss Mitchell started to send the kids who did the best to "set up." Mick couldn't really see what they were setting up, because he was trying to focus on Miss Mitchell's cards. Even so, he kept getting things wrong.

When Mick, Miss Paisley, and a tiny boy were the only ones left, a girl with dark hair appeared at the edge of his vision. She was a few inches shorter and a few years younger than Miss Mitchell, but she had the same intense expression and the same bright alley rat eyes. Really bright. She was wearing an instisuit and heavy shoes but somehow moved silently across the creaky wooden floor.

She started talking to Miss Mitchell. Mick managed to make out something about a "vault" and an "intruder." There might have been something about a "bored, narrow grave," which sounded ominous.

Miss Mitchell cocked her head and asked a short question drowned out by the sounds of kids clanging at things in the distance. The dark-haired girl said something, and Miss Mitchell asked another short question.

Mick couldn't move closer because he was stuck resting on one knee and two hands, with his other leg sticking out behind him. But he did turn his head to see and hear better.

Miss Mitchell asked something about Miss North. The dark-haired girl shook her head. They nodded at one another, and the dark-haired girl turned away, walking swiftly and silently past Mick.

Out of the corner of his eye, he noticed Miss Mitchell nod and return her gaze to him, Miss Paisley, and the little kid. Maybe out of pity, she called a halt to concentration. "Course," she called out.

"Course" turned out to be an obstacle course. "Set-up" had apparently been packing the running track with obstacles—boxes, steps, ropes, and other items seemingly pulled at random out of an angry garden shed. They covered all but one curve of the track.

The students lined up at the start. Alison, Dolly, and Owl were chatting away at the middle of the line. Mick put himself at the end of the line so he could watch the others go first, and Leech took a place directly in front of him. "Don't try to be champion on your first day," Leech said. "That's how you get hurt. Also, Miss Mitchell moves the obstacles sometimes whilst we're on the course, so keep a sharp lookout."

Miss Mitchell called "go" for one kid at a time. Fast and graceful, the oldest kids went first, hardly slowing for the obstacles. When it was his turn, Mick struggled, but the silver lining was that he never really got going fast enough to get hurt.

After course, the kids helped return the obstacles to the wall beneath the windows before Miss Mitchell produced a rag-stuffed leather ball and divided the kids into two teams. One team tied bright red sashes over their shoulders, and everyone started kicking each other's shins while trying to guide the ball into small goals at either end of the court. Mick liked soccer okay, but he was exhausted, so he lurked at the fringes of the game, catching his breath and protecting his shins. Most of the kids were pretty good, and Leech was excellent.

After the game, Mick complimented Leech on his soccer.

"'Soccer' is a connan, since association rules football doesn't yet exist," Leech said. "Of course, everyone here calls it 'footie,' which is also a connan, and so far we haven't broken the future."

Mick found that reassuring. If he wasn't getting conned or

going crazy and he really was in the past, he didn't want to break the future. He needed it to be there when he went back.

After showering, Mick tugged on his instisuit, tied his brogues as tight as they'd go—still too loose—and followed Leech across the lobby of the Great Hall, detouring slightly to contemplate the stern marble faces of James Gunn, Edward Forsyth, and the Institute's other fancy dead guys.

Soon, he and Leech were standing on the top floor in front of Miss North's office, which was near the big room where he'd met her and the Vicar his first day at the Institute.

Leech knocked on the door. "We're only just in time," he told Mick, "In future, don't stop to gawp. Miss North is most particular about punctuality."

A rebellious voice in Mick's head said he wasn't going to worry about these people's rules and schedules. As far as he was concerned, anything he did in 1853 was 171 years early, and nobody had the right to tell him he was late for anything.

As he entered Miss North's office and fell under her piercing gray gaze, he decided to test that outlook on somebody less scary.

"One moment," she told them, putting her head down and pulling up the sleeves of her plain gray dress to finish writing something.

Miss North's office was grimly elegant, with a sturdy oak desk, a separate table for drawing, and a high-backed leather chair tucked in the corner. There were three small chairs in front of the desk, and Mick took his cue from Leech by settling into one of them.

On the white plaster wall behind the desk were a half dozen portraits of serious-looking women that Leech had mentioned were former Girls' School headmistresses. While Miss North continued writing, Mick stared at the portraits, half-expecting them to magically come to life. The one in the corner behind Miss North seemed likely to have some criticisms.

With a nod and a flourish, Miss North set down her pen, looking up at them. "Have you selected a name for yourself?" she asked Mick.

"Yes, ma'am."

"Miss," she said.

"What did I miss?" he asked, confused.

She smiled slightly. "In this time and place, a married woman without a title is called 'madam,' or 'ma'am.' An unmarried woman or girl without a title is called 'miss.' I am unmarried and therefore a 'miss.'" She paused. "With something amiss, at my age, many would say."

"Oh," Mick said. "What about men? Or boys?"

Miss North shrugged slightly. "'Mister.' And you have chosen to be Mister...?"

Mick took a deep breath. "Mitchell Edwin Gunn." The name had come to him that morning when he'd looked at the bust of James Gunn. He thought it was a pretty good one. "Mitchell" shortened to "Mitch," which sounded a lot like "Mick." And "Mitch E. Gunn" sounded like "Michigan," which was stuck in his head after his connan conversation with Leech. Plus, Miss Mitchell had been nice to him during condy. So it all sort of fit together.

"Welcome to the Forsyth Institute, Mr. Gunn."

"Thank you." The new name felt weird.

"There was little fervor in that 'thank you,'" Miss North said.

"What's fervor?"

"Excitement,"

"I'm sorry, ma'am. Miss."

"You needn't apologize. I daresay you have little cause for excitement, at least happy excitement. Doubtless you regard stepping into that glow-orb as the worst possible stroke of bad luck."

Mick realized he was nodding and stopped.

"Nevertheless," Miss North continued, "I need to impress upon you that in many ways, you are a fantastically fortunate boy." She smiled in response to Mick's skeptical expression. "Mr. Charles, after remembering your posture, kindly identify for Mr. Gunn a half dozen ways in which he may count himself fortunate."

Leech came out of his slouch. "Yes, miss. Let's see," he began. "You're lucky it's no earlier than 1853. You're lucky we found you before some cutpurse did. You're lucky you had any clothes on at all when you arrived. Some don't. You're lucky you dropped where people speak your language. You're lucky the Institute exists so that you're not begging for crusts and sleeping in an alley."

"One more yet, Mr. Charles," Miss North said.

Leech winked at Mick. "You're lucky to have me as your model for gentlemanly dress and deportment."

"Cheeky, Mr. Charles," Miss North said.

"Yes, miss," Leech said cheerfully.

"You should also," Miss North said, "consider yourself fortunate to have survived the drop. Some don't."

"Really?" Mick asked.

Faces grim, they both nodded.

Miss North said, "I asked Mr. Charles to discuss your drop in terms of fortune, and so he did, competently enough. But there was perhaps not as much blind luck as all that."

"What's that mean?" Mick asked.

"To begin with," she answered, "although people do indeed die or suffer injury in a time alley, it is uncommon. Mishaps seem to happen primarily in one of two circumstances. First, an alley rat is injured along the way—not by the alley itself, but by someone or something they encounter in one of the way-worlds."

"Way-worlds?" Mick asked.

"Intermediate points encountered as one is pulled from the future to the past," she said. "They seem to be part of the real world rather than the world of the alleys, although no one is entirely certain. Not all alley rats stop at way-worlds, but many do. Some even stop at several."

Several? Mick had lost count of all the ones he'd gone through. He asked, "What's the other way to get hurt?"

"Being a passenger," Miss North said. "Unlike alley rats, arrows can pass right through a time alley and never notice. But if an arrow is touching a rat when the rat enters the aperture, the arrow can be pulled in as a passenger and will travel back in time with the rat. And if the passenger loses connection with the rat, she may get left in a way-world. And many passengers become quite ill after dropping, even fatally so."

Miss North let that sink in. "So, in truth, although you were indeed quite fortunate to survive, once you stepped into that glow-orb, fortune was not the only consideration. Now, Mr. Charles, comment on the fact that Mr. Gunn dropped in 1853."

"Yes, miss." Leech screwed up his face in thought for a moment. "It means there is roughly a nine in ten chance he stepped into the glow-orb between 1953 and 1983."

Mick opened his mouth to say it had been way later than that but managed to stop himself. Miss North nodded in slight approval.

"And why is that, Mr. Charles?" she asked.

"Because nearly seven in ten rats drop between one hundred and one hundred and ten years before their late points. And most of the rest drop between one hundred ten and one hundred thirty years before."

"Could Mr. Gunn have arrived from two hundred years in the future?"

Leech snorted.

"Why not?"

"The Shroud, miss."

"Explain."

"It's, well, it's the *Shroud*, miss."

Miss North raised her eyebrows.

Leech blushed and tried again. "Well, it's … sort of the edge of the time map. Nobody has a late point after the Shroud. At least, nobody we know of."

"Why not?" Mick asked.

"Nobody knows," Leech said. "It may be when magic dies. Or when a new magic takes over. Or the world is eaten by a giant albatross."

"Mr. Charles," Miss North said sternly.

"When is it?" Mick asked. "The Shroud?"

Leech said, "Most likely July or August of 2024."

Mick got goosebumps. He'd stepped into the shimmer in August 2024.

Miss North made Leech walk through why it wasn't such dumb luck that Mick had ended up when and where he did. Alley rats mostly dropped in big, powerful cities like London, and usually in certain neighborhoods within those cities. That was part of the reason the Forsyth Institute existed. A lot of rats had dropped in London over the years, and some of them—

including Edward Forsyth—had become rich and influential and used their money and influence to build up the Institute to find and help other rats.

Mick was pretty sure Leech had said some other stuff too. But his brain kept circling back to the fact that his late point was basically the same time as the Shroud. That had to mean something.

CHAPTER 10

A FLICKERING FAWKES

Until lunch, Mick wandered about the Institute, trying to build up a mental map. To his surprise, he found himself in a corridor outside the nursery.

Miss Weathers was sitting outside one of the nursery doors, her nose in an enormous book. Aggressive children's singing was forcing its way through the door.

"Greetings, young dropper," she said without looking up. "Mr. Phillips is with the children, and I fear that I'm not over-fond of 'My Roses Blossom the Whole Year Round.'"

If that was what the toddlers were singing, Mick wasn't fond of it either. "Who's Mr. Phillips?"

"The choirmaster."

After a while, the singing fell quiet. Miss Weathers cocked her head for a moment and opened the door enough to poke her nose in. A man's voice said something, and she opened the door all the way.

Most of the little kids had wandered over to the play rug

beside the tall windows, but two were still listening to Mr. Phillips, who was standing in the middle of the room, singing a short melody in a clear, sweet voice. One of the kids, a tiny redhead, sang it back perfectly. The other, a slightly bigger blonde girl who might have been almost old enough for kindergarten, made up her own notes. Fortunately, she stopped when she spotted Miss Weathers.

"Miss Ellen!" the little girl cried, pointing enthusiastically at Miss Weathers and then walking determinedly where her finger led her.

"Julia," Miss Weathers said with exaggerated gravity. "This is a friend of mine, Mr...."

"Gunn, I guess," Mick said.

Miss Weathers nodded. Little Julia seemed to mull this over, as if deciding whether she approved of the name.

Mick looked back and forth between Julia and the redheaded girl, wondering which one Emilia would sound like when she could sing.

Julia said earnestly, "Miss Ellen, the children were good as good before songing. But then there were *difficulties*."

Miss Weathers kept the grave expression on her face. "Thank you, Julia. I shall consult with Mr. Phillips."

Julia nodded soberly. Without another word, she turned and trotted to join the other kids on the play rug. The redheaded kid hugged Mr. Phillips' leg before following Julia.

"Mr. Gunn, was it?" Mr. Phillips asked. "We've not met, I don't think?" He was a short, round-faced man, whose thick, wavy hair flopped gently as he spoke. "I'm Mr. Philips. My vocation is listening to students sing, but I also listen to them talk. The Institute is not a bad place for a child—quite the contrary. But I'll warrant you've had a hard journey here. If you ever want to discuss that, or anything else, don't hesitate to visit my classroom. Or if you want to sing about it. I find nothing so soothing as a song."

"Thanks," Mick said, not sure what to do with that.

"Well, I've trespassed upon your sultanate quite long enough, Miss Weathers." Mr. Phillips said. "Thank you for your patience. And now I must go force some red-eyed grinds to raise their voices in song. Perhaps I could rouse their spirits by teaching them something scandalous from the Penny Gaffs."

Miss Weathers laughed. "I daresay the Vicar wouldn't approve."

Mr. Phillips laughed too. "No, nor Miss North, and hers is a wrath to be avoided. A pleasure making your acquaintance, Mr. Gunn."

After the music instructor left, Mick chatted with Miss Weathers briefly and watched the toddlers play. It was nice to see, but also sad, because it made him think about Emilia. And about when he'd been a toddler and had both of his parents around. He mumbled something at Miss Weathers and headed back for the Great Hall.

Realizing it was almost time for lunch, he made his way down to the dining hall, where Leech had saved him a seat in their usual spot beside the Most Particular Eater, who nodded slightly at Mick as he sat down. They were also across from Miss Paisley, the surly ribbon girl, who pretended that they didn't exist.

"Mitch E. Gunn," Leech said. "Clever. What nickname would you like? 'Gunner'? You could do a great deal worse. 'Leech,' say."

Mick nodded. "Gunner" actually was pretty good.

"Excellent," Leech said. "Have you heard about this afternoon's alley?"

Mick shook his head.

"We're meeting Miss North in the lobby in an hour and a half to greet an alley," Leech said. "Well, Miss Atkinson's team is doing the actual greeting, but Miss North wanted us to come."

"That sounds interesting. Let me know how it goes," Mick said.

"You're to come with us," Leech said.

"Me? Why?"

"I'd imagine Miss North wants to introduce you to alleys," Leech said. "And probably to make sure you aren't alley blind."

"What if I am?" Mick asked.

"You aren't. It's very rare for a rat to go alley blind so young."

Mick knew that "rare" didn't mean "impossible," but he also knew he couldn't do anything about it either way, so he tried not to worry. "How do they know there's going to be an alley?"

"Caterwauling."

Leech explained that, in the normal world, "caterwauling" meant "cats howling" or just "loud, unpleasant noise." In the world of time alleys, it was a sign there was going to be a time alley. Sometimes, it actually was cats howling. But it could be dogs barking, or even weird cold spots or unnatural winds. Anybody could notice a caterwauling, even arrows. Leech said there were also "stirrings" that only alley rats could sense.

"Like what?" Mick asked.

Leech shrugged. "Odd sensations. Shocks that feel almost like static electricity. Skin crawling like you've brushed against a ghost. Anyhow, since the caterwauling came so early, it'll be a drop alley." Before Mick could ask, Leech explained, "An alley that might bring a dropper from the future. With lift alleys—which lift you up and take you to the past—you're lucky to get ten minutes' warning."

After lunch, they went back to their room and changed into their baggy, itchy, and uncomfortable outside suits. At least Mick's tie was purple. He liked purple.

There was a rectangle of polished silver metal nailed to the door that gave a dim reflection. Leech looked at his face and necktie knot and nodded approvingly. "Children whose fathers engage in respectable professions," he said.

"Huh?"

Leech reached into a well-worn satchel sitting atop his dresser and pulled out a book. He flipped through the pages until finding the passage he wanted. "'When engaged in duties outside the walls of the Institute,'" he recited in an accent that sounded uncannily like the Vicar's, "'unless instructed to the contrary, students shall take care to dress in a respectable but unassuming manner, in keeping with the fashion among children whose fathers engage in respectable professions.'"

Leech put the book back in his satchel and pulled the satchel's strap over his shoulder. "These clothes we wear outside are meant to make it look like our families are prosperous, but not truly wealthy," he said. "We should look like the children of doctors or lawyers, not of lords and ladies."

"Why?"

"We need to look respectable enough to be treated politely but not so elevated that we draw too much attention and cannot patrol properly. Well, and these clothes are already expensive. The Institute would be beggared if we all went about in silks and satins."

Mick suddenly remembered bumping into his mom and

spilling fruit punch Gatorade on her favorite silk blouse because he'd been drinking it while tossing a football to himself. She'd stared at him for a long time, grabbed him by the hand, and walked him over to his dad before going upstairs to her bedroom. His dad had said she was probably going to list Mick on eBay.

He always missed his mom. Honestly, he missed his dad too, no matter how mad he was at him.

Mick used his heavy sleeve to wipe away the tears blurring his eyes. He could tell that Leech was pretending not to notice.

They were the first ones to reach the lobby, so Mick killed time by looking at the marble busts again. One was James Gunn, the architect whose name he'd borrowed. Gunn had a mustache the size of Tennessee. Another was Edward Forsyth, who had given his name to the Institute. He had no mustache but did have fearsome sideburns that looked ready to wrestle with his ears for control of his temples. The bronze plaque beneath his bust said in ye olde lettering: "Edward Forsyth (1741-1810), Viscount of Caithneck, Son of Denis, Earl of Conigsbury. He brought order and vision to a grateful institution, and to the very sands of time. *Si non esset, invenire eum oporteret.*" Mick assumed it was Latin. When people used foreign languages to be fancy, it was usually Latin or Greek, and Greek letters looked like fish, or eggs wearing belts.

Leech elbowed Mick in the arm. Mick followed Leech's gaze across the Great Hall. Dolly, Alison, and Miss North were walking briskly toward them, Miss North slightly in the lead, the other two on either side.

When they were together, Miss North quickly inspected their outfits before giving a small nod of approval.

"Are your satchels properly equipped?" she asked.

The other kids said, "Yes, Miss North."

Mick shrugged.

"Mr. Charles?" Miss North asked, inclining her head at Mick.

"As he's not a street, miss, no items are in fact required. Even so, Mr. Gunn's satchel contains the required items for a street specified in *Hyde's Practical*: three calling cards for the Institute, a lesser fieldbook, two pencils, a penknife, and an appropriate amount of ready-penny, viz, one florin, one shilling, and thruppence. Optional copy of *Wilson's London Guide* not included as none was available."

"Indeed," Miss North said blandly. "Were you aware of that, Mr. Gunn?"

Mick didn't want to get Leech in trouble, but he was pretty sure that Miss North already knew he had no idea what was in his satchel. He shrugged again.

Miss North looked hard at Mick, then at Leech. "Do you know what a florin is, Mr. Gunn?"

"A flower?" Mick guessed.

"Mr. Charles, having the correct items does Mr. Gunn no good if he does not know what they are."

"Yes, miss," Leech said.

"A florin, Mr. Gunn, is a small silver coin worth two shillings. Spent wisely, it is enough for several wholesome meals. Mr. Charles will ensure that you know the common coins and prices of common goods."

They could all hear the unspoken *or else*.

"Yes, miss," Leech said meekly.

"And you, Mr. Gunn, until you learn which horses are likely to trample you, which people would cut your throat for sport and which would charge a guinea, you will be careful and quiet.

You will stay close to me, and you will not speak unless instructed. Understood?

Mick nodded.

"Good. Time alleys can be dangerous. London can be dangerous. You are about to encounter both at once. Do keep your wits about you."

It was an overcast day but not too cold or wet, so they set off walking. The Institute was in a pleasant, leafy neighborhood where most of the buildings were red brick or gray stone. If it hadn't been for the horse-clop and wheel-rattle of carriages, Mick might have thought he was in one of the older fancy Chicago neighborhoods, maybe Lincoln Park since everybody was so pale.

Miss North and the kids were talking technical about the alley. It felt like the Star Trek gobbledygook somebody said before phase-inverting some tachyons, crawling through some tubes, and blowing up a Borg cube. He wondered if he was the only person in 1853 who knew about the Borg. That would be really depressing. Though not as depressing as not having a real toilet.

After they had walked a ways, the houses got closer together and less leafy. Everything started to smell a bit, though not nearly as bad as wherever he'd dropped a couple days before. Had it really been only a couple days?

A scraggly-haired girl a little taller than Alison, wearing dirty clothes and carrying a few bouquets of sad flowers, stepped out of a side street. "Flowers, missus?" she said in a loud, complaining tone. "Fine poppies for a fine lady?" She thrust one of the wilting bouquets toward Miss North. As she did, she said quietly, in a calm tone, "Aperture Seven. Opens within a quarter hour." Beneath the dark hair and filthy face, her eyes glinted an intense alley rat green.

Miss North ignored the flowers but gave the girl a small coin. The girl curtsied and thanked Miss North in the loud, complaining voice before wandering away.

As they resumed walking, Leech pressed close to Mick and whispered, "Gail Atkinson. Cleverest kid at the Institute, except perhaps our Alison. Sure to be a don someday."

"Why do all the alley rats have those eyes?" Mick whispered.

"What eyes?" Leech whispered back.

"Silence and alertness," Miss North said from up ahead.

Mick had no idea how she'd heard them.

They walked another block or so before turning. Even before they turned, Mick knew they were near the time alley. The street seemed unnaturally bright, so there had to be a shimmering coming from somewhere other than the gloomy sun lurking behind the haze of cloud and smoke. There, he thought, turning to a spot across the street, in front of a store. Across a large window was written, "John Reed & Sons, Tobacconists," and in front of it was a bright, yellow and orange shimmering globe. Mick realized he was also hearing a faint alley song.

On the sidewalk nearby, a woman in a puffy dress was pushing a wheelchair with two big wheels in the front and a small one in the back. It had a protective fabric canopy that covered its occupant except for a pair of trousered calves and the silvery flash of a cane handle. It looked like the sort of quirky chair Tía Julieta would have wanted. As the woman and the chair passed through the shimmer, it flared so brightly Mick had to close his eyes and turn his head. When it was safe to look again, the woman and the wheelchair had disappeared into the crowd. Mick watched in fascination as the shimmer kept growing and getting brighter, though not as bright as the flare.

The other kids and Miss North were watching too. From the opposite side of the street, so was the dirty flower girl, Gail Atkinson. Other than his group and Miss Atkinson, nobody seemed to notice the shimmering. A man with a bushy beard, possibly John Reed or a son, stood in the doorway of the store, his face half hidden by the shimmer, the other half veiled by smoke from his pipe.

The alley song was now quite loud, and Mick felt the same tugging sensation he'd felt when the alley had appeared in Chicago. It wasn't until Leech pulled him back by his collar that Mick realized he'd started to step toward the alley.

After a minute or two, the shimmer stopped growing, and Mick's goosebumps got stronger. Something was about to happen.

A gangly man with a large brown sack slung over his shoulder sauntered toward the shimmer. The sack covered the man's face, but from the way he moved, Mick guessed the man had no idea he was walking into something. Mick half-wondered if he should warn the man, but the man continued through the shimmer unharmed and unaware.

For a moment, the tension continued to build, and then a sort of lightning bolt streaked across the shimmer, which went dark for an instant, like a TV losing power for a second. Then it flickered a few more times before disappearing for good.

"Fox," Leech said, with a disappointed tone.

At a discreet gesture from Miss North, they turned and walked back the way they had come.

As they walked, Miss North asked Mick a few questions

about the shimmer—shape, size, colors, brightness, whether there had been any rings around it. Not wanting to accidentally say something dumb, Mick kept his answers short.

Miss North nodded and said, "We may confidently conclude that you are able to see alleys satisfactorily, Mr. Gunn."

Mick sighed with relief.

"Miss March, observations, if you please," Miss North asked.

"Glow-orb. Size Five, un-ringed. Vibrancy six, primary solar yellows, secondary whites, flat sheen," Alison said.

"Not a Seven?" Miss North asked.

Mick remembered that Miss Atkinson had said something about a Seven.

"No, miss," Alison said.

"Mr. Charles, Miss Tee, do you concur?"

"Yes, miss," they both said.

"That wasn't right, was it?" Dolly asked. "It didn't feel like a fox until the very end."

"We shall discuss it further at the Institute, Miss Tee," Miss North said, her tone cutting off further discussion.

"What's wrong with first names?" Mick asked Leech. He was realizing that in 1853 London, almost everybody, even kids, was "Mister," "Miss," or "Missus." For kids, as far as Mick could tell, the only exceptions seemed to be for really young kids, other kids on your patrol team, close friends, or certain people with nicknames. "Why is everybody 'Miss Whatever'?"

"Not 'Whatever,'" Leech corrected. "'Thingummy.' 'Miss Thingummy.'"

"There's no way that's a word," Mick said.

"It's very much a word," Leech said. "The English have a word for everything. Except giving your country back."

Mick had always thought of Ireland as being sort of

England's little brother, only with leprechauns, but he was starting to realize he'd missed something. He'd have to ask Leech about it when Miss North wasn't glaring at them.

Back at the Institute, Miss North led them briskly to the room where Mick had first met her and the Vicar. This time, the Vicar was sitting at the big map table, surrounded by stacks of dusty books. In one of the stacks, Mick recognized the dull brown color of several journals from the Room of Future Present.

The Vicar looked up at them, removing a pair of gold-rimmed spectacles and rubbing his nose between his eyes. "Another damp squib?"

Miss North nodded.

"So many, of late," the Vicar said. "The spotter was Miss Atkinson?"

Miss North nodded again. "She and her team correctly predicted the time and place of the glow-orb. But they predicted a Seven, and it was a Five. There was no frame."

"My word," the Vicar remarked, more to himself than anyone else. He put his spectacles back on and stared at the trees and roofs visible through the long bank of windows. Then he took them off again and put them right back on. His expression was worried.

After a moment, he said, "Well, that is a perplexity, is it not?" He rose to his feet and smiled, though it didn't make him look any happier. "And when confronted with a perplexity, I find tea a great comfort."

The Vicar led the way to the couch and chairs. Even before they settled in, a teenaged girl appeared from a side door. She set a tea tray on the coffee table before nodding respectfully at the Vicar and disappearing through the side door.

The Vicar pushed tea and cookies on everyone, and Leech managed to scarf a few extra cookies before Miss North could stop him.

Nobody spoke for a bit, which made Mick a little nervous. Eventually, he dared to ask, "What's so bad about a fox?"

Leech tilted his head and looked at Mick. "Out of curiosity, Gunner, how are you spelling that?"

"F-o-x," Mick said.

Leech and Dolly laughed, and the others smiled.

Mick flushed with confused embarrassment.

"It's f-a-w-k-e-s," Alison explained. "Named for Guy Fawkes."

"He tried to blow up Parliament, but the gunpowder didn't explode," Leech explained. "Alas."

Miss North frowned at him, but Leech just smiled back politely.

"Why does it matter?" Mick asked.

Leech grinned. "I just don't want you imagining a fox trotting out of an alley with its tail up."

"Not foxes," Mick said. "The alley. Why does it matter that it's a fawkes, or a damp squid, or whatever you call it?"

"Squib," Dolly said.

"*Whatever* you call it," Mick said.

"I'm afraid," the Vicar said slowly, "that it is one of those cases where it matters because we don't know whether it matters."

Mick sighed loudly and then blushed a little. He'd meant to sigh on the inside.

"I'm not being deliberately paradoxical, Mr. Gunn," the Vicar said. "I simply mean to say we don't know whether it's important, not for certain. But it is a most curious thing, and we rather suspect that it might mean something, perhaps something not altogether good. We had got quite successful at predicting which alleys would be fawkeses. But of late, well ..."

"Okay," Mick said. He could understand that they didn't like being wrong. Or being surprised. Some surprises were pretty awful. You might think you were pulling your sister out of a weird light, for example, only instead you were falling a couple centuries back in time and learning about foxes that aren't foxes while getting ambushed by your own underwear. You might think you were tired of your chores and your boring uncle and your runaway dad, that you didn't want to go try to make more new friends at another new school. But then you found out that your new school wouldn't start for a hundred and seventy-one years, so you couldn't go even if you wanted it to. And then you learned that you wouldn't mind taking out the trash and doing some fractions, if you just got to go home.

CHAPTER 11

DISARMING THE RAT TRAP

Finished asking questions, the Vicar and Miss North shooed the kids out of the room.

After turning a corner, Leech let out a long series of tsks. "Always hoarding the biscuits for themselves, adults." He reached into the front pocket of his jacket and pulled out a bunch of cookies. He handed one to each of the kids before popping the last one in his mouth. Everyone scarfed them down.

"I don't understand what's going on," Mick said.

"Naturally," Leech said. "Americans are thick as Tewkesbury mustard."

Dolly punched Leech in the shoulder. He winced, despite wearing ten pounds of jacket.

"Thanks," Mick told Dolly.

"What don't you understand, Gunner?" Alison asked. "Do you like 'Gunner,' by the by?"

Mick shrugged about the nickname and tried to organize his thoughts. "It's just, the Vicar keeps saying that nobody really understands how time travel works. So why are he and Miss North so worried about fawkes alleys?"

The group had ambled to the rail overlooking the Great Hall. Leech looked at the Great Clock. "Drat it. I've not finished Mr. Victor's reading. Must dash." He turned nimbly and trotted toward the stairs.

Dolly looked at Alison, who was staring into space. "Don't you worry," Dolly told her, "I'll sort Gunner out."

Alison stared a few seconds too long before jerking her attention back to Dolly and Mick. "Thank you."

Mick followed Dolly to what turned out to be the library, if you went in the front door. The library's reading room was high-ceilinged and well-lit by tall windows but not all that much larger than the Sixers' common room. Although there were some older students scattered among the mismatched tables and desks, squinting intently at books, most of the seats were empty.

Dolly led him to a small table in a lonely corner, where they sat down, facing each other in uncomfortable chairs. "I'm pleased you're not alley blind."

"What happens if you're alley blind?"

Dolly frowned. "It depends when it happens. If you were already alley blind, so soon after dropping, we would probably lose you to Orphans."

That didn't sound good. "Orphans?"

"The School for Orphans of the Empire. It's quite a good school, actually, but they don't study time-travel there. They mayn't even discuss it, as so many of the pupils are arrows."

"You said that it depends when it happens. Could I still go alley blind?"

"We all could," Dolly said, shrugging. "But it's most unlikely to happen for many years yet. Most rats have unusually keen alley sight for the first few hours or days after an alley, and then it fades to a normal level and stays the same for years. Usually at least until age fifteen or sixteen. Some rats do go alley blind then."

"What happens if you go alley blind then?"

"Choir practice," she said.

"What?"

"We say that pupils who go alley blind then have more time for choir practice."

Mick shuddered at the memory of the toddlers singing "My Roses Blossom the Whole Year Round."

"Most rats don't go alley blind so young," Dolly said reassuringly. "Most of us never go alley blind at all, in fact. Starting around age eighteen, most rats' alley sight does start to weaken, but most rats have some alley sight left at age twenty-five. And they say if you have any alley sight left then, you'll have it the rest of your days."

Mick nodded. Not long ago, he didn't know alley sight existed, but now he was really worried about losing his.

"We ought to discuss fawkes alleys," Dolly said. "Yes?"

After Mick nodded, Dolly explained fawkeses and why they had people worried. The problem was they were happening too often. There had always been fawkeses, but they were supposed to be rare—usually one or two out of ten alleys. The other alleys opened all the way like they should and then closed down like they should. Sometimes, they even brought a dropper.

"Like me," Mick said.

Dolly nodded. "But lately, so many alleys are fawkeses. Something odd is afoot."

"Something bad?"

Dolly thought for a moment. "When it comes to alleys, odd things are often frightful things. Near the end of the Protectorate, for almost two months, one fairy path in two dropped a corpse. Or parts of one." She shuddered slightly. "And sometimes odd things mean that the rules have changed. Until 1767, a few talented rats could shuttle the alleys. Travel through time deliberately, that is. But then, just days after All Hallows' Eve, it suddenly became impossible. Nobody knows why."

"Nobody here knows anything, do they?" Mick said. He realized he sounded bratty. "Sorry."

"Quite all right," Dolly said. "The Vicar is always saying that none of us knows much, and I expect he's correct, though Alison is determined to know everything. She already knows more than most grinds, and she's three more years till her sorting exams. That's why they made her a thane when she was so young."

"Thane?"

"The student in charge of a street team or greet team."

"Which are you?"

"We're streets. Alison, Leech, and I. Though Alison will likely be a greet next year."

Mick wondered if they knew how silly it all sounded. Greets and streets. Fawkeses and glow-orbs. "What's the difference?"

"Streets patrol for signs that alleys might open. Greets, well, greet the alleys that do open."

"So why was it you guys when I dropped? Not greets?"

"By the time we spotted the signs, it was too late to summon greets."

"Why?" Mick asked.

Dolly scrunched up her face. "Well, it's a very large city, and we cannot possibly cover all of it, not even in our main patrol areas. We sometimes miss alleys. It was fortunate we found yours, really. That day, we were assigned to patrol beyond the usual sequences to the southeast. Because of all the fawkeses. We were turning north, to stop at the Society for Chronal Fancy before returning to the Institute. That's when Leech happened to sense a stirring for your alley. We had already patrolled that area not a half hour earlier, and none of us had noticed any stirrings or other signs. Not even Leech. Don't tell him I said so, but Leech *is* awfully good at sensing stirrings."

Mick nodded. "So the signs were late for my alley?"

Dolly nodded.

Mick thought about it. "But how would you know what late is? I mean, since you don't always see alleys open? Maybe you only see the ones that take a long time to open or that stay open extra long. Or only the ones that do a light show and make cats howl. Maybe most alleys just open and close, and you never know about them."

She tilted her head. "It's difficult to explain, but usually there are signs, and we can predict what will happen. Alison was most distressed that we missed your signs."

Mick remembered the faraway look in Alison's eyes just before they'd left her. "Is that why she's so worried about the fawkeses? Because they're weird?"

Dolly thought before pursing her lips and nodding. "Gunner, I shall tell you this because I don't wish you to pain Alison by mistake. It isn't a secret, precisely, but please don't discuss it carelessly."

She fell silent again, and for a moment it seemed like she might not tell Mick anything after all. Eventually she whispered, "Alison had a twin brother. He dropped out of a fawkes. Alison and her brother were very young when they were pulled into their glow-orb, five years of age, I believe. Miss North says the glow-orb was Alison's, and her brother was a passenger."

"Wait—so people *can* come out of fawkeses?"

"It's ever so rare," Dolly said. "Their alley was disturbed in some manner. Alison and her brother both came to London about five years ago, but were separated then. Her brother dropped, but she was pulled back into the alley and then dropped in Manchester about seven years ago."

"Two years before her brother?" Mick asked. *Yikes.*

Dolly nodded. "Fortunately, her brother dropped somewhere with a view of Westminster Abbey. Alison didn't know what it was, but she remembered it and could describe it. Alison remembers things with exceptional clarity. Someone told her it was in London, so she came here by herself. It's a very long way, especially for such a small girl. And most dangerous."

There were half-formed tears in Dolly's eyes. Mick wondered if she was thinking of Alison or herself. His eyes started to moisten too.

"And then," Dolly said, "she searched London until she found where she had been separated from her brother."

"How?" Mick asked.

"I don't know," Dolly said. "I should imagine she remembered where the buildings were and where the sun was, that sort of thing." Dolly paused. "She looked for him there every day."

"For two whole years?"

Dolly nodded. "She didn't know his drop date, you see. It might have been before hers or after hers. She had to search the city for him in case he was already there, and she had to go every day to that spot at the right hour in case that was the day he would finally drop. She told me once that she remembered her brother's face, that he was in terrible pain, and she couldn't bear to think he would drop out of the alley all alone."

"Why didn't the Institute help her?"

"The Institute didn't know about her. She dropped in Manchester, mind, not in London. And, of course, she didn't know about the Institute, either."

Mick tried to imagine what he would have done if he'd dropped by himself, without a clue. If he hadn't even known the Institute existed. Alison had found her way to London and then found somewhere to sleep and something to eat for two years. He wasn't sure he could have done that, and she'd been a lot younger than he was.

"But she found him?" Mick asked. "When he dropped out of the fawkes alley?"

Dolly's eyes grew wet again. "She did. There was a greet team waiting for him. But he dropped out and died straight away. That's when the greets realized Alison existed, when she knelt on the cobbles and started pressing at his chest. I've heard it was as though she wanted to make his heart beat."

Mick guessed they didn't have CPR where Dolly came from. When she came from. He also guessed that wasn't really the point.

They both sat silently, and the library's quiet felt like the silence at a funeral.

Then Mick pressed onward. "Now I get why Alison hates fawkeses. But why are the Vicar and Miss North so worried? "

Dolly frowned. "Some say fawkeses are alleys that were supposed to have somebody in them but then collapse because they're empty." Her mouth scrunched up. "Miss North and the Vicar are worried because we aren't certain *why* they're empty."

"What's that mean?"

"Well," she said, "some say that a fawkes is empty because nobody was lifted at all. But others say that a fawkes is empty because the alley rat *was* lifted, but somehow sloughed off."

"Sloughed off?"

"Fell out of the alley in the wrong place or time, as Alison and her brother did. Only what happened to her is most unusual. When people slough off, it's usually because they've died," Dolly said. "So they say."

Mick let that sink in for a moment. "So everybody's worried about the new fawkeses because kids might be dying?"

Dolly nodded.

They sat silently for a while, and Dolly took his hand on the table. He squeezed back.

"I ought to find Alison," Dolly said, letting go of his hand and standing up. "We should prepare for tomorrow's patrol."

"Thanks for explaining all that stuff," Mick said.

"You're most welcome," she said, gathering her satchel and bustling toward the door.

It sounded like they would start giving Mick tutorials soon enough and that he would eventually go out on patrol. But not yet. So, since Dolly and Alison were preparing for patrol and Leech was in tutorial, Mick had time to kill. He went back to the Tory Six common room, but there wasn't anything for him to do there. He was too old to join the little kids clustered around a table, apparently trying to get a marble out of a glass bottle. And he was too young to join the grinds battling stacks of books.

He decided he wanted to figure out how to get in and out of the Institute on his own, just in case. The Institute had been good to him so far, but if that changed, he didn't want to be a prisoner. Besides, everybody at the Institute kept telling him it was impossible to go back to his real life and that he shouldn't even talk about that life. To get home, he might need to go somewhere people didn't believe that the future should remain locked up behind an unbreachable wall of deadly fire.

He began by exploring escape routes in the room he shared with Leech. He lowered the rope ladder and eventually figured out how to lock the bottom in place so it didn't flap around when he climbed it. After reaching the top and scraping some knuckles, he managed to loosen the window latch and swivel the window up and out far enough that it held itself open.

He pulled himself up onto the thick stone windowsill, lying on it and poking out his toes until his foot crunched on the fine gravel below and he could slide onto the roof. He knew it was against the rules to be up there by himself, but it didn't sound like a rule people really cared about.

It was chillier than it had been when they'd seen the fawkes, and he could see his breath, a wispy echo of the fog hiding most of London. In a couple directions he could make out scraps of what looked like huge parks, and in another direction, he thought he could see slices of the big river—the Thames. Peeking through the fog here and there were hints of how big the city was, sullen blotches of gray and red, dark slicks of damp stone stretching to the horizon.

Part of Mick still held out hope it was all just a dream. But being up on the roof and seeing everything, hearing the clattering carriages and the shouting drivers, feeling the cold air on his skin, smelling the complicated and often unpleasant scents of the city, from the whiff of dirty water to the harsh scent of coal smoke, he knew it was real—London, 1853, everything.

He wandered around the roof. There were none of the air conditioning units he remembered from Chicago roofs, of course, but there were vents of various kinds. And lots of chimneys, skylights, and cisterns, which were basically huge wood and metal buckets on stilts with copper pipes dropping out of them and into the roof.

It was a big roof, which made sense. It was a big building, covering most of an entire, irregularly shaped block. Mick had already forgotten most of the names of the surrounding streets, but he remembered the street on the shortest side was Little Castle, which was a fun name. And accurate—the Institute really was a little castle. There was even a turret on the opposite edge of the building. The parts of the block not covered by the main Institute building were covered by its garden, its separate kitchens, a pair of service alleys notched into the main building, and a standalone building that Leech had said was the servants' quarters. People had told him the Institute had fewer servants than most buildings of its size and prestige, but it still apparently needed a pretty big building for them.

Mostly, the Institute and its related buildings were themselves the barrier against the outside world, but at the edge of the property beyond the garden, on either side of the servants' quarters, was a tall, slick stone wall topped with iron spikes. On the nearer part of the wall was a pair of iron gates, a small one for people, a bigger one for carriages and wagons. Beyond that wall, on the other side of the street, a tall, skinny building ran across the width of the entire block, presenting a flat, window-less face to the Institute. Leech said the building was home to the laundry that did the Institute's washing, the butcher that provided meats to its kitchens, and all sorts of other businesses, everything from lawyers to accountants to a coffee house and even some offices connected to something called "the Project" that was somehow related to the Institute.

Mick's explorations brought him to the thigh-high stone wall at the inside edge of the roof, where he could survey the garden and the gates. The carriage gate was open while an undersized young wagoner and some kids from the kitchens were unloading a wagon, but Mick knew from Leech that the gates were usually locked, so he probably couldn't go out that way. He might be able to slide down one of the drainpipes to the service alleys. But he'd *really* need to get out before he tried that. It was a long way down.

Maybe he could climb the carriage gate, using its iron bars like a ladder? It was pretty tall, though.

"Plotting your escape already?" asked a voice behind him.

Mick stepped away from the edge and turned around. It was Miss Emmet.

"Not really," he said.

She gave a gentle humph. "Have you selected a name yet, young sir?"

"Mitchell Gunn. But kids are starting to call me Gunner."

"You could do worse," she said. "So, Mr. Gunn, if you aren't planning an escape, why are you up here?"

"Trying to figure a way out, miss. But not to escape. Just to, well, to know a way out, I guess. In case there's a fire or something."

"Or something, indeed," she said. "Most wise, Mr. Gunn." She tilted her head at him. "Have you found your escape route?"

Mick shook his head.

She smiled. "Well, if there's ever an actual fire, you will use the fire escape just over there," she said, pointing to the corner of the Institute opposite the carriage gate. "It leads to the Little Castle service alley. Or perhaps the one, there, that leads to the Charles Place service alley. But lowering a fire escape causes a frightful clamor. Far too noisy for someone seeking to … not escape. Some students have been known to climb the carriage gate. I couldn't do so until I was some years older than you appear to be, but I was a small girl and never an acrobat. I didn't tell you that, by the way. Students are prohibited to exit the Institute without permission, and a respectable librarian such as myself would never discuss doing so."

Mick nodded to show he understood.

"You know the main doors, of course?" she asked.

He nodded again.

"The keys for the boys' and girls' doors and corresponding gates are hung on large hooks beside the duty wardens' doors, and the wardens and Mr. James protect them most jealously. There are no other doors in the student wings, I'm afraid, except those leading to the garden. In case of a fire, a student could break a window on the ground floor. Or even the first floor. But there are no other *doors*."

She'd made a big deal out of emphasizing "doors" and was now holding his gaze with her eyebrows raised.

"Is there some way out that isn't a door?" he asked.

"What an extremely clever question that of course I cannot

answer, being a very respectable librarian. Changing the topic altogether and merely making idle conversation, I find myself reflecting on performing sanitation duties when I was a student —that's 'dumpwaiter duties' among the children today, I believe."

Mick blushed slightly.

"When I was a girl, Headmistress Potts relished assigning sanitation duties to students who displeased her."

"Miss North wasn't the headmistress?" Mick asked.

"Dear me, no. Miss North was a student then as well, and then a don, of course. Anyway, most, ah, muck ends up in the chromium steel tanks hidden over there, and the night soil man takes it away in his cart." Miss Emmet pointed toward the far side of the garden at a squat, rounded building with a tin roof that poked above an arc of tall hedges. "We use some for fertilizer, so do avoid frolicking in that compost pile beside that unattractive shed."

Excellent advice, Mick thought.

"But before the muck reaches the tanks and the night soil man, much of it goes down to the cellars by dumbwaiter. Your namesake James Gunn wisely wished to create healthful air currents to and from the cellars, to prevent noxious miasmas, and of course to make the cellars a little less fragrant. Thus, throughout the cellars are a number of vents of varying sizes that communicate with the outside. When I was a girl, one could clamber into a particular large vent that opens onto the Little Castle service alley. Of course there's a grille covering it, but some dreadful children found the grille rather easy to unlatch from the inside. And after you've returned and are safely out of the vent, you can latch it again. If you're a dreadful child, of course," she said, raising her eyebrows conspiratorially.

"Dreadful," Mick said solemnly.

She grinned at him. "And now I fear I must return to my duties. And you ought to come with me, as you aren't permitted to be up here alone. Though, with favorable breezes, it is a pleasing spot to get a breath of fresh air. And on a clearer day, one can see the city spread out in all its squalid glory."

"I should close the window. To my room." Then he remembered how he was supposed to show respect. "Miss."

"Ah, of course. Return here afterward."

After Mick did so, Miss Emmet led him through a door that she locked behind them and then down a steep, narrow flight of stairs where something banged against the wall from the other side.

"The dumpwaiter," she explained.

They went down some more stairs until they reached the library's floor. "Here we part ways, young sir. But this stairway will take you down to the cellars." She then gave him directions to the vent she'd told him about. "Just to be absolutely certain that you don't accidentally slide out that vent," she said, winking.

"Yes, miss," Mick said, putting on his best attending-holiday-Mass face.

Hardly getting lost at all, Mick found the vent, which turned out to be in a half-hidden room coated with dust and cobwebs. In the dim light creeping through the dirty windows near the ceiling, Mick could see the vent, which was basically a big circle in the wall between the high, barred windows. There was a sturdy set of mostly empty shelves beneath it, which Mick used as a ladder until he was staring straight at the vent. Like Miss Emmet had said, there was a heavy grille, but it had hinges on one side, so Mick just swung it open. Although it was the sort of ancient ironwork that should have creaked creepily, it made no sound. Maybe kids had been spraying the 1853 version of WD-40 on it so they could sneak out.

Mick clambered into the vent and pulled the grille shut behind him with his toes. He couldn't latch it that way, but he didn't want to lock himself out anyway. The vent itself turned out to be made out of some dense metal. It curved up before dropping down. Mick squirmed until he was resting his belly on a curve, his torso hanging down so that his hands touched the outside grille. From this position, he could unlatch that grille easily and sort of shove it to one side while he slithered down and out like a squishy, slow-motion Slinky.

Mick nervously listened and looked for problems, but nobody stuck a head out of the Institute to yell at him as he carefully got to his feet. He was in an alley, with the Institute rising above him on both sides. In one direction, the alley dead-ended. He trotted the other direction until he reached the mouth of the alley, where there was nothing between him and the city.

Reminding himself that he'd promised not to leave the Institute, he returned to the vent. It was hard work worming his way back in and closing the outside grille behind him, and he thoroughly banged his knees and elbows. But he didn't care.

Back inside, he started to push the inner grille open but jerked his hand back when he heard a rustling sound from the storage room. He remained still, wondering if some teacher was getting something off a dusty shelf. Or just waiting there to bust Mick for sneaking out.

Wondering how much noise he'd been making, he held his breath and peered through the grille. He thought he saw something move and then stop, maybe a person lurking by the door.

Then, maybe, there was movement again. But whatever he saw was shadowy and blocked by shelves, so he couldn't be sure what it was, or even whether it was anything.

He waited a long time, breathing shallowly and staring hard, but there were no more sounds or movements. He pushed open the grille, climbed down the heavy shelves, and crept out of the room.

As he climbed the stairs out of the cellar, he felt better than he had since stepping into the glow-orb. Being able to get out of the Institute wasn't the same thing as being able to get out of 1853, but it was a start, and he felt less like a rat in a trap.

CHAPTER 12

GODDESS OF MEMORY

A few days later, Leech's alarm clock crawled into Mick's skull and clanged until his eyes ached.

When Leech finally turned the alarm off, Mick curled up with the scratchy blanket over his head for a while before reluctantly facing the morning chill. He shoved his instisuit and brogues into his satchel and shoved himself into his condy and mocks.

Mick was still among the worst at concentration and course, but at least he had started to notice some of Miss Mitchell's surprise changes. That day, Miss Paisley was in front of him and, as usual, had a couple nimble moments, including side-stepping a box on wheels that appeared out of nowhere. But she refused to pay attention to Miss Mitchell, so she tripped a couple times over sneaky obstacles and then spent the rest of condy rubbing her knee and shooting nasty glances at Miss Mitchell.

Before dashing off to read something before his tutorial

with Mr. Victor, Leech showed Mick to the Scriptorium, the room where kids wrote their future journals.

Mick wandered around to inspect the room. Like all rooms on the ground floor that Mick had seen, it had high ceilings and a lot of windows. There was a big desk in a corner that formed a triangle with the walls. In the middle of the room, a few heavy armchairs formed a circle, their backs to a huge marble sculpture of a woman in a toga, with a bunch of smaller people clustered at her feet and climbing the toga. At first, Mick thought it was a weird version of Snow White and the seven dwarves. But when he looked closely, he realized the smaller people were toddlers.

"The goddess of memory and her daughters, the nine Muses," said a nearby voice.

Mick looked up to see a little old man closing a heavy door behind the desk. It settled into place, blending invisibly into the wall. The old man began walking toward Mick. "The Muses inspire people to write and study. History, poetry, and so forth. That one's astronomy," he said pointing to a girl holding some marbles in her open hand that were probably supposed to be planets.

Mick liked the man's voice. It was a little raspy and surprisingly deep but also kindly and full of life, much like his eyes. His frizzy gray-white hair, mostly on the sides and the back of his head, seemed to be living a cheerful life of its own.

The old man had reached Mick by then and held out his hand, which Mick shook. "You're Mr. Gunn?"

Mick nodded.

"I'm Mr. Hartnell, the archivist, for my sins." He pointed to one of the walls. "This way, if you please."

Mick followed the old man to the wall, which also turned

out to have several half-hidden doors, identifiable only by their brass knobs. He opened one of them, gesturing that Mick should go in.

Mick stepped into a room hardly bigger than a closet except for being quite tall. Large windows at the very top filled it with light. A sort of deep, thick shelf running from wall to wall served as a desk.

"Sit, sit," Mr. Hartnell said, crowding into the room behind him.

There was only one chair, a battered wooden thing that looked like it belonged on a curb with a "FREE" sign taped to it. The desk was equally battered, little grooves and dips worn into its top by years of wrists and elbows.

"Shuffle over a bit, if you will," Mr. Hartnell said.

Mick moved his chair over so Mr. Hartnell had space to stand beside him. The old man lifted the strap of his worn satchel over his head and then set it on the desk.

Mr. Hartnell produced a metal box that he set on the desk with a solid thunk. From an inside pocket of his jacket, he extracted a small metal key attached to an iron ball and handed it to Mick. The iron ball was surprisingly heavy.

"Don't lose the key. There's no copy."

Mick nodded.

"Forty-seven," Mr. Hartnell said, pointing to the key, the ball, and then the box. "047" was stamped on each. "Do remember that to spare me digging out the ledger. That ledger is beastly heavy, and its lock is surely possessed by malign spirits."

Mick nodded again.

"That was a jest about the malign spirits," Mr. Hartnell said. "This new building is much too full of light, marble, and mathematics to countenance the supernatural. The old building, now, that had a bit of puckish magic to it. Puck was a right bastard, mind. Counterfeit crabs, kicked stools, missing journals, and the rest. We're better off without him, in the main."

Mick knew most of the words Mr. Hartnell had just used, but he wasn't sure he understood any of the ideas. He had no idea what any of it had to do with hockey, for starters. But it seemed like the sort of thing that he could nod at without needing to understand.

"No, in this building," the old man continued, shaking his head disapprovingly, "when you find books scattered about and doorknobs scratched and dented, you can rest assured that the culprit is not a mischievous fairy. Open your box, if you will."

Mick turned the key in the lock and lifted the lid. Inside was a thick, plain black notebook. At Mr. Hartnell's instruction, he flipped through it to make sure its pages were blank.

When Mick had finished flipping, Mr. Hartnell said, "That is now your journal."

Mick had expected the journal to look like the ones in the Room of Future Present. Mr. Hartnell saw his expression and asked him to explain. Mick told him about helping Miss Emmet shelve the books.

The old man nodded. "A true librarian's soul, our Miss Emmet," he said. "But the future journals you saw in that room aren't the original journals, and the copies look different to the originals. Here in the Scriptorium, we safeguard journals that are still being written. Once completed, journals are locked deep in the Vault until enough time has passed that they describe the past rather than the future. And then they are copied out, and those copies are stored in safe places, including the Room of Future Present, whilst the originals go back to a slightly less deep part of the Vault."

Mr. Hartnell showed him how to use a dip pen. Unsurprisingly, it required dipping. Specifically, Mick dipped the pointy steel pen into an inkwell and then wiped the extra ink off on the inkwell before scratching out a few words and then doing it all again. Once he had mostly stopped dropping globs of ink and accidentally poking the pointy pen through the paper, Mr. Hartnell pronounced him ready to begin writing his journal.

"What should I write?" Mick asked.

"At the center of the first page—just here," Mr. Hartnell said, pointing, "write your newly chosen name in full and the date of your late point—day, month, and year. Ensure that all of it, especially the year of your late point, may be easily read. And do write out the name of the month, in letters, not numbers. And of course, do *not* include your real name, on this page or anywhere else." He raised his eyebrows to check that Mick understood. Mick nodded. "Good, good," the archivist continued. "After that, you ought to write anything you remember about the future. The aperture you came through. Any way-worlds through which you passed. Describe them for other people, not for yourself. If you can write, 'It was twice as tall as me, and I'm—' How tall are you?"

"Four-seven," Mick said.

"So, ideally you would say, 'It was about twice as tall as me, and I'm four foot seven.' That's much better than 'it was taller than me' and not saying how much taller or how tall you are. And when you are unsure about something, say so. Honest, clear, and exact. Honest, clear, and exact, my boy, first and always. Virtues in life, virtues in journals. Describe what people eat, where they find shelter, how they stay warm. Describe the roads, the entertainments, the clothes, the books, how information is recorded, how conversations happen, any of that. Who runs the world, who runs your city. How people travel from one place to another."

"So … everything," Mick said.

The old man laughed merrily. "Correct, milad. We're trying to figure out if the future can change, you see. So we want people to remember everything. You can't really do it wrong, so long as you do your utmost to be …" He looked at Mick expectantly.

"Honest, clear, and exact?" Mick guessed.

"Just so," Mr. Hartnell said with a grin.

"And nobody will read it until—" he stopped. He'd almost said "2024." "Until the year I stepped into the alley?"

"The following year, to be exact."

"And honest and clear?" Mick asked.

With a smile, Mr. Hartnell showed Mick how to latch the door once he was alone in the writing room and insisted that he do so to protect his journal's secrecy. Mick was supposed to write until the hour struck and then lock his journal in the box before unlatching the door.

And so, Mick tried to write everything he could remember about the glow-orb, the buck, the scared rabbit, the plunges into cold and confusing waters, and all the rest.

He managed to push the pen's steel nib slowly and blotchily across the journal's thick pages all the way to seeing Alison's, Dolly's, and Leech's shoes in the stinky alley. When the clock struck quarter till, he started writing about the future. He wrote about ballpoint pens and wireless keyboards and voice recognition, all of which were better than the stupid stab pen and gloopy ink. Then it was time to lock the journal in the surprisingly heavy box, unlatch the door, and walk to Mr. Hartnell's desk.

"Safely locked?" the archivist asked, taking the heavy box and shaking it to confirm that the notebook was inside. "Good lad."

Mr. Hartnell rose from his chair and walked a short distance along the wall. He placed a key in a discreet keyhole and turned it. To Mick's surprise, a section of wood paneling folded out, revealing a bank of metal drawers that looked a lot like the safety deposit boxes in a heist movie. Each drawer was just big enough to contain the box that had Mick's journal inside it. Mr. Hartnell locked the drawer and then closed and locked the paneling too.

It seemed like a lot of trouble for a bunch of kids' journals. Mick was pretty sure the only people who might care about his journal were his family, and they'd never get to read it. Mick realized that if he couldn't get back home, then as soon as his family realized he was missing, they would think he'd only been gone for a day, then a week, then a month and so on and that he might come back at any minute. But, really, he would be long dead, nothing of him left but a fake name on an old headstone in a London graveyard that they'd never be able to connect to him.

He realized he'd been staring blankly at the paneling and blinked a few times.

"Back from your brown study?" the archivist asked.

"My what?" Mick asked.

"A daydream, but a gloomy one."

"Oh," Mick said. "I was wondering why all the locks for kids' journals."

The old man breathed out, a slow and thoughtful process

that made his cheeks shake slightly. "Knowing the future, even scraps of it, even shards of it mixed higgledy-piggledy among heaps of nonsense, as it is in children's journals, well… That can give one real power. And wicked people who want power are willing to hurt others to get it. No need to tempt the wicked. Now then, young sir, this has been a pleasure, but I've other duties, as, I'm sure, do you."

Telling grown-ups that you didn't have anything to do quickly turned into having a bunch of chores, so Mike just nodded and walked out, trying to look like a kid with lots of other duties. On the stairway, he passed a few kids who checked their pocket watches to avoid making eye contact. Maybe if he wanted to look busy, he should get a pocket watch.

Or he could do what some kid did while Mick was in the hallway on the way to visit Miss Weathers in the nursery—just duck out of sight in one of the alcoves for the busts of half-important people gathering dust in an unused hallway before Mick could even see who it was. If nobody could see you, you didn't have to look busy.

Leech was already teasing Mick that he went to visit Miss Weathers so often because he had a crush on her, but the truth was that Mick just found her relaxing. She reminded him of Tía Verónica—smart, serious, happy to tell him about gross diseases, and not vampire pale.

The toddlers were asleep, lying still on little cots by the window. They were clumped in a pleasant patch of sunshine, like cats in old-fashioned clothes. Mick giggled a little.

Miss Weathers was sitting in her usual chair, lost in a heavy book. "A pleasure to see you, Mr. Gunn," she said without looking up. It was spooky how she did that.

"You can call me Gunner. It might even keep kids from giving me some stupid nickname."

"Simply because they try to give you a stupid nickname doesn't mean you must accept it."

"Do you have a nickname?" Mick asked.

"Years ago, some children tried to give me one. I declined."

"That worked?"

"My refusals occasionally took the form of fists to the throat," she said blandly.

"Like, *fists* fists?"

"Only until they stopped using the nickname," she said. "Which was no time at all." Her accent changed, and she suddenly sounded very different. "There are some hard weans in Queen Victoria's London I'd not wish to cross, but you'll not find them inside these walls."

Mick made a mental note not to call Miss Weathers names.

He sat with her for a while, enjoying not having to talk. But eventually he got fidgety and returned to the vent in the basement that led outside. He squirmed in and out of the building several times. He felt better now that he could do it pretty smoothly and not hurt himself much. They said he couldn't leave 1853. If he really was stuck in the past, he didn't really want to leave the Institute. But he wanted the option. His time alley had taught him that he couldn't always control where—or when—he went, but it had also taught him that he'd definitely rather have control than not.

CHAPTER 13

A REMARKABLE ALLEY SIGHT

Over the next few weeks, Mick settled into something like a routine. Leech's horrible alarm clock would wake them both, and they would go to condy, except some Sundays, when Leech went to Mass at St. Clare's. Leech mostly didn't go to Mass. He was always saying that religion was "a heap of twaddle." But then sometimes he'd get up early and go to St. Clare's because religion was *his* heap of twaddle. Mick's mom had basically done that too. She'd made fun of the archbishops and complained about creeper priests until suddenly she was bringing Emilia home from getting baptized and daring his dad to say something about it. A lot of kids went to church more regularly than that, though. In 1853, people went to church all the time. The Vicar gave an Anglican sermon in the Institute's spacious chapel for anybody who wanted, like Dolly and Alison. There were other services at the Institute for different religions. You could also go somewhere else. Some students went to All Souls, the largest nearby church.

Students didn't have to go to condy daily, and at a certain point, it apparently became optional or maybe semi-optional for students who got good enough, especially girls for some reason. But that was a long way off for Mick, who went to condy at least once a day, even on the weekends, when he didn't have to go at all. Eventually, he started to get better at concentration and course and didn't feel as embarrassed in front of Allison, Dolly, and Leech. He even started having enough energy left over to enjoy soccer. Pretty soon he was better at concentration and course than Miss Paisley, which he decided was a victory because she'd been at the Institute almost two years.

After condy, he took horrible cold showers and ate tasty hot breakfasts. Then he usually went to the Scriptorium to write in his future journal, which he mostly liked because it gave him time to think, though sometimes thinking about the future made him a bit homesick. And Mr. Hartnell was always cheerful, even the day that the Scriptorium was closed because some idiot had tried to open its outer door with the wrong key and jammed the lock.

If Mick had free time after writing in his journal, he'd explore the Institute a bit more, maybe visit Miss Weathers or Miss Emmet. At first, visiting Miss Weathers in the nursery had the perk of letting him use a particular egg-shaped mirror on a cabinet near the windows. It had a stand that let Mick swivel it up or down, and it was clearer than the other mirrors he'd found, so he could use it to check on the alley rat glow behind his ice tea eyes. With some people, like Miss Paisley, the glow was so faint that Mick sometimes wasn't sure it was there. With others, like the Vicar, Miss North, or (especially) the fake flower girl, Miss Atkinson, it was so bright it should have shone through their eyelids when they blinked. His own glow seemed really bright too. For a while, every time he went to the nursery, he checked to see if it was getting brighter or dimmer. But he stopped after Miss Weathers made fun of him for supposedly flirting with his own reflection.

Most days, though, he didn't have any free time after writing in his journal because he had tutorials. Lots of tutorials. Because he wouldn't be on a normal schedule until Trinity term started, his tutorials were unofficial, scheduled at the convenience of the professors and designed to get him up to speed on certain basics. His tutorials were often with Miss North, sometimes with Miss Emmet, and occasionally with another random professor, including the scary Mr. Victor.

Miss North was the most no-nonsense teacher Mick could imagine. She didn't care whether he was right or wrong. She didn't care whether he was happy or sad. She only cared whether he focused on his lessons. And if he didn't, she'd give him a look that terrified him every bit as much as Mr. Victor did. Maybe more.

Luckily, it was usually easy to pay attention to Miss North. She mostly talked about interesting things. She started with a history of alleys and alley rats, and time travel history was more fun than regular history. Mick learned about the founding of the various schools with various names that eventually became the Institute. The schools had started in 1592 in a little house at the outskirts of London, and then in 1652 it had gotten a slightly bigger house slightly closer to the center of London. Then came "generous patronage of Edward Forsyth," starting soon after the Collapse that let the school take over a large building not far from Big Ben and the Houses of Parliament. Finally, in 1806, the Project had taken over that building, and the school had moved to the current building and had been renamed for Edward Forsyth.

After taking care of the history, Miss North's lessons focused on how time alleys worked, which Mick knew he needed to learn about so he could go back home. Sure, everybody kept *saying* it was impossible to travel forward in time at all and extra impossible to avoid the birth flame in order to return to his real life. But they also kept admitting nobody really *knew* anything. Mick didn't intend to take "no" for an answer from people who admitted they didn't know the answer.

To teach Mick to recognize various forms of time alley apertures, Miss North relied on *Broome's Taxonomy*, an oversized book of beautiful color pictures that were painted by hand because there weren't any color photographs in 1853. Mick doubted apertures would show up in photographs anyway. If you could photograph apertures, he'd have seen pictures of them all over social media—no way that wouldn't go viral. Because each copy of *Broome's* was hand-painted, no copy had exactly the same pictures. The glow-orbs in Miss North's copy were crisper than the ones in Miss Emmet's, and the fairy paths in Mr. Victor's a little yellower. Much the same was true for *Clayton's Supplemental*, a smaller book that added to, and sometimes argued with, *Broome's*.

Sometimes, usually around lunchtime, Mick got to go outside with Leech. Mick wasn't yet allowed to go on regular patrol (patrol without an adult present), but Leech was helping him get used to the non-time alley parts of 1853 London. How to walk without getting run over by carriages. How to hail a cab or pay for the omnibus. What people's clothes (and horses, and carriages, and houses) told you about what they did for a living and who their parents were. He was slowly learning to tell which accent was which, though he wasn't close to being able to imitate any of them. Sometimes, the Institute gave Leech enough money to buy them lunch on the street, usually a hot baked potato or some bread, and Mick was getting good enough with 1853 coins to handle the purchases.

After lunch, Mick had more tutorials, usually with Miss Emmet in her office or one of the library's back rooms. She often left him alone to look at *Broome's* and *Clayton's*, though sometimes she made him sort books while she lectured on history or London or alleys. Sometimes she even snuck him a little sliver of something sweet that one of her student "spies" had bought in a shop.

One day, he was with Miss Emmet, shoving a last bit of shortbread into his mouth, when Dolly appeared, her face excited.

"Aperture expected in"—she checked her pocket watch—"eighty-six minutes. Miss North says we're to greet it. You too, Gunner."

Miss Emmet waved Mick on his way. After changing, he and Dolly went down to the lobby. Alison was already there, and Leech sprinted across the lobby so that he arrived several seconds before Miss North.

Miss North scanned them briefly and continued toward the girls' door without breaking stride. Alison and Dolly followed her, and Mick and Leech trotted out the boys' door and met them on Little Castle.

Someone had already hailed a cab for them. In the cab, Miss North and Alison faced forward, the others backward. Once the carriage was rolling, Miss North said, "Miss March, if you please."

"Fairy Eight," Alison said. "Greens and blues. Signs since half twelve. Aperture quarter past three."

She was speaking quietly and omitting as many words as possible to make it harder for eavesdroppers to understand. *Hyde's Practical* recommended that, though Mick doubted it was necessary that day. He could barely hear her over the clopping and clattering from horses and the wheels. The cabbie would have needed wolves' ears.

The cab soon deposited them at their destination, a couple blocks from where the aperture was supposed to appear. The neighborhood seemed a little seedy but not terrible. The 1853 London version of Uncle Dan's neighborhood, maybe.

"Now, Gunner," Leech said as they walked, "if it turns out to be a horse kick alley, do be sure to get as close as possible so that you can see all the phenomena."

Mick rolled his eyes. He wasn't falling for that one. Even he knew that horse kick alleys were extremely rare and mostly invisible. Usually, the only visible part of a horse kick alley was a hazy frame that appeared right before it opened. Of course, even if alley rats didn't see a horse kick alley, they would find out it was there just before it closed, when it sent out a shock-wave. The shockwave only affected alley rats, but if they got close enough to a powerful enough alley, the shockwave could knock them over or even knock them out.

After a couple blocks, the group turned the corner, and Mick saw the shimmer of an aperture starting to form in an overgrown lot between a house and a pawnshop.

Miss Atkinson, the greet who had been at Mick's first alley, was standing across the street from the aperture. She was wearing her dirty flower girl disguise, begging people to buy her limp bouquets as they dodged past her on the sidewalk. No, on the "pavement," Mick reminded himself. Miss Atkinson was also doing a good job pretending not to see the huge, hypnotic rectangle glowing in the vacant lot across the street. The other three members of her greet team, all about her size and age, were standing on the far sidewalk, just a few yards away from the aperture, with their backs to it. Unlike Miss Atkinson, they were dressed respectably.

As Alison had previewed, the aperture was a mix of greens and blues, faint but slowly getting brighter. It lay flat on the ground, which meant that Alison had also been right that it was a fairy path. It was a big one, which made sense since it was supposed to become an Eight. Mick now knew that apertures went from One to Ten, Ten being the largest. Apparently there was a lot of argument over how big each size really was. Apertures weren't easy to measure, since they usually grew as they opened. But for fairy paths, the rule of thumb was a foot longer and half a foot wider for every size you went up. So a fairy One was about a foot long and six inches wide, which meant it wouldn't produce any droppers unless actual rats started time-traveling. But it wouldn't take long to squeeze a kindergarten class through a fairy Ten.

Mick thought the aperture was starting to "frame up" (grow a solid border), though he wasn't totally sure. According to the books, a lot of the times an aperture didn't frame up until a few minutes before opening, and they usually didn't open until they were full size. But it was far enough along that he heard the familiar song and felt the familiar tug—the desire to step toward it. Into it.

He asked Leech what time it was.

"Still about ten minutes," Leech said.

"Alison was right," Mick whispered.

"About what?" Leech asked.

Mick shrugged. "Colors. Magnitude. Time of aperture," he said.

Leech gave him an odd look.

"Describe what you see, Mr. Gunn. Quietly," Miss North said. "Cross here, children," she said loudly. "To the milliner's."

Mick knew better than to stare at the aperture while they were crossing the street. That would be too obvious. Also, he'd probably trip over a loose cobble. Everyone said the streets of London were dangerous, and it turned out that included the actual, physical streets and their treacherous cobblestones. Once they had crossed the street and taken up position about thirty or forty feet from the aperture, the kids turned to face the aperture. Miss North stood next to Mick but turned mostly away from the aperture, pretending to look for something coming up the road.

Trying not to stare too obviously, Mick described it all to Miss North. It was better not to stare, anyway. It was bright enough to hurt his eyes a little if he stared, and the closer he looked, the more it called out to him with a song that hummed right inside him. No wonder he'd reached into the glow-orb back in Chicago.

"And that is all quite clear to you?" Miss North asked when he'd finished describing everything.

"All except the frame," Mick said. "That's a little fuzzy—wait." The fairy path now had a clear frame, dark blue with little sparks of white and yellow shimmering inside it. "No. It's framed up for sure." It was quite beautiful.

"When did you first notice the aperture?" Miss North asked.

Mick shrugged. "When we turned the corner." It was taking a lot of willpower not to walk straight into the fairy path.

The other kids were staring at him.

"Miss Tee?" asked Miss March. "Do you concur?"

"I don't—well... I suppose, as much as ..." She trailed off, looking flustered.

Mick wondered if Dolly was trying not to say that he was being an idiot. But Dolly was a balls-and-strikes kind of kid—if you were being dumb, she'd say it, just like she'd say if you were being smart. Besides, if he'd been that wrong, Leech definitely would have made some joke already. But Leech was just looking slowly back and forth between Mick's face and the aperture.

"What?" Mick asked him.

Alison asked him a couple questions about things he'd said, and Mick realized she was taking notes. He blushed a little—that meant she thought what he was saying was important. You weren't supposed to take notes outside the Institute about anything involving time-travel unless it was important, and even then the notes had to be in a coded shorthand that Mick hadn't learned yet.

Suddenly, the fairy path shimmered all over and then grew almost dull again, just before a bright line began running up and down its length, getting faster each time, like when his Uncle Dan's scanner had lost control right before burning out. Mick started to step toward it, but Leech grabbed his arm.

The path went dull and lifeless, like a sullen tarp, and Mick thought it had died out. But then it flared back alive like the finale of a fireworks show, so bright that Mick closed his eyes and turned away.

When he opened them again, the aperture was gone. Once the fireflies had cleared out of his vision, he could see a dropper who hadn't been there before: a mostly naked kid with long, blond hair, sitting on the grass, hugging his or her knees. Knowing that sometimes alley rats died during the drop, Mick held his breath until he saw the kid's head move side to side warily as Miss Atkinson's greet team slowly moved closer.

Miss North waited until the greets had helped the kid struggle into an overcoat and stand up. Then she nodded to herself and stopped pretending to be looking down the road. She turned and began walking back the direction they had come from.

Mick and the others fell in behind her. A heavy carriage clattered along the otherwise quiet street, dull and black like the inside of a sack. As it passed, Mick realized it was the Institute's own carriage. He risked a quick look over his shoulder and saw the greets helping the new dropper into the carriage.

After walking five or ten minutes—Mick was really starting to want a pocket watch—they hailed a cab as well. It was a boring ride because Miss North wouldn't let them speak. Back at the Institute, Miss North took Alison's notes and told Mick to follow her to her office.

Wondering what he'd done wrong, Mick followed Miss North upstairs. He soon found himself sitting in front of her desk, weighed down by the dour stares of the former head-mistresses on the wall behind her while he dipped the flat blade of a pen into an inkwell and scratched out everything he could remember about the fairy path. A few ink-smudged moments later, he handed the paper to Miss North, who compared it with Alison's notes.

"You saw all these details?" she asked him, gesturing to his notes and Alison's.

Mick nodded.

"And the line that"—she looked at Mick's notes—"swung

back and forth just before everything went dark for a second.' How rapid were its movements, would you say?"

"Slow at first, like…" he looked up at the portrait of the grim-faced, white-haired headmistress hanging over Miss North's shoulder. "Like, if that painting was the fairy path, at the start, the line went from the top to bottom maybe this fast." He raised his finger slowly from the bottom of the picture to the top. "But right before it went dark, it was going too fast for me to be sure it was even moving, you know?"

Miss North gave a thoughtful "humph" and looked back and forth between Alison's neat pencil notes and Mick's messy ink notes. Then she closed her eyes for a long time.

"Miss North?" he asked.

Eyes still closed, she raised her index finger, holding it in the air, her elbow resting on the desk.

Mick waited quietly. Then waited some more.

Just as he was starting to wonder if Miss North had fallen asleep, her eyes opened and her hand lowered to the desk. "Mr. Gunn, I trust that you're being altogether honest with me as to what you can see."

"I am," Mick said. He knew he sounded annoyed, but he didn't care.

Miss North nodded. "And you're not straining to be helpful? Saying that you're certain that you saw something when actually you only *might* have seen it?"

"I'm not making stuff up," Mick said, even more annoyed. "It was right there. Everybody saw it. You can't make stuff up if everybody's looking right at it."

Miss North chuckled. "And yet many do, often with great success."

"Not me," Mick said.

Miss North smiled slightly at him. "I believe you, Mr. Gunn. I just need to be certain. You know, of course, that some have better alley sight than others?"

Mick nodded.

"For example, some in our party didn't see the frame at all."

Mick stared at her. "No way." That was like... like... not seeing the big ugly gold frame on the portrait behind Miss North.

"Miss Atkinson slipped her notes to Miss March, and I can report that of all of us, only Miss Atkinson saw a line of light. She did not see it so clearly as you. She said that there was a moving blur, followed by a flickering of sorts. And Miss Atkinson may have the most acute alley sight at the Institute."

"Is that good or bad?" Mick asked. "That I saw all that stuff."

Miss North laughed. "On balance, I rather think it's for the good. It's usually better to have a talent than not, and you certainly appear to have a rare talent."

Mick had never had a rare talent. He was good at some things, especially school. But he wasn't great at anything. It would be pretty cool to be great at something for a change.

"However," Miss North said, emphasizing it hard enough that Mick figured his face had shown his thoughts, "we shall need to test your abilities further. And I shouldn't wish you to —" She broke off at a knock at the door. "Enter," she called.

It was Alison. "The Vicar asked me to fetch Mr. Gunn if it's quite convenient."

"Certainly. Thank you, Mr. Gunn. Miss March, do please inform the Vicar that Mr. Gunn's observations appear to be quite accurate."

Mick and Alison went next door to the solarium, and Alison tugged the thin bronze bell pull. The Vicar's muffled voice said to enter. Alison put her hand on the knob but didn't turn it. She put her other hand on Mick's forearm then seemed to think for a moment. Eventually, she whispered, "Did you really see all of that? About the alley?"

Mick nodded.

She nodded thoughtfully. "I suppose it will all turn out for the best." But she didn't sound convinced.

Chapter 14

The Hoodie Ghost

I n the solarium, the Vicar was standing side by side with someone at the big table, both of them leaning over the map of London with their backs to Mick.

"Vicar," Alison called out.

The Vicar turned to face them. Then so did the other person, a girl with extremely bright alley rat eyes. Miss Atkinson. There was no sign of her flower girl disguise, and her instisuit was crisp and clean. *She must change clothes really fast.* Mick would still be fighting with his shirt. *Wait... Yep, that was her.* Seeing Miss Atkinson in her instisuit, he realized that she was also the dark-haired girl who'd whispered to Miss Mitchell during condy not long after he'd first gotten to the Institute.

The Vicar and Miss Atkinson were both staring at him, their heads tilted slightly. He wondered if they knew that they matched.

Alison looked at the Vicar. "Miss North said to tell you that Mr. Gunn's account of the aperture was quite accurate."

The Vicar and Miss Atkinson seemed to realize that they'd been staring. They both straightened their necks, and the Vicar smiled kindly.

"Thank you, Miss March. And thank you for joining us, Mr. Gunn."

The Vicar led them to the sofa and chairs by the fireplace, where there was tea in thin cups and cookies on fragile plates because it was the Vicar and it was London. Mick had to admit that tea was growing on him, and he was already a fan of the cookies. The biscuits. Whatever he was supposed to call them.

After tea and a chat, the Vicar let Alison leave. She looked a little relieved.

The Vicar led Miss Atkinson and Mick back to the big table, where he had them try to find a good match for that afternoon's fairy path in *Broome's*. They stood, shoulder to shoulder, flipping through the big pages. Miss Atkinson lingered on a couple that weren't terrible matches. But Mick knew they weren't right. They didn't have the little stars in the frame. Miss Atkinson eventually reached the same conclusion.

"You seem quite definite in your assessments, Mr. Gunn," the Vicar said when Mick and Miss Atkinson had finished looking. "Even more than our Miss Atkinson, who is one of the most definite young people I have encountered in a long career of rather definite young people."

Miss Atkinson nodded slightly, as if to say that she was confident for a reason.

Mick shrugged.

"Well, we shall have to consider adding a note to the appendix, shan't we, Miss Atkinson? Truth be told, it's well past time the Society set the plates on another edition."

Mick knew from a book his dad had written that an

appendix wasn't just an organ nobody needed. It was also something that you stuck at the end of a book. "An appendix to what?" he asked.

"*Clayton's Supplemental*," Miss Atkinson said.

"Mr. Clayton won't mind?" Mick asked. "Or is he dead?" Most of the books at the Institute sounded like they'd been written a thousand years earlier by thousand-year-old people.

Miss Atkinson and the Vicar both chuckled.

"What?" Mick asked.

The Vicar smiled kindly. "I am Mr. Clayton," he explained. "Each morning I manage to ascertain that I am not deceased."

"I should inform you if you were, Vicar," Miss Atkinson said. Her tone was perfectly sincere, but a smile flickered at the edge of her mouth.

Mick felt that somebody really should have told him the first time they'd given him the book that the Vicar had written it. He tried to remember if he'd said anything mean about it where the Vicar could hear.

"Do sit, children." The Vicar said pointed to the chairs in front of them as he began walking around the table.

Mick sat next to Miss Atkinson. The table was meant for adults, so it almost came up to his collarbones. Still, in the large windows on the other side of the table he had a nice view of a blue sky, wispy with clouds above and wavy with breeze-blown trees below, like a picture of spring in a baby book.

The Vicar sat down across the table from them. "Mr. Gunn, you appear to have a most remarkable alley sight. That will require certain amendments to your studies. You will be obliged to spend rather more time outside the walls than most pupils at your stage of education. This is at once regrettable and necessary."

"Regrettable?" Mick asked.

"You might—reasonably enough—expect that if you busy yourself with additional patrol duties, we would excuse you from some of your studies. Unfortunately, that often will not be possible. Being able to see alleys is useful only if one understands what one sees, and such understanding comes only with study."

Mick sighed. So he was going to get the same homework, just with more chores on top.

The Vicar said, "I shall inform Miss North that adjustments must be made. You will continue to work with Miss March and her team, but you will also find yourself seconded to Miss Atkinson's team, quite frequently, I expect. Understood?"

"Except for what 'seconded' means."

The Vicar smiled. "Temporarily reassigned. Miss Atkinson, does that present problems for you?"

"Provided he's not a hopeless ignoramus, no, sir." She looked at Mick. "We haven't time to nursemaid ignoramuses."

The Vicar laughed merrily, and Miss Atkinson blushed faintly. "I didn't wish to be rude," she said.

Mick nodded. He got where she was coming from.

"Do try not to be a hopeless ignoramus, Mr. Gunn," the Vicar said with a smile. "I'm remembering a very different young boy who was a rather notable ignoramus. Not hopeless, though it was a near-run thing. He had unusually good alley sight too. He was not a fair-featured boy, nor a prodigy of physical or mental feats. But he was a very gifted spotter, which encouraged him to become a piece of puffed-up vanity. He spent several months making a gala of his abilities and refusing to learn a deucèd thing from his professors—or his failures."

"Was it you?" Mick asked. The Vicar seemed too nice to talk about other people that way.

The Vicar nodded. "In a moment of preening witlessness, I very nearly led a dear friend to his death. It is quite a useful thing to see the alleys clearly. But it is also quite a useful thing to have long arms if one must retrieve items from the top shelf in the larder. And having good alley sight or long arms is not a substitute for cleverness or kindness or endeavor."

A little later, Miss Atkinson led Mick out of the solarium toward the Great Hall. Pausing at the top of the stairs, she said, "For me, it was picking apples."

"What?" Mick asked.

"The Vicar's sermon about having long arms. When he gave it to me, it was about apples on high branches. Still, 'tis good advice. You can't learn anything if you think you know everything, and if you can see alleys better than the rest, it's easy to walk around thinking you know everything."

"Is that what you did?"

She nodded. "I was insufferable. Until the third or fourth thrashing, that is."

Mick flashed on his Uncle Dan playing Pro Skater in his boxers. She probably meant a different kind of "thrashing."

Miss Atkinson turned to look at him. "The third or fourth ass-whuppin'," she said, in a surprisingly American accent. Something Southern.

He wondered if she was American too. It was really hard not to ask. Also, he had a hard time picturing her getting beat up.

"Quite a few children were needed to administer the thrashings," she said, her accent back to prim, Vicarish English. "So do avoid being provoking. It leads to thrashings."

"Got it," Mick said.

"On the other hand," she said, smiling, "I've become Day Prefect. Time herself whispers hints about the order of things in my ear, whilst most of my tormentors have left the Institute to eavesdrop on lordlings' halfwit broods or drag their tatty cuffs through inkwells in some windowless counting room. So I am glad to have good alley sight and a properly ordered mind."

Mick hadn't gotten all of that, but he'd understood enough. He smiled back.

"And on that theme, I really must attend to my duties as Day Prefect," she said, turning and starting down the main stairway of the Great Hall.

Mick recognized the tone of somebody bringing the conversation to an end, but he tried to get in a couple more questions. "What's a Day Prefect?" he asked, jogging at her heels as she glided down the stairs.

She tilted her head at him and then smiled. "The student given charge of the daylight greet teams."

"Oh," Mick said. "Is there a Night Prefect, too?"

She shook her head. "Nighttime is the province of the dons. The rest of us generally work in daylight—from dawn till don, if you will."

Leech had tried to explain the dons to Mick a couple times. He'd made them sound like a group of college-age students who spent half their time reading really thick books and the other half doing super-spy stuff. "The dons are, like, nerd ninjas?" Mick asked.

She chortled. "That's a rather good way of phrasing it. Pity it's a connan. I rather expect it would please Clarissa Mitchell."

"Miss Mitchell? The one who teaches condy?"

"The same. She also leads the dons' midnight shift."

They were nearing the second floor. Or the first floor, in

British. "But why is it the dons? Who are in charge of nights, I mean."

Miss Atkinson stopped abruptly at the bottom of the stairway. "Miss North doubtless told you of the terrors of London?"

Mick nodded.

"Do you believe her?"

Mick shrugged. "Sure."

"Well, that's London in the daylight. Imagine it in the dark."

Mick hadn't thought of that. It was spooky enough inside the Institute when everything went to candles and oil lamps, like the whole place was holding a flashlight under its chin to tell a ghost story. He was okay with letting Miss Mitchell handle the ghost stories on the dangerous side of the wall.

Sounding American again, Miss Atkinson said, "Nerd ninjas come in handy when you got a bunch of creeps with razors lurking in the shadows." Then her English accent came back. "Now, pray pardon me whilst I attend to my duties."

She started to go but stopped herself after a half-step. "As you're to be seconded to my team, you should call me Gail. We aren't as formal as some teams. I shall call you Mitchell, unless you object."

"Could you call me Gunner?"

"I could, and I shall. Now, Gunner, I truly must attend to my duties."

After Miss Atkinson—Gail—left, Mick found himself drifting to the library. He picked his way through the newspaper racks and study tables and walked past Miss Harvey, the teenager at the circulation desk, who smiled at him in recognition.

Miss Emmet was in the messy back room where sturdy tables sighed under heaps of books that seemed to be growing toward the ceiling, as if the trees they came from had taken root a second time. She was standing with her back to him, sorting big stacks into smaller stacks, holding one-sided conversations with certain books about whether they were "miserable little bores," "charming little chappies," or "gilded misses with spines of steel." She did this whenever she organized books, and Mick had never heard her repeat a phrase.

Mick stood quietly, enjoying the cheerful little phrases. Sometimes, Miss Emmet reminded him of his mom. Not enough to feel homesick, but enough to feel a little less lonely and scared.

"Here for quidditch?" Miss Emmet asked over her shoulder.

"Huh?" Mick asked. "Pardon me?" he said in proper English.

"Messing about with magical *Broome's*," she said. "Quidditch. *Harry Potter and the Athlete's Foot.*"

Mick laughed. "But isn't that a—"

"Connan?" she asked, looking at him over her shoulder. "Too right it is. Trot about where I can see you, like a civilized youth."

Mick obeyed. As he went, he asked, "But aren't you supposed to not—" Mick paused. He didn't want to sound like he was criticizing. "Not give away your late point and everything?"

"'And everything,'" she quoted in an amused tone. "Two days ago, you announced to me that you were 'here for' a certain page of *Broome's*. Last week when I said that many believe that the capital of China has the most alleys in the world, you asked, 'How come it's Beijing?'"

Mick waited patiently. Although Miss Emmet sometimes seemed to be saying random things, she'd secretly be building to a point. It was like reverse Jenga—dropping blocks into a jumbled pile until everything imploded into a tidy tower.

Maybe that was what she was up to with all the books. Maybe one day, she'd push one last book into one last messy pile, and they'd erupt into a space elevator. Or a time elevator. He realized Miss Emmet was staring at him with one eyebrow raised. He wished he could do that.

"You've no notion what I mean, have you?" she asked.

Mick shook his head.

"A great deal of what alley rats do their first year or two after dropping is a ruddy connan," she said. "And even decades afterward, many shed connans like perspiration on a summer's day. Not great drops, but a visible sheen, nevertheless. And I, milad, can spot a connan like you can see a ring on a Ten. 'And everything' and 'here for' are connans. So is saying 'Beijing' rather than 'Peking.'"

"Oh," Mick said. "Sorry."

She waved her hand. "It can't be helped. And, yes, it's important to minimize one's connans. Reduce their number and, well, their conspicuousness. But, really, that's the best we can hope for—inconspicuous anachronisms. Because there will be anachronisms. We are all of us very much out of time."

Mick thought at first that she meant they had run out of time. Then he realized she meant "out of time" like being out of place—that they were all in the wrong time.

Mick thought that over. "But aren't you—we—supposed to not talk on purpose about Harry Potter and stuff?"

"'And stuff,'" Miss Emmet said, smiling.

Another connan, he assumed. "But aren't we? So people won't know exactly when we come from?"

"We do need to keep quiet about that, at least until we know whom to trust. But the future is also our past, and we must be able to discuss our pasts with others, else we shall all go quite mad. Besides, I never said it was *my* future. There was a girl in my tory, one who had only recently dropped. She took comfort in storytelling, so she told Harry Potter stories to us girls. I was only eight or so, which was the perfect age. She was a rather good storyteller, too, and those stories were ripping good fun that carried us all through a particularly dark and dreary winter. So perhaps I knew the stories before I dropped. And perhaps I didn't."

"I see," Mick said, proud of himself for not saying, "Okay."

Miss Emmet glanced up from her sorting long enough to give him a quick, lopsided smirk. He was pretty sure that she'd somehow heard the "okay" he hadn't said. "*Have* you come for quidditch, then?" she asked.

Mick shook his head. "Not really."

"Well, then, you must have come to help me sort a few hundred books."

Mick sighed. He'd walked right into that one.

Miss Emmet laughed. "I shan't make you sort books if you've come here for another purpose."

"The Vicar and Miss Atkinson say I'm supposed to become a spotter. That's what they're called, right? Spotters?"

Miss Emmet nodded.

"So I think I need to learn about how things work out there. But that book you loaned me is super-boring." He realized that maybe Miss Emmet liked the book. "A little boring, anyway." He blushed.

Miss Emmet winked at him and said, "Mr. Cunningham *is* a little super-boring."

Phew. "So I was thinking," Mick said, "maybe the journals? In the Room of Future Present?"

Miss Emmet smiled and led him to the Room of Future Present, unlocking the door for him before returning to her work. There were a few dozen 1852s, all of them copied from the originals in impressively neat handwriting. He picked some off the shelf and sat down to skim them, quickly setting aside the ones written by little kids who didn't remember anything outside of their own houses and the ones that were all "me, me, me" and no 1852. One seemed promising until he realized it was about Edinburgh. Eventually, he found a good one about London and took it back to one of the big chairs in the middle of the room, where he tugged off his brogues and settled in with his knees against his chest.

Jane Yates, the girl who'd written the journal, was interesting. And she'd been nearly twelve when she'd stepped into a lift alley near the Tower of London, so she remembered 1852 clearly. Her descriptions of 1738 were pretty interesting too, although life back then hadn't been easy, especially for a girl. At some point, her life started to feel real to him, like he was living it. Then he popped out of it, back into the Room of Future Present, and realized he'd been dreaming.

When he'd dozed off, the room had been warm with late afternoon sunlight but now was nearly dark. He could see Miss Emmet gliding along the wall of books, her back to him. She stopped right where he'd taken Jane Yates' journal off the shelf.

But no, Miss Emmet would have been using a lamp. And this person was too small to be Miss Emmet. And was wearing a hoodie. Well, not a hoodie. Whatever an 1853 hoodie was. Gray clothes from top to bottom, including the hood.

Sometimes, when Mick woke halfway in the night, he'd feel

143

like a ghost was hovering at the foot of his bed, and he'd be paralyzed. Even though he'd know it wasn't real, he'd be paralyzed. He'd know that, if he really wanted to, his body still worked. But he somehow couldn't quite make himself move, so he'd either fall back asleep into nightmares or wake up completely, and there'd be nothing there. This felt like that, but when he tried to wiggle his fingers, they moved easily. He was awake.

Which meant there really was somebody standing there.

From far off, Mick heard door hinges creak. The hoodie ghost turned its head toward the noise and then turned its whole body and tiptoed quietly to the door, which was open a crack. The hoodie ghost stuck its face through the crack and squeezed through the door.

Mick stood up and stared, but the hoodie ghost was gone.

Soon after that, Miss Emmet walked through the open door, holding a lantern so that she could read the open book she carried as she walked.

"I think I saw someone here just now," Mick told her. "A student, I think. With no lamp. In a hood."

Miss Emmet looked at him, tilting her head a tiny bit. "And not one of the student aides? Miss Harvey, perhaps?"

"I don't think so, miss. They don't wear hoods, do they?"

"Not as a rule, no. Which way?" she asked. "To the back?"

"Yes."

Miss Emmet set down the book and bustled in that direction, holding the lamp in front of her. Mick caught up and jogged at her heels.

The corridor branched in two. One branch had nothing but locked doors. The other led to the sorting room. Miss Emmet looked around and then moved quickly, almost running, toward the back door. The corridor was empty, however. The key was in the lock, and the door was unlocked.

Frowning, Miss Emmet slowly locked the door.

She led Mick back to the sorting room, asking him more questions about the hoodie ghost, but all he could say was that the person had been wearing gray and looked more like a student than a professor.

She nodded. "Well, goodness knows I snuck about this drafty heap of rooms more than my fair share as a student. But I don't think I ever wore a hood when doing so." She paused. "Isn't it time you attended to your lessons?"

Mick could tell that she was shooing him out so that she could think about the hoodie ghost. So maybe he should think about it, too.

CHAPTER 15

THE SQUAD AND THE SNOBS

A few days later, at the start of Trinity term, Alison, Leech, Dolly, and Mick were gathered around the table finishing lunch while they planned for the afternoon's patrol. It would be the first time Miss North let Mick go on patrol without an adult, so Alison had convinced Miss North to let the team eat lunch in the study attached to Miss North's office while they prepared him.

Leech had somehow gotten his hands on extra lunch, so they were as stuffed full of food as Miss North's study was stuffed with books and maps. Alison was always saying that kids at the Institute ate way better than almost everybody in London, and Mick was definitely never weak from hunger. But that afternoon might have been the first time since dropping in 1853 that he'd felt actually, truly full. He was feeling good about that, and he was feeling even better that he'd finally convinced the others to call their street team "the Squad." They'd needed some sort of name. So many kids at the Institute were on patrol teams that just saying "the team" got confusing.

Mick felt nervous about his first patrol. So all through lunch, even when the rest of the Squad had been goofing off, he'd been studying *Hyde's Practical*. The introduction said the old version had been called *Reade's Practical*, but then in 1851 Elinor Hyde had completely rewritten it. Some older kids still used *Reade's* because they were used to it, but the Squad said Reade was an idiot who would get you into trouble, and a lot of kids said, "Read Hyde; hide Reade."

Hyde's was really useful. In addition to explaining how to spot stirrings and caterwaulings and other alley signs, it explained how London worked. There was even a separate version, called *Wilson's London Guide* (which Elinor Hyde had written under the pen name "E.H. Wilson"). *Wilson's* was an actual tourist guide, without any mention of time-travel, that a lot of arrow visitors to London apparently also used.

Mick was grateful for the guides. Before getting sucked into the shimmer, he had spent a lifetime learning how Chicago worked, how the future worked. And a lot of that was useless in 1853 London. Or worse than useless—confusing or even dangerous. Without even knowing he was doing it, he would get himself in trouble making an assumption based on 2024 Chicago. He'd assume he knew how to walk to the corner without drawing attention. How to buy food at the store. But he didn't, not in 1853 London. There were so many little things that he didn't know that he didn't know, and then suddenly he needed to know them, sometimes urgently. He hated standing on some street full of snorting horses, indignant facial hair, and ye olde shouting while he tried to figure out whether some inexplicable hunk of 1853 was used to peel potatoes or start fires or give psychic commands to llamas.

Hyde's and *Wilson's* gave him some key basics that any arrow Londoner his age would have learned simply by growing up in the right time. Which neighborhoods were fancy and which were dangerous. How to pick good baked potatoes from a cart, how to talk to the police, that sort of thing. The *Wilson's* section on coins had been a lifesaver. In 1853 London, coins were basically the only way to buy anything, and they made no sense. You'd think the penny would be the least valuable coin, but that was actually the half-farthing (eight to the penny). The pound was the English version of the dollar, and there were 240 pennies in a pound because 100 would've made too much sense. And then there were groats and shillings and florins and a bunch of different nicknames for the same stupid coin, and sometimes you said "pence" instead of "penny," and half the time you weren't allowed to say words the way they looked ("twopence" was pronounced "tuppence"). It was like the whole coin system was designed to make you too scared to buy things.

And, if you were a girl, it was like the whole city was designed to make you too scared to leave home. The introduction said Elinor Hyde had rewritten the *Practical* partly to explain how to look and act like a regular girl of the era but still be able to do your job. There was a whole chapter on how to keep your dress from sabotaging you during patrol. Mick was glad he didn't have to worry about dresses. He was still losing battles to his underwear.

One thing he definitely knew he didn't understand was a little section before everything else in *Hyde's*—in nearly every book he'd seen so far in the Institute. The "Disclaimer." It said that the publisher was the Society for Chronal Fancy and that the book was one of many works of fiction by members of the Society. *Wilson's* didn't have it, but it was published by a different publisher and, on the surface, had nothing to do with time travel.

Mick read the Disclaimer aloud to the others as they finished lunch. "It's not all made up though, is it?" he asked. "Time travel?" He felt stupid asking the question aloud. But then, not a day went by that he didn't ask himself whether time-travel was a hoax or a delusion.

"Time travel is quite real," Alison said. "But the Institute puts the Disclaimer at the start of every book it publishes, even the most accurate ones."

"Why?" Mick asked.

"Human nature," Leech said. "In theory, students and professors are forbidden to take books about time travel outside of the Institute without permission."

"Because books like *Hyde's* could reveal our secrets," Alison explained.

"Or embarrass the Institute by making us look like a lunatic asylum rather than a boarding school for the children of gentlemen and members of the professional classes," Leech said. "And the bastard children of the peerage. Mustn't forget them."

"And we're supposed to be two boarding schools, boys and girls," Dolly added. "Of course, that's a lot of botheration, so we don't do it. Except," she added grudgingly, "for the dratted separate entrances."

Mick nodded. The girls' door was only open 10:00-5:00 Monday to Friday, but during those hours, no matter how inconvenient it was, Alison, Dolly, and all the other female students, dons, and professors were supposed to use the door to give arrows the impression that the boys' and girls' schools were a lot more separate than they actually were. Sometimes they ignored that rule, but they ran the risk of getting chewed out. Boys definitely weren't allowed to use the girls' door when it was open.

"To return to Gunner's question," Alison said primly, "even though they oughtn't do, sometimes rats take books about time-travel where an arrow might see them. The Disclaimer protects the Institute in case that happens."

"So," Mick asked, "the books are about real things, but the Disclaimer says they're made up so that people won't think we're crazy?"

The others nodded.

"Is the Society for"—he looked at the Disclaimer again—"Chronal Fancy, is that fake too?"

"It's real," Alison said. "It must be, in case anyone ever investigates. They have offices off Devonshire by Great Ormond. Regular meetings, public lectures, and so forth. The Vicar often attends."

"But why are we talking about the Disclaimer," Leech asked, "when we should be talking about the Mysterious Interloper?" Leech had immediately named the hoodie ghost the "Mysterious Interloper" and had been trying without much success to get the Squad to discuss it at every opportunity. "You're a fortunate fellow, Gunner. All I ever get at the library are headaches."

"Just think how much worse it would be if you actually read a book," Dolly said.

"I'm not foolhardy," Leech said primly. "I'm not going to expose myself needlessly to all those nasty little words."

Alison laughed. It was a clear, warm sound that Mick wasn't sure he had ever heard before. Could that be right? He'd really never heard Alison laugh?

Dolly asked Mick, "You're still certain the intruder—"

"Mysterious Interloper," Leech interjected.

"—the intruder was a student?" Dolly finished asking.

Mick shrugged. "It was pretty dark. But probably. She was too short to be an adult."

"She?" Dolly asked. "It was a girl?"

Mick shrugged. He hadn't really thought about that until that instant, but it seemed right, even though he was pretty sure the Interloper had been wearing trousers, not a skirt.

"I do find it intriguing that Miss Emmet seem troubled about the intruder," Alison admitted. She was lost in thought for a moment before saying, "But we must prepare for this afternoon."

They brushed their lunch crumbs off the table so they could lay out the Plan, the Institute's map of London. There were copies of the Plan throughout the Institute, including small copies in *Hyde's Practical*. Miss North's study had a big version rolled up onto a long stick hanging on the wall, and Alison plucked it down and laid it on one side of the table. Leech and Dolly unrolled it and weighed it down at the edges with little bean bags to keep it from curling back up.

They took Mick through the Plan. After spending a lot of time on the neighborhoods near the Institute, they made him go over London's important bridges, roads, buildings, and neighborhoods. As usual, he did pretty well with stuff near the Institute and with the really important bridges and such but struggled with more distant parts of the Plan.

After Mick finished regular London, Alison made everyone do the Squad's daily alley rat tour of the Plan, especially the alley clusters. The clusters were crucial because time alleys usually appeared somewhere in one of the clusters. From one point of view, London was a big cluster, and so were other huge cities like Peking, Tokyo, Constantinople, and Cairo. The clusters all seemed to be in big cities, though that might just be because nobody was there to see rats who dropped in a forest or a sheep pasture.

Each city had its own clusters. London had between five and fifty, depending which professor was insisting that there was only one reasonable way to count them. Alison made Mick focus on the fifteen or twenty that *Hyde's Practical* said were worth worrying about. He was getting pretty good at the clusters. The basics, anyway. There was some fancy stuff that got more complicated: a few clusters moved around a bit day to day but kept their centers anchored ("twiving"), and some migrated steadily in one direction ("drifting"). But that was minor stuff that streets and greets could ignore, except for Scholar's Playground, which twived up to three hundred yards a day and seemed to have started drifting too.

Learning the clusters would have been easier if the names made more sense. Each cluster had an official name, but people, especially kids, often used nicknames instead. Most of the nicknames sounded like jokes: "Figgy Pudding," "Work to Death," "Mrs. Grundy's Parlor," and so on. (And some *were* jokes because Leech kept inventing nicknames like "Her Majesty's Derrière" just to mess with Mick.) Sometimes you could figure out the nicknames by looking at the Plan. Figgy Pudding got its name from being near Fig Lane. Work to Death's center was between a workhouse and a cemetery. But sometimes the nicknames were mysterious. Mick had no idea why Figgy Pudding was also called Coleman's Doorstep.

Institute streets and greets mostly patrolled only two clusters: Museum and Park. Those were by far the busiest in

London and had been for decades. And there was another one, Grays Corrections (the third busiest), that they handled sometimes. At first, Mick had been surprised that the Institute handled so few clusters. He'd vaguely assumed that the Institute handled all of London. But that was before he had realized how big London was and how long it took to get around the city, especially since the fastest way was usually running, unless you had a horse.

After they reviewed the clusters, they looked at the "outposts," which were small offices and townhouses where the dons lived when they were outside the walls. The outpost dons always pretended to be doing some kind of arrow business— accounting, tailoring, anything boring and forgettable—but they were usually doing something relating to time travel, including patrolling clusters that the Institute couldn't.

Only after Mick went over arrow London and alley rat London one more time with almost no mistakes did Alison say he was ready to patrol.

And, after all that, Mick's first patrol turned out to be boring. A few stirrings but no alleys, not even a fawkes. Mick wasn't sure whether he was disappointed or relieved.

As Trinity term got into full swing, Mick fell into a rhythm. He started his days with condy, followed by breakfast. Then, once or twice a week, he worked on his future journal, which could still make him homesick, although chatting with the good-natured Mr. Hartnell usually cheered him up. After that, it was reading something, often *Broome's* or *Clayton's* to learn about alleys or *Hyde's* and *Wilson's* to learn about London. Sometimes he read histories to learn about England and its empire. The

English really liked taking their cannons to new places. Reading was often with Miss Emmet, and being around her made him less homesick. Also, he valued the unofficial little tips she snuck into their lessons—shortcuts and where to stand on the roof for the best views, or how to use lamps so that they didn't waste oil or sputter. She had really good tips on everything except getting around London.

After tutorial, he ate lunch with the Sixers. Then he usually went patrolling with the Squad. The Squad taught him how to blend in, and patrol itself taught him how navigate London, in part by motivating him to study the Plan a lot harder so that he wouldn't have to depend on other people for directions. Sometimes he still caught himself reaching for his phone to check Google Maps, but of course he didn't have a phone, much less satellites feeding GPS data to it. Instead, he had a pocket watch, courtesy of Miss North ("This remains the Institute's property, Mr. Gunn, so do take care"). Whenever he found himself reaching for his phone, he pulled out his watch instead. He wondered how many of the students who were always checking their watches were doing the same thing.

Some afternoons, or even some evenings, he went on patrol with Gail and her greets. It was unusual for somebody as new and as young as Mick to be out with a greet team. Greets were usually older than streets and knew more about time alleys. But Mick had better alley sight than them, even Gail. So he could be useful.

Patrolling with Gail's team was a mix of good and bad. He liked Gail. She was funny in ways that snuck up on you but also really smart and calm. Unfortunately, her greets—Daniel, Flora, and Stephen—were obnoxious. He'd started to think of them as the Snobs.

The Snobs were smart and worked hard, but everything was a competition for them, and they got cranky if they weren't winning. And since they couldn't beat Mick at seeing alleys, they picked on his weak points. Like, they wouldn't shut up about how he didn't know about things like French history or Latin. If they were at condy with him, they mocked him for being slow during course. But they were two or three years older than he was, so it wasn't impressive that they were faster.

He definitely didn't like the Snobs, but he'd dealt with worse. And they were scared of Gail, so they mostly acted okay when she was watching. Which she usually was.

And sometimes they got so grouchy that they went from annoying to amusing. They all had glowing alley rat eyes, not especially bright but still obvious. So the surly expressions on their faces when they got extra grumpy made them look like anime villains, like they were going to reach into their satchels and pull out Pokémon or enchanted daggers.

After patrol one day, Mick told Gail how funny the Snobs looked sometimes. She'd laughed. "'Glowing eyes.' A fine way to describe that sort of angry baby envy."

Mick realized that Gail hadn't understood what he'd meant by "glowing eyes." So she couldn't see alley rat eyes. And if she couldn't, maybe he was the only one who could. He realized he'd never heard anybody mention the eyes. He meant to ask Gail about it, or maybe Alison, but it got lost in the shuffle because he had so much to learn.

And he did learn. He learned a lot about London. He also learned about alleys, though not nearly as much as anybody wanted. There weren't enough alleys to learn from. Every time he went out with the Squad or the Snobs, he got excited, hoping that he'd see a dropper come out of an alley, though of course he also got a little scared that a dead kid would fall out, like Alison's brother. But there weren't any droppers for either of Mick's teams. Most days nothing happened.

It wasn't supposed to be that way. Everyone was saying that the alleys were acting oddly—more fawkeses, more empties, fewer droppers. He could feel people starting to get worried.

One day, Mick and Leech were on the roof with a bunch of other Sixers, washing grime off some skylights under the prefects' supervision. Mick was yet again wishing that the Institute would hire people to clean up and not make the students do it. He'd used to think the same thing at home, but his mom had always said that chores built character. Leech and the others said it was a bit about building character but mostly because you couldn't keep secrets from servants, who went everywhere and saw everything.

Mick rubbed tiredly at the skylight. It was hard to keep the rag clean, and it felt like he was just painting the glass with watery dirt. "Doesn't the Queen have a million secrets?" he complained to Leech. "And a million servants?"

Leech laughed. "Her secrets involve ministers and treaties and … and normal secrets. She's *supposed* to have such secrets. If someone steals her secrets, he's a traitor, and he'll be locked in the Tower. If someone steals our secrets, we're lunatics, and we'll be locked in Bedlam."

Mick's Plan lessons automatically flashed through his mind, showing him the Tower of London and Bedlam insane asylum, nearest clusters and all. He was a little proud of himself for how well he remembered everything, but then he felt a stab of sadness that he could see the map of London with his eyes closed but had only a vague idea what his Chicago looked like on a map. He wasn't even sure he could have found where his family had lived before his dad left and his mom died. Not that their house would even be built for another hundred years or more.

The prefects called out that the windows were clean enough, and Mick gratefully tossed the rag into the dirty pail. Soon, they were dressed for patrol and back on the streets.

Before he'd started patrolling, Mick had half-imagined that the Squad had a routine beat, like old-school cops with brass badges and batons, or maybe steampunky time cops pushing wheelbarrows full of whirring, glowing alley-detection contraptions hidden under piles of hay. But their only technology was notebooks and pencils, and their patrol routes changed daily. True, there were about a dozen standard "Sequences of Plan Stations." Each sequence was a route that street teams followed to cover the main parts of each cluster, and each had "stations" along the way, sort of like stops on Chicago L lines. But streets never patrolled a sequence from start to finish. On any given day, they were sent to the stations that the professors or dons thought would be the most productive.

The Squad—well, Alison—always got their instructions from the warden of the day on a skinny slip of paper called the "rasher." The rasher required them to patrol certain stations, while others were "tpg," which stood for "time permitting." The phrase meant "if there's enough time," but it made Mick picture Time as a stern-faced goddess who permitted or denied puny human requests. Maybe one day Goddess Time would permit him to go back home.

That day, the Squad was mostly in the western Park cluster

sequences, starting at Cambridge Square and skirting the reservoirs on their way north. They moved slowly enough to search for alley signs but tried never to linger long enough to draw attention. On patrol, they had to look like they were doing regular 1853 kid business. Otherwise, people started asking them questions, and then they couldn't do their job. That was why every time they went out, Alison got a little money from the warden so that they could stop to buy something from a cheesemonger, a baker, a stationer, or some other shopkeeper or street vendor. It was good camouflage. Mick was pretty sure that it also saved the professors and dons from doing their own errands.

It was important not to get so caught up patrolling that you let yourself be targeted by criminals. The Institute and its alley clusters were mostly in good neighborhoods, so if you went out in daylight and in groups, the risk of violence wasn't too terrible. But fancy clothes didn't stop crooks from grabbing your money. If anything, they made you look like you had more money to grab. From her years living on London streets, Alison was probably the best of anybody at the Institute, including the professors, at spotting potential trouble. Dolly was pretty good. Leech was remarkably bad. Dolly liked to point out that Leech had gotten his pocket picked all the time before he joined Alison and Dolly's team.

Thieves were another reason to get friendly with the cops. Alison knew where the usual constables patrolled and would bring them little treats—roasted chestnuts, baked potatoes, hot cups of coffee, that sort of thing. Today, it was Constable Archer, a friendly but slightly dimwitted young man whose round face sprouted oddly distributed patches of hair, as if different parts of his beard had gotten in an argument and weren't talking to each other.

Alison handed the constable the sweetened prunes from the Welsh costermonger's stall that he liked. She and Leech chatted with the constable for a bit. Leech was a natural mimic and sometimes matched the accent of whatever arrow they were speaking to. But if it was somebody he was going to see again, like Constable Archer, Leech used an accent that sounded like the Vicar's.

Mick didn't talk to Constable Archer, or any of the cops. Mick still sounded American, and *future* American at that. The professors had given him a quick bio he could use in an emergency ("My father is a physician in Surrey, and my mother is with the angels"), but until he sounded English enough, he wasn't supposed to use it. In fact, he was supposed to avoid talking with outsiders longer than it took to buy a baked potato. If somebody official pressured him to talk, he supposed to look scared, say he wasn't supposed to talk about his family, and, if he absolutely had to, say that the professors would explain everything. That was fine with Mick. His mom had never really trusted cops, and some of that had rubbed off on him, even though Alison said not to worry too much about Constable Archer and the other usual police officers because the Institute paid their wages. At first, Mick had thought she was kidding, but Miss Emmet said it was true. The Institute gave money to the mayor, or alderman, or something, and got extra police in the neighborhood—friendly ones who weren't the brightest candles in the chandelier.

That day, Constable Archer hadn't seen anything interesting, so the Squad moved on. A while later, they were standing in the skimpy shade of the sad trees lining Bryanstone Square.

"Any stirrings?" Alison asked, like she did every fifteen minutes on patrol.

Everyone looked at Leech, who was extremely good at sensing stirrings. Leech shook his head.

Alison sighed. Usually, that was exactly what happened: nothing. When nothing was happening with time alleys, Alison sometimes taught Mick a bit about streetcraft—how to spot gangs of pickpockets or other crooks when they were pretending not to know each other, how to tell when what sounded like random whistling was actually signals from those gangs, that sort of thing. But it had been a boring patrol even for pickpockets and coded yelling. They were done for the day and had done a lot of walking for a lot of nothing, so they were footsore and annoyed. Still, it was a beautiful afternoon, so they decided to take the long way back to the Institute, skirting the southern edge of Regent's Park.

Dolly wistfully asked to go to the Botanic Gardens. Alison's pocket watch said they didn't have time, but she did let them stop for spice-cakes at York Terrace, which cheered Dolly up. The spice cakes came from Mayor Cakes, an old man with a bright red face and a bright red cart that he parked outside the entrance to the park. Mayor Cakes had gleaming white hair and a dirty brown coat, and Mick sometimes thought that if the Mayor brushed his teeth as carefully as he polished his cart, his teeth would look more like his hair and less like his coat. Then again, maybe not. Leech said that most Londoners brushed their teeth with "ground up rocks, nonsensical herbs, or nothing at all." Mick suspected the toothpaste they used at the Institute was a connan, but he was all for anything that kept his teeth from looking like Mayor Cakes'.

Mick liked the Mayor's spice-cakes okay, even though they

didn't have enough currants. Dolly *loved* them. Most of the time, Dolly looked like she was afraid to step too hard anywhere because the ground might be booby-trapped. But when she truly enjoyed something, she transformed. She probably would smile only a tiny, private smile, but her entire face—her entire body—relaxed, and she let her feet rest firmly on the ground. Mick was glad to see it that day, as always. Somehow, it felt like if Dolly could find little moments of delight, things might work out for him too.

The next day's patrol was much the same. The Squad's route took them slightly farther south into the sequences, to the Uxbridge road at St. George's chapel, and not quite so far west, but they still bought a couple things at shops to look like normal kids on normal errands and still made sure to give Constable Archer some prunes. Constable Archer warned them that a gang of teenage pickpockets from Whitechapel had been spotted in the area. Alison gave a thoroughly ladylike gasp and thanked the constable for protecting her, giving no sign that she'd warned the Squad about the gang a couple hours ago, when she'd first heard them whistling to one another. Their next stop was Mayor Cakes. Dolly nearly hopped with glee when Alison said they had time for the Botanic Gardens. But that didn't apply to Mick, who had to hustle over to Fitzroy Square to meet Gail and the Snobs.

He arrived a minute early, according to his watch. Of course, every watch in 1853 had its own opinion, even though the alley rats tried to synchronize them to the Great Clock. 1853 churches had the same problem. Every hour, or even every fifteen minutes, the churches rang their bells, and none of them agreed what time it was. Back in the Institute, that usually wasn't a problem because the loudest bells were almost always from All Souls Church on Langham Place. But out on the streets, there were a lot of churches, and the winds and echoes carried the sounds of their bells from surprising directions.

Gail was already there when Mick arrived. Like Alison, Gail was never late. Unlike Alison, she never looked worried about it. Or about anything. She always looked calm and just a bit amused, like she was remembering a good joke she'd heard months earlier. Daniel and Flora were there too. Daniel looked disappointed that Mick was on time. Daniel always liked to point out when Mick was late, according to somebody's watch, in somebody's time zone.

Mick was still exchanging greetings with the others when Stephen appeared, jogging toward them on Grafton Street. He was coming from the northeast, which was a little weird, since the Institute was in the other direction.

Gail reached into her battered leather satchel to extract the "greet sheet," the square of paper setting the day's itinerary. Unlike streets, greets didn't have to worry about the patrol sequences. Instead, they got lists of places to inspect based on what the streets were reporting—where a potential alley was, how strong the signs were, and predictions about when it might open. Gail mostly ignored the predictions unless they came from one of the handful of dons or professors whose predictions were sometimes right. She said the most reliable ones came from Miss North, Mr. Victor, and Miss Mitchell.

Street teams like the Squad mostly worked in threes, and they stuck together for safety because they were younger. Greet teams like Gail's usually had four members but often split into pairs to cover more ground. Today, though, the list was pretty short, so they stuck together, with Mick mostly just trying to stay out of their way.

They started with a faint stirring in the Cumberland market, but if it was going to turn into an alley, it wouldn't be for another day or two. Daniel said one day; Flora said two. They bickered about it until the next stop, a false alarm in Mornington Crescent. A friendly young man who sold baked potatoes on Arlington Street said there had been a bunch of dogs barking, but it turned out a fox had been running through gardens near the train tracks. On Phoenix Street near Clarendon Square, Gail, who had at least as good a feel for stirrings as Leech, swore that she felt a recent alley. Mick thought he could see a faint orangey mist swirling like the last bits of a smoke bomb, which *Clayton's* said might mean a large fairy path had closed recently. But there was no sign of a dropper, so they moved on.

Eventually, they entered the cemetery near the Foundling Hospital. A fog was creeping across that part of the city, though fortunately not the sort of pea-souper that occasionally made the Institute cancel patrol because the air was too thick to see through and too toxic to breathe safely. Mick could still see through that afternoon's fog, though it did make the cemetery feel extra creepy.

In a patch of grass and gravestones not far from the foundling girls' school, Mick spotted a whirlpool of irregular white and yellow bands, like a large, swirling puddle covering grass, graves, and the pathway. The white bands were spiraling inward clockwise, and the yellow bands were spiraling outward counterclockwise. It was the first whirlpool Mick had seen in real life, and the whites of the whirlpool and the whites of the fog were blurring together in a way that made him slightly dizzy.

They all stood, pretending to look mournfully at the headstone in front of them. He could tell that the other kids could now see the whirlpool too.

"Gunner?" Gail prompted.

Mick tossed out the fancy language from *Broome's.* "Whirlpool, circular with no discernible ovoid tendencies. Primary bichromatic, ivory and canary. No visible frame, no frame haze. Bright inward spirals, interwoven and color-corresponding, conflicting spins. Estimated outer diameter of aperture fourteen feet—no, it grew, maybe fifteen or sixteen. Bright diameter twelve or thirteen feet. So, Eight tending to Nine." He waited, squinting, to see if the outer diameter would grow any more. Nope. "Outer diameter steady."

Gail looked slightly away from the whirlpool in case anyone was watching them, though Mick knew she was keeping a close eye on it. As he did the same, an old woman carrying a bouquet of flowers walked right through the whirlpool. She was a little creepy and ghostly, the fog hiding her legs below the knee and slightly blurring the rest of her. Mick shivered. In a graveyard, the last thing you wanted to see was someone who looked like a ghost.

When Gail told the Snobs to agree or disagree with Mick's description, there was a long silence. Maybe the Snobs really were thinking, but probably they didn't want to admit they couldn't see everything Mick saw. Which was so stupid—it didn't bother him that they were better at a lot of alley rat stuff than he was. Or that Gail was better at everything than he was, except seeing alleys.

Eventually, the Snobs quietly confirmed what Mick had said.

Not long after that, the whirlpool's spirals sputtered, like bike wheels where the rider kept flicking the brakes on and off. Then they paused and switched directions.

"Spin variation," Stephen said. His voice went up a little at the end, like a question. So he'd noticed that something had changed but wasn't sure what.

"Reversal?" Gail asked. "Inner and outer spirals?"

"Both," Mick confirmed.

"Flora," Gail asked, "time till opening?"

Flora scrunched her forehead, trying to do the math. The books said you had to pick the right "formula," which was misleading. Mick wasn't a math whiz, but he knew that with a real formula, you got the same answer every time you plugged in the same numbers. With alleys, sometimes you got ten as the answer, sometimes you got twelve or twenty. Occasionally, you got a gerbil named Stanislaus doing a drum solo. Alleys were predictable sometimes, but only sometimes, and you couldn't even predict when they would be predictable. And even if you found a predictable alley, you needed to pick the right formula, which was really hard for most people. You had to know the size, color, speed, patterns, and the rest. Which most people couldn't see nearly as well as Mick.

Of course, once you picked the formula, you had to be able to do the math, which Mick definitely could not. The easy ones required algebra; the hard ones needed calculus and a couple supercomputers.

"Three minutes," Flora said. "Approximately."

Gail hit her stopwatch, and Flora recited the name of the formula and the relevant variables. The part that Mick could understand sounded right. Stephen and Daniel both said they agreed with Flora, although Mick was pretty sure Daniel had no clue. He was better at sneering than at math.

Just after three minutes, there was a bright flash before the whirlpool slowed. The yellow spiral stopped moving; a little later, the white one did too. It flickered a few times and then disappeared, leaving only wisps of fog and silence.

"Motherfawkser!" Gail said.

Technically, it wasn't a swear word. But it was close enough, and all of them wanted to swear. There really was something wrong with the alleys… and maybe with the kids trapped inside them.

CHAPTER 16

A DEATH IN THE ALLEYS

After Gail, Mick, and the Snobs reported the graveyard fawkes to a frowning Miss North, there was still time before dinner, so Mick stopped at the nursery to say hi to Miss Weathers and solemn little Julia, who still called him "Miss Ellen's friend." After that, he went to condy. He thought about running course. Sometimes Miss Mitchell would set up an obstacle course for herself and a few other dons, and she let Mick use it if he stayed out of the way. Her courses were honestly too hard for Mick, but he used them anyway because he wasn't allowed to set one up for himself and because he was tired of the Snobs making fun of how slow he was at course. But Miss Mitchell wasn't there, and Mick didn't know any of the dons who were running course.

Leech was playing pick-up footie with Owl and some kids not too much bigger than Mick, so Mick joined in. Mick was good enough not to embarrass himself, Owl was tough and absolutely refused to get pushed around, and Leech was as impressive as always. Leech didn't run faster than the other kids, but he reacted quicker. And more calmly. And he had eyes in the back of his head when he played soccer, which was weird since he was such an easy target for pickpockets. Mick and Leech played so long that they had to skip showering to get to dinner on time. Miss Paisley, who was sitting next to Leech, scarfed her dinner and left early, not bothering to take her plate to the sideboard.

"Now we know how to chase her away," Leech told Mick. "Your condy stench."

"You smell worse," Mick said.

"I smell fairer than the roses in the Botanic Gardens," Leech said indignantly. "And you, Miss Particular Eater?" he asked the tiny Miss Winchwood, who was sitting across the table from him. "Does my friend's stench distress you?"

Miss Winchwood silently continued her particular eating. Mick was starting to admire her focus.

The next morning, Mick spent a little extra time running course while the other kids played footie. Not too far from the start of the course, he saw Miss Paisley glaring angrily at the universe as she held her arm, which she said she'd hurt coming down the stairs to condy. She looked like a grumpy cat meme.

After showering, Mick went to a make-up future journal session, but the Scriptorium's outer door was locked. He knocked several times, louder each time, but got no answer from Mr. Hartnell.

Mick was tempted to treat this as free time and maybe go sit on his favorite bench in the garden. But when Miss North found out—and Miss North always found out—she would act like it was his fault Mr. Hartnell had locked the door, and then she'd probably give him extra lessons.

So, since he was supposed to see Miss North for a tutorial after his journal session anyway, he went straight to her office. She didn't answer his knock either, and as he turned away from the door, he found Miss Emmet standing there.

"She's not answering?" Miss Emmet asked.

Mick shook his head.

"Unfortunate," she replied. "But you are ahead of your time, I believe?"

"Yes, miss," he answered. "I came early because the Scriptorium was locked."

"That'll be the pirates, I expect."

"Miss?"

She smiled. "You've not heard the rumors, I gather."

Mick shook his head.

"Rumor has it that pirates tried to raid the Scriptorium," she explained. "Presumably they had to portage their boats up Wardour Street, which seems unduly strenuous to me. But, then, the ways of pirates are not my ways."

Mick wasn't sure what all the words meant, but her tone was joking. "So it wasn't pirates?" he asked.

"Hardly."

She started walking away from Miss North's office. Mick fell in behind her, realizing they were headed to the library.

She said, "It could have been burglars, I suppose. There have been reports of cracksmen in the neighborhood. But I doubt it."

Mick knew from listening to conversations with policemen

that "cracksmen" were burglars who targeted fancy houses. "Why?" Just a few days earlier, Constable Archer had said something about cracksmen stealing the silver from a home right across the square.

Miss Emmet didn't say anything. Mick waited patiently before asking again.

"Presently, Mr. Gunn, presently."

But it wasn't very present. She didn't speak until they were in her little office. "You believe you asked a simple question. But you actually asked me several complicated questions."

"Miss?"

"In fine houses, burglars tend to rely on help from servants or tradesmen. But we aren't a typical fine house. We have very few servants, in comparison with schools of similar size and prestige. We rely on students—and dons and professors—a great deal more than most such schools."

Mick thought of all the chores he had to do. Miss Emmet laughed, and Mick realized he was frowning.

"You understand why, of course?" she asked.

"Because we can't say no." He smiled a little to let her know he was kidding. Mostly.

She smiled. "There's more truth in that than one might wish. But that isn't the primary reason."

"Leech says it's because people can't keep secrets from servants," he said.

"Mr. Charles is correct. The more servants who sleep and work within our walls, the more people know where we keep our jewels. The more people who know, the greater the risk one of them will tell a burglar."

"We have jewels?" Mick asked.

"Figuratively," Miss Emmet said.

"But the Institute does have servants," Mick said. "Mr. James. And the caretakers."

"Despite appearances, Mr. James and the caretakers are not traditional servants," Miss Emmet said. "They are all alley rats. Indeed, most of them are former students of the Institute. Buildings this large and complex require knowledgeable and skilled laborers and craftsmen to function, and we daren't hire anyone who isn't loyal to the Institute. Mr. Willard, the head caretaker, is an especially loyal and capable man."

Mick nodded. Now that he thought about it, Mr. James' eyes and most of the caretakers' eyes did have the alley rat glow. "But there's also Mrs. Robbin," he said, "and the other cooks, and the kitchen kids. And lots of outsiders come. The laundresses. The costermonger and his wife. The coal man. The baker. The butcher and his apprentice—"

"But none of them ever enter the main building," Miss Emmet pointed out.

Mick realized that was true. Deliveries never made it past the kitchens, which were right beside the gate in a building detached from the rest of the Institute. The cooks and their helpers carried food deliveries into the kitchens, and the caretakers or students brought the other deliveries into the main building. When things needed to go out, students or caretakers brought them out of the main building and left them at the gate or, in the case of dirty clothes, wheeled them across Forsyth Place to the laundry. And the night soil man never even came inside the walls—he pulled his cart into the service alleys to drain the cisterns.

"That's why Mrs. Robbin, the other cooks, and the kitchen kids never come inside the main building," he said. They cooked all the meals for the Institute, but they always wheeled the food carts to an outer door of the dining hall, and some Institute kids pushed it the rest of the way. Mick felt silly for not having noticed all that earlier.

"And why their quarters are in a separate building that has no door within the walls and no windows facing the garden and main building," Miss Emmet said.

"What about the man who fixed the Great Clock a couple weeks ago?" Mick asked. "The skinny, really tall one?"

Miss Emmet nodded. "We occasionally are obliged to grant entry to skilled tradesmen. But they too are loyal to the Institute. For example, Mr. Yardley, who fixed the clock, also happens to be a graduate of the Institute." Miss Emmet stared at him intently. "Has anyone mentioned the Project to you?"

"I've heard of it," Mick said. "But I don't understand it."

"Little wonder. We don't speak of the Project much here," Miss Emmet said. "Among alley rats, it isn't a secret, precisely, but we are secretive by nature."

She fell silent. It felt like this was one of those situations where the less Mick asked, the more he'd learn. He forced himself to keep quiet and wait.

Eventually, Miss Emmet asked, "I assume you've noticed that students at the Institute still have their alley sight, in the main, especially the younger ones?" she asked. "And that those who go alley blind often leave for other schools? Demeter Academy, St. George's, Lady Grenville's, Orphans?"

Mick nodded. Demeter Academy was basically a school for farming and shop class on the far side of the Thames. The others were closer to the Institute. St. George's and Lady Grenville's were fancy boarding schools, one for boys and one for girls. Orphans was where you went if you had never had decent alley sight, and many of its students were arrows. In fact, Alison had arrow friends there, older kids she'd lived on the street with after coming to London. Dolly said that Alison had harassed the Vicar and Miss North until they had gotten her friends into Orphans and thus off the streets. Alison visited them every Sunday, even when the Squad had Sunday patrol.

"The Project runs those schools too," Miss Emmet explained. "It runs quite a few other things as well. Our tradesmen are almost always alley rats, often carefully selected graduates of Orphans. So they're loyal to the Project. Unlikely to spread our secrets, especially to burglars."

"What is the Project?" Mick asked.

"That's the most complicated question of all," she said. "There have been alley rats for hundreds of years. Possibly thousands of years. But in England, so far as we are aware, they did not band together until the late sixteenth century."

Mick nodded. He knew that.

Miss Emmet continued. "And those bands were modest at first. I suspect they were essentially a means for their members to reassure one another that they were not lunatics, that they had indeed somehow fallen from the future into the past."

Mick nodded even impatiently. He knew that too.

She chuckled at his impatience. "Difficult though it is to be dropped in the past, there are advantages, including knowing the future. Of course, alley rats drop as children, so it's exceedingly rare that they are expert in the sciences or the history of the future. But simply knowing that something is possible is a tremendous advantage."

"How?"

"Suppose that you were a gentleman of means deciding whether to invest in a new invention. If a man came to you and told you that he was devising a heavier-than-air flying machine, would you call him a madman, or would you hear him out?"

Mick wondered if she was trying to trick him into a connan.

"Mr. Gunn, I am confident the Wright brothers' first flight occurred many decades before your late point. We needn't be coy."

Mick nodded.

"So, even though you are not an engineer and cannot judge this man's plans for a flying machine, you might give him some money in exchange for a share of the profits, mightn't you? He might not be the one to invent the airplane, but you know that *somebody* will be. An arrow, of course, couldn't know that."

Mick started to see where this was going.

"Now," Miss Emmet continued, "let us say that the inventor were a woman with the same idea. Would you consider investing? What if the woman were the same color as me, or darker? Would you still?"

Mick nodded.

"So, compared with the typical arrow, as an investor you would be more likely to succeed and far more likely to make money simply because you know what can be done. And who can do it."

"But that would be a mortal anachronism, right?" Mick asked. "Paying somebody to invent the airplane now, instead of when it's supposed to get invented? That would change the future a lot."

Miss Emmet shrugged. "Well, it does seem that the future is surprisingly resistant to change. But, yes, what you describe likely would be a mortal anachronism. It would certainly be a connan. However, connans didn't trouble most alley rats until at least the end of the previous century. That's part of how we know the future is hard to change. Earlier alley rats ran absolutely dreadful risks. If it were easy to change the future, they would have changed it a thousand times over. Or possibly destroyed it altogether. But, now, connans *do* trouble us. Today, we wouldn't invest in the flying machine before its time. Still, we do know that its time is coming and when. And we shall start planning accordingly. It happened with the railroad and the docks. It is happening now with the telegraph."

"The Institute is doing all that?"

"The Project is doing all that. And using some of the proceeds to fund the Institute, just as it funds the other schools I mentioned."

"But I thought— Didn't the Institute's money come from whatsisname? Edward Forsyth?"

"Only some of it. And he wouldn't have had the money to give in the first place if it hadn't been for the Project."

"Wasn't he rich because he was a nobleman?" Mick asked. But then he realized something. "Wait—he was an alley rat, right?"

Miss Emmet nodded.

"So how was he the son of an earl from back then? Of *anybody* from back then?"

Miss Emmet laughed merrily. "He wasn't. My suspicion has always been that the Forsyth line itself was originally a fiction, though of course one later sanctified by law and privilege. There are other possible explanations, of course," Miss Emmet remarked. "What they have in common is the Project."

She looked at him intently before continuing. "For centuries, the Project has been silently guiding, discreetly nudging and twisting arms. Clever young alley rats, especially those with little talent for seeing alleys, are sent elsewhere to learn. If they're young men, particularly clever and sufficiently pale, they go to Oxford or Cambridge or perhaps one of the universities in town. Others attend one of the Project's own Societies. Learning, making friends among the 'better' classes. Rising, rising."

Mick got only some of that, but she sounded a little bitter by the end. "Why only pale young men?" he asked.

She laughed. "One day, dark fingers may chisel that question into the cenotaph of the British Empire." She smiled. "There are many answers to your question, but the simplest is: that's how it is. In this place and time, pale men are treated better than pale women, than darker men, and, especially, than darker women." She pointed to herself. "Even those of us who wouldn't be considered very dark at all, in other places and times."

Studying apertures, Mick had learned the word "monochromatic." It meant "having only one color," and it described the Institute and London pretty well. At the Institute, he was one of the darker-skinned kids, but back home his mom's cousins had joked about how light-skinned he and Emilia were. At least until his mom and Tía Julieta had chewed them out for doing it.

Not everybody was vampire pale, of course. Miss Mitchell. Miss Weathers. Stephen the Snob. The Sixers girls' prefect, Miss Dylan, and a few other Sixers, and some kids in other tories. There were even a few professors, like Miss Emmet. As for London, it was too big and too messy for clean rules. London had people from all places and races, especially if you went down to the docks where tall ships brought goods and people from around the world and carried them away again. But in the tree-lined, relatively healthy parts of London, "monochromatic" was pretty accurate. And even with pale people, English people found ways to create a pecking order. Irish people, like Leech, and Welsh and Scottish people were every bit as pale as Englishmen, and Mick couldn't tell any of them apart, except sometimes by accent. But, as Leech often pointed out, that didn't stop most English people from treating them as inferior races.

Mick sighed. Every time he started to think he was settling okay into 1853, something would remind him that he was far from home, surrounded by strange and dangerous people with strange and dangerous ideas. Sometimes, it made him want to give up and hide under his cot.

It came to him in a flash. "That's why you don't go out much, isn't it?"

Miss Emmet looked startled.

Mick blushed. "Sorry."

She smiled faintly and reached across her desk to pat his hand. "Don't be. Most people don't notice. I even allow myself to forget, sometimes."

They sat in awkward silence for a long time.

Eventually, Miss Emmet said, "We have wandered rather far afield from your question about burglars, haven't we?"

Mick nodded.

"And why might I have told you all that about the Project?"

"Because it's important?" Mick guessed.

"True so far as it goes," she said. "But why tell you now?"

Mick thought. How had they gotten started on all this? Pirates. And then something about burglars trying to break into the Scriptorium and why Miss Emmet didn't think servants or tradesmen— "Oh," he said.

"Yes?"

"If it wasn't burglars from the outside trying to break in,"

Mick said, letting it sink in, "it was one of us, right? Someone from the Institute, or at least from the Project?"

"Indeed," Miss Emmet said. "And I'd much prefer pirates. Pillaging is less frightening than betrayal."

When Mick returned to Miss North's office, he found a note dangling from a ribbon tied around the doorknob: *My tutorials cancelled to-day. Pupils shall continue their lessons as appropriate.*

On patrol, Leech and Dolly said they had never heard of Miss North canceling a tutorial. Alison remembered that Miss North had canceled a tutorial years earlier. Miss North had spent the day in the infirmary after being stabbed by a would-be mugger. "The dons said she broke both his kneecaps and stood over him until the police arrived," Alison said proudly.

Nothing happened on patrol. During streeting, Alison gave Constable Archer sweet plums and asked him about any burglaries nearby, but he hadn't heard anything. They saw no alleys, not even a fawkes. Leech felt a faint stirring near the mews opposite Montague House, but it faded without doing anything interesting. Greeting with Gail and the Snobs was equally fruitless.

At dinner, everybody was gossiping about whatever had happened at the Scriptorium. The younger kids babbled about pirates and time ghosts. The older kids argued about how the cracksmen had gotten in. Depending who told the tale, Mr. Hartnell had beaten a dozen burglars to death with a journal safe or the burglars had stabbed him a dozen times in the heart. It was hotly debated whether he had survived the dozen stab-bings or had died and returned as an unholy vengeance wraith.

The next morning, Mick's tutorials went back to normal.

Patrol was routine too, until the Squad was on patrol one afternoon. On the last station of the sequence, on Princes Street near Hanover Square, the Squad found a glow-orb Seven a half hour from opening. It was a short jog to the Institute, so Dolly ran off and came back a quarter hour later with Miss North and Gail. Gail explained that Daniel was in tutorial, and Stephen and Flora had checked themselves out of the Institute.

Pretending to be doing something else, they all waited impatiently for the glow-orb to open. It started as a monochromatic light blue but quickly turned multiple blues and whites, crisply ringed in dark blues. Mick narrated the changes while Alison and Gail took notes. Gail was so good at taking notes that she was writing down both what he saw and what she saw, all in code, all without looking down at her pad.

As always, it was odd to see people walk cluelessly through the glow-orb. When the swirling had changed direction several times and sped up, a woman with frizzy hair in a frizzy fur coat casually strolled through it.

"How can she not notice it?" Mick wondered aloud.

"Who?" Leech asked.

Mick looked at Leech to see if he was kidding. Leech shrugged. By the time Mick looked back, the woman had wandered out of sight. Then the glow-orb suddenly stopped swirling and turned ocean blue. Then it turned darker from top to bottom and then bottom to top. The familiar wink.

A fraction of a second later, a dropper appeared, slumping to the ground.

Ignoring a hansom cab that nearly ran her down, Alison rushed across the street, Gail close behind. Then everybody else reacted.

The dropper was lying on the pavement, and Alison was on

her knees, clutching the kid by the shoulders. It looked like a boy about Mick's age, his clothes tattered and his hair wild.

Gail was kneeling beside Alison, one arm around her shoulders. When Gail looked up at Miss North and shook her head, Mick realized the boy was dead.

Mick remembered how Alison's brother had died. He felt sick for her.

Miss North looked at Alison and then at Gail, jerking her head toward the Institute. Gail forced Alison to let go of the boy and stand up with her. Dolly and Leech positioned themselves on either side of Alison, each putting an arm around her waist and nudging her toward the Institute.

Gail nodded at Stephen and Flora, who had appeared out of nowhere. "The carriage," she said. They nodded and took off running.

Miss North reached into her satchel and withdrew a cotton sheet or blanket, which she draped over the dead boy, up to his chin. She smoothed his hair a little.

A few passersby had begun to gather.

"The lad," Miss North announced, "is sadly subject to fits and fevers, so let us hope that it is nothing contagious." Her tone expressed some doubt, however, and the passersby edged backward and remembered urgent business elsewhere. This process repeated itself twice more before the Institute's carriage arrived. Miss North, Gail, Stephen, and Flora gently lifted the dropper into the carriage, and Miss North climbed in beside him.

"Meet me in the solarium in half an hour," she told Mick and Gail. "The others need not attend."

The carriage clattered off, and Gail and Mick stared at each other before shrugging and starting toward the Institute.

"Stephen and Flora showed up fast," Mick said.

"Telegraph," Gail said.

The telegraph was like steampunk texting. Pressing a switch in certain patterns electrically sent words over wires. But it was pretty new in 1853.

"The Project has a secret telegraph network," Gail explained. "Stations hidden all over London. It has for decades, even back when it was probably a connan. Greet teams and dons use it regularly. I shouldn't tell you until you're a greet. But it's foolish to hide it from you when you patrol with us so often."

Mick thought back on all the times the Snobs had wandered away and come back with more information. All the times that some street urchin had run up to Gail's team with a paper message that Gail had said was from the Institute, no matter which direction the kid had come from. He should have figured it out. No wonder the Snobs thought he was an idiot.

"We're skilled at deception, greets," Gail said, reading his mind. "Do take heart. You'll soon be as untrustworthy as we are."

Mick laughed a little, which was probably what she'd wanted.

In the solarium, the debriefing among Miss North, the Vicar, Mick, and Gail went as usual, with tea and biscuits for everyone and worried frowns for the adults.

Gail presented her notes and Alison's notes about what Mick had said, and then Mick answered some follow-up questions.

"Tell us again about this woman in the fur coat, Mr. Gunn," Miss North instructed.

When Mick finished, Miss North asked Gail, "And you didn't see her?"

Gail shook her head.

Miss North and the Vicar looked carefully at one another. "I'm afraid we shall need the others after all," the Vicar said. "Including Miss March, do we think?"

Miss North nodded sadly.

The Vicar tugged the bell pull. A don appeared within moments, disappearing again in search of the others. Stephen and Daniel came a few moments later, and Leech, Dolly, and Alison arrived shortly after that. Alison was moving gingerly, her eyes red from crying.

Once everybody was present, the Vicar and Miss North asked everyone if they had seen the woman in the fur coat. Nobody had.

"Perhaps Mr. Gunn is mistaken," Stephen said.

Mick glared at him. They'd just watched a kid die, and Stephen was still trying to make Mick look bad.

"Perhaps," the Vicar replied, unconvinced. He then walked Mick through everything that Mick could remember about the woman, including the way she had disappeared when he turned away for a moment.

"Have you ever seen the woman before?" Miss North asked.

Mick shrugged. "I don't think so. Did she mess up the alley somehow? Is that why the boy..."

He trailed off, aware of Alison's grief.

Miss North shook her head. "Highly doubtful. Alleys do not affect arrows, and arrows do not affect alleys."

"Right, right," Mick said. "Like the old woman with the flowers at the cemetery." He thought back. "Or like that woman with the wheelchair at that first alley I went to. The fawkes at the tobacconist's."

The others started to talk over each other.

"One at a time," Miss North said.

Taking turns, the kids all said that they didn't remember any such women, except Gail, who might have seen the old woman at the cemetery.

"Perhaps Mr. Gunn is mistaken," Stephen said again.

"Describe these ladies, if you will, Mr. Gunn," the Vicar instructed.

Mick did, pausing often to close his eyes while he tried to summon up memories.

"So the first lady, wheeling the chair, you didn't see her until the glow-orb had already appeared, correct?" the Vicar asked Mick.

Mick nodded.

"And she seemed indistinct?" Miss North asked. "Owing, you assumed, to the shimmer of the glow-orb?"

"I gue— I suppose," Mick said. He looked at the Squad to see if they understood why the adults were asking so many questions. Alison didn't seem to notice. Leech and Dolly shrugged.

"The second lady, at the burial grounds," the Vicar continued. "You say you could only see her above the knees, owing to the fog?"

Mick nodded.

"Miss Atkinson," Miss North said, "you said that you might have seen this old woman 'out of the corner of your eye'?"

Gail nodded.

"Yet Mr. Gunn says that he saw her when she passed through the whirlpool, with fewer than three minutes until full aperture. Is that correct?"

Gail nodded again.

"Miss Atkinson," Miss North asked, "are you in the habit of failing to keep an aperture under observation immediately before it opens?"

"Certainly not." Gail sounded a little offended.

"And the fog was not so thick so as to conceal this woman from your view?"

"No, miss."

"And thus?" Miss North asked.

Gail frowned and then got it. "Ah. I should have seen her directly, at some point. And for some length of time. Not for merely an instant and not merely out of the corner of my eye."

"Quite," Miss North said. "Yet you remain certain that you saw her only fleetingly?"

Gail thought. "I don't know as I'd say 'certain.' I believe I saw her as she crossed the whirlpool, but not clearly and not for any length of time."

"Mr. Gunn?" the Vicar asked.

Mick thought back. He remembered the old woman walking through the whirlpool, looking like a ghost because the fog was hiding her legs. "I definitely saw her. But only when she was walking through the whirlpool."

The Vicar and Miss North looked at one another, eyebrows raised.

Mick looked down at the coffee table and noticed that there was still a large pile of biscuits on the tray. Leech was apparently too worried to plunder them, which made Mick worried too.

"Was it the same with all three ladies?" the Vicar asked. "You remember seeing them only within the aperture?"

Mick hadn't thought about it that way, but the Vicar was right. Mick nodded.

The Vicar and Miss North looked at one another again.

"This has been most instructive," the Vicar said, his face solemn. "Children, if I might make a suggestion—please go outside and find somewhere pleasant to be for an hour or two." He gestured to the windows covering much of the solarium's outer wall. "It's rather a splendid afternoon, and sunshine is a soothing balm after such ... events."

The whole meeting had made Mick nervous, and being kicked out so the grown-ups could have a mysterious discussion made it worse. But he did feel a little better when he looked down and saw that nearly all the biscuits had disappeared, presumably into Leech's pockets.

Gail and the Snobs went one way, the Squad another. The Squad took the Vicar's suggestion to go outside. With help from Dolly and Mick, Leech herded Alison toward Regents Park, making her eat the Vicar's tea biscuits as they went. They bought roasted nuts for Alison and Mick from a big-headed boy in a threadbare waistcoat and then spice-cakes from Mayor Cakes for Dolly and Leech. Since the Botanic Gardens were closed to the public that day, they strolled aimlessly through the park while munching their treats.

The Vicar had been right: it was a beautiful day. Much too sunny and warm for a kid to die on the dirty paving stones of Princes Street. None of them were talking much, not even Leech. Mick knew they were all freaking out about the boy's death, and they all knew that Alison was thinking about her brother.

For a long time, they just sat squeezed together on an iron bench, smelling the roses and listening to the birds singing in the tall trees. Mick savored being out in the sun without having to hunt alleys or deal with the Snobs. When he closed his eyes, he felt like he was in Kosciuszko Park, back when he was little and his mom was alive and his dad was around. That kind of memory usually made him feel sad, but it didn't that day. Maybe he'd used up all his sadness.

Eventually, Alison broke the silence. "Thank you."

Mick opened his eyes.

"Thank you," Alison said again, her voice trembling a bit. "You are marvelous friends. I wish that I had known you when my brother…"

In another surprise, Dolly turned and hugged Alison ferociously. It was a normal kid thing to do, but they weren't normal kids, not really. Maybe it was 1853 or maybe it was being at a school for time-weirdos, but they didn't do much regular kid stuff.

Alison laughed and then hugged Dolly back. A little while later, Dolly pulled away, looking slightly sheepish. Leech reached across Alison to hand Dolly the last biscuit and pat her arm. Mick patted her on the shoulder.

They sat quietly again.

"They weren't there," Alison said out of nowhere.

"What weren't there?" Leech asked.

"The women."

"I promise I saw them," Mick said.

"I don't doubt that you saw them," Alison said. "But they weren't there. That's what Miss North and the Vicar believe, anyway."

"What?" Leech asked.

"They weren't in the real world, I mean to say," Alison explained. "They were part of the alleys, somehow. That's why only Gunner saw them."

"Gail saw the one with the flowers," Mick pointed out.

"But only just," Alison said. "You have the best alley sight at the Institute. Miss Atkinson may have the second best. You two are the only ones who saw any of those women, and you're the only one who saw all three. That only gives sense if those women were part of the alleys. Besides, if they weren't part of the alleys, at least one of us—or one of Miss Atkinson's team—would have seen at least one of them."

"But how?" Dolly asked.

Alison shrugged unhappily.

They sat quietly again, listening to the birds.

"Echo phantasms," Alison said to herself. "Yes, echo phantasms."

"Do you think?" Dolly asked.

Mick leaned to catch Leech's eye. Leech shrugged.

"*An Anatomy of Apertural Oddities?*" Alison asked Leech.

Leech shrugged again.

"Honestly, Leech," Alison said.

"What are echo phantasms?" Mick asked.

"Occasionally," Alison said, "a lift alley will show a... a sort of echo of the person who stepped into it."

Mick thought about it. "But I saw the women in *drop* alleys."

Alison nodded. "Then again, they were fawkeses that shouldn't have been fawkeses. So something went wrong. Perhaps whatever went wrong caused an echo phantasm."

"Is that possible?" Leech asked.

"I don't know," Alison admitted.

Leech said, "So what are we to do about it?"

They thought it over.

After a while, Dolly said, "I say we get more spice-cakes."

Leech stood up, tugged Dolly off the bench, and hugged her so hard she started hitting his shoulders, but she was laughing too much to get any strength into the blows. Alison smiled a little, then looked sad. Then she saw Mick looking and smiled sadly.

He smiled back, his emotions as conflicted as her expression.

CHAPTER 17

ON THE TRAIL OF LADIES UNKNOWN

After the break-in at the Scriptorium and the dead kid in the fawkes, everybody at the Institute started acting weird. During condy the next morning, Miss Paisley and Owl—who usually kept politely to himself unless he had a question for Alison or unless Leech managed to get under his skin—argued for five solid minutes over who was distracting whom until Miss Mitchell sent them to opposite corners of the gym. Miss Paisley just kept walking and didn't come back. During breakfast, a couple greet teams from Tories Two and Five got into a shoving match about eggs. Mick couldn't do his make-up journaling session because the Scriptorium was still closed.

When Mick arrived for tutorial with Miss North, Alison was waiting at Miss North's door. She entered before Mick, striding straight to Miss North's desk and launching into her theory about echo phantasms.

Miss North heard her out expressionlessly. "Thank you, Miss March."

Alison waited, obviously expecting more.

"And now," Miss North said, "Mr. Gunn has a great deal to learn."

"But—"

"Miss March," Miss North said crisply, "if you please."

Alison stood there for a moment, indignant. Then she squared her shoulders and walked out. She shut the door behind her more loudly than necessary, though it wasn't quite a slam.

Miss North looked at Mick. "She is distraught, as is only natural."

The tutorial proceeded as if nothing had happened the day before. Although Mick knew that Miss North and the other professors had to be thinking about the dead kid in the fawkes and the mysterious women in the apertures, they weren't talking to the kids about it.

Later, Alison was, unusually, a few minutes late to meet in the Great Hall for patrol. While Leech and Dolly bickered to pass the time, Mick stared at the plaque about Edward Forsyth. Life was just weird. And unfair. One kid gets sucked a century into the past and ends up a nobleman. Another one ends up dead in front of a hat shop.

Alison rushed them through patrol, practically chucking Constable Archer's baked potato at him without stopping to talk. They finished early, stopping at a quiet intersection in a respectable neighborhood just north of the British Museum.

"Do you have to patrol with Miss Atkinson's team now?" Alison asked Mick.

He shook his head.

"Good." She took a deep breath. "Who wishes to get into trouble?"

Leech's hand shot up. Dolly and Mick looked at one another quizzically.

"Trouble?" Dolly asked.

"Well," Alison said. "I suppose it rather depends on whether we're caught."

Dolly frowned. "Caught doing what?"

"Going off sequence," Alison said. "I'm going to inspect where Gunner saw the ghost ladies."

"Why?" Dolly asked. It was a fair question. Although greets had a lot of discretion about where they went on patrol or otherwise, the professors hated when street teams went off sequence.

"To determine whether he saw echo phantasms."

"But what can we learn?" Dolly asked. "The apertures closed long ago."

"I wish to inspect the sites again," Alison said.

Dolly frowned. "Surely, *you* remember them perfectly."

"Nobody's memory is perfect," Alison said.

"Besides," Leech added, "Alison can only remember what she saw. She didn't see the cemetery site. And perhaps at the others she didn't see the thing that matters. Whatever it might be."

"Can you see doing dumpwaiter duty until Michaelmas?" Dolly asked Leech. "Because we shall be if we're caught going off sequence."

"Sure, and the trick to being caught," Leech said, "is don't."

"I'll go," Mick said. He felt like it was his fault that the Princes Street dropper had died. If he'd realized earlier that he was the only one seeing the women, maybe somebody could have figured out what was happening and saved the kid.

Dolly continued pointing out all the reasons not to go, but that didn't stop her from walking briskly east along Bernard

Street with the rest of them. Pretty soon they were at the cemetery near the Foundling School, where Mick had seen the whirlpool and the ghostly old woman with the flowers. Alison made him show her exactly where the whirlpool had been and where he and the others had been standing.

"And you're certain you saw the old woman only inside the whirlpool?" Alison asked.

Mick was standing where he'd been when he'd seen the whirlpool. It was a bright, clear day, and everything had looked different in the fog. He closed his eyes and tried to bring up a clear memory. "I think so," he said, opening his eyes. "I think I saw her the first time there"—he pointed to a crumbling stone cross headstone—"and the last time, um..." He scanned the graves until spotting a bright white headstone. "About there," he said pointing. "I guess I thought she must've turned off onto Heathcote Street there, or maybe the little alley."

"She was on that path, there?" Alison asked, pointing to the narrow dirt footpath winding through the graves thirty or forty yards away.

Mick shrugged. "I think."

"Leech," Alison said. "Walk the path to and fro. Slowly."

Leech did so.

"Did it look like that?" Alison asked.

Mick concentrated. "It's not quite right," he said. "He's going behind those gravestones. The woman went in front of them."

Alison told Leech to come closer. Eventually, they figured out the path the woman had taken: straight through the whirlpool.

They'd been right. The woman had been in the whirlpool, not the real world.

Alison and Dolly speculated about what that might mean

until Alison abruptly walked away without checking if the others were following her.

Mick, Dolly, and Leech looked at each other and shrugged before hustling to catch up.

The Squad followed the broad bustle of Grays Inn Lane for a ways before taking a couple more streets to the tobacconist's where Mick had seen the first woman pushing the wheelchair into the glow-orb. That had been early in his time in London, when everything had felt like a theme park. But now he was getting used to narrow, bumpy streets with horses instead of cars. He preferred horses; they were more fun to watch, even if you did have to make sure they didn't kick you in the head or plonk five pounds of poop on your foot.

Standing across the street from the tobacconist's again, Mick remembered seeing the yellow and orange glow-orb and the woman pushing the wheelchair. She'd appeared at the edge of the glow-orb. Then it had flared so brightly he'd had to close his eyes. By the time he'd opened them, she'd been gone. Back then, he'd thought then she'd just disappeared into the crowd. But now he doubted it.

He explained what he remembered, and they agreed it really was looking like the women had been inside the alleys.

Dolly pointed out that Leech was risking being late to tutorial with Mr. Victor. Leech looked at his pocket watch and swore.

Alison led them to Victoria Street and hailed a cab. Soon they were clattering along the wide course of Holborn Street until the driver stopped where Oxford met Wells. Leech hopped out of the cab and left at a sprint.

Alison paid the driver absently. She was staring off into

space and kept doing so as they walked to where the boy had died.

There, they stood across the street from the milliner's, looking at where the glow-orb had appeared. With Dolly and Alison on either side protecting him from pushy pedestrians, Mick closed his eyes, remembering. The glow-orb had been a mix of shimmering blues and whites, with navy rings. It got brighter. Then the woman in the frizzy coat with the frizzy hair appeared. But were they actually frizzy, or just blurry from the glow-orb's shimmer?

In any case, Mick was getting pretty sure he'd never seen the frizzy woman outside of the alley. It was starting to look like a pattern, for sure.

He told Alison and Dolly, who nodded in agreement.

Unlike the previous two stops, Alison had barely said anything. Her face was tight as she stared at the pavement in front of the milliner's.

Dolly put a hand on Alison's forearm.

"Are they the same woman, do you think?" Alison asked at last.

Mick shook his head. "Different ages. But sort of the same face. Relatives, maybe?"

"We must tell Miss North," Dolly said.

"I hope she'll listen," Alison said.

Be careful what you hope for, Mick thought.

Miss North listened carefully and did not like what she heard. She glared at the three of them. "You do understand that you went off sequence?"

They all nodded, keeping their eyes down.

"And I presume Mr. Charles joined you on this ... excursion?"

"He had a tutorial with Mr. Victor," Alison said.

It was accurate without being exactly true, which was close as Alison came to lying.

"Miss North," Alison said, "I'm the thane. If we oughtn't have done it, it's my fault."

Miss North her eyebrows. "'If?'"

"We did learn something most important," Alison said defiantly. "It's almost certain that the women were in the alleys, not in the ordinary world. Surely—"

"I have been devoting considerable effort to devising ways to show Mr. Gunn the alley sites so as to learn more without coloring his memories," Miss North said. "That is now impossible."

Dolly and Mick winced. Alison pressed on. "I do apologize, Miss North. Truly. But Gunner remembered. He did."

Miss North sighed. "Miss March, normally you are an exemplary student. And I understand that this recent death is particularly painful for you. But your… zeal does not place you above the rules. What you did today interferes with our efforts to understand the poor boy's death. And to prevent future deaths. I am displeased, and I am disappointed."

Dolly looked like she'd been slapped. Mick felt like she looked.

Alison looked sad but unbowed. "I understand, miss."

"Each of you, including Mr. Charles, is barred from leaving the Institute, for any purpose, under any circumstances, for two weeks. If your behavior is beyond reproach during that time, I may then permit you to resume your streeting duties."

"No patrol?" Dolly asked, aghast. Realizing she had spoken aloud, she raised her hand to her mouth.

"Indeed not," Miss North said. "And you three shall spend

the next two weeks doing such tasks as may be required in the kitchens or the cellars. Report to Mrs. Robbin tomorrow at your normal patrol time."

Mick winced.

"And you, Mr. Gunn, shall explain to Miss Atkinson why you cannot patrol with her team for two weeks at least."

Mick winced again. "Yes, miss."

Miss North stared at them for a while. "Children, you meant well, which is in your favor. But you must also *do* well, according to your capacities. And you can do much better. A certain amount of foresight is required of pupils at the Institute, and your actions today demonstrate a dismaying lack of that virtue. You are dismissed."

A little later, the Squad was in the Sixers' common room, at a small table beside the empty fireplace, away from the studiers and the game players. Leech was so grateful they'd covered for him that he wasn't even rubbing in that they had punishment duty.

"I can tell Miss Atkinson for you," Alison offered to Mick. "I am to blame, really."

It was tempting. But it wasn't Alison's fault, not really. She hadn't forced him to go. "I'll do it," he said.

"I do hope we haven't lost Miss North's trust," Alison said.

"We haven't," Dolly said. "She doesn't hold grudges. If we don't do anything foolish in the next two weeks, she'll simply treat it as a lesson learned."

Alison reached across the table and took Dolly's hand gratefully.

Mick thought it was interesting how, when Dolly was

thinking about herself, she went around half-flinching, as if the whole world were an ambush. But when she was thinking about other people, she was a lot more confident. And her confidence was justified—she saw the big picture really well. She just couldn't see herself in it, somehow.

"So they're echo phantasms?" Leech asked. "You're sure?"

Alison nodded. She lifted a thin book from the stack that she had retrieved from her room and opened it. She passed it to Leech, pointing to a passage. Dolly and Mick leaned over to read too. It was a long footnote about echo phantasms and how they appeared just before lift alleys closed, showing an image of whoever had stepped into the alley earlier.

"*Lift* alleys, however," Leech said.

"Perhaps it works for drop alleys too," Alison said.

"How?" he asked. "People step *out* of drop alleys, not *into* them."

"What else could it be?" Alison asked.

They all sat quietly for a bit.

"Nobody saw the ladies at all, not even before Gunner did," Dolly noted. "If the ladies were in the real world earlier and stepped into the alley before Gunner saw them, why didn't *anybody* else see them when they were in the real world?"

"Perhaps no one had got there yet," Alison said.

"At the first one, Miss Atkinson's team was there at least an hour before the alley opened," Leech pointed out.

"And the last alley didn't open till after Miss Atkinson arrived," Dolly added. "The lady couldn't have stepped into it before it was open."

Alison shrugged again. "I don't know what's happening. But it has something to do with echoes. And it must be related to fawkeses, and the dropper who…"

She couldn't bring herself to say *who died*.

"I think that's right," Leech said, "But—"

"But what?" Alison asked sharply.

Leech looked at Dolly for support.

Dolly said, "But it's best we do what Miss North said, isn't it? The dons and the professors, they know more about this than we do. Fawkes alleys, echo phantasms. All of it."

Alison's face took a stubborn set. "I shall do it alone, then," she said.

"Do what?" Leech asked gently.

"Never you mind, Leigh Charles," she said. "Never any of you mind." She lifted her stack of books and stomped away.

After a glum conversation with Dolly and Leech, Mick went to the lobby of the Great Hall to wait for Gail to return from patrol. He had to tell her he was grounded, and he didn't want to have to go to her tory to do it. Rip off the Band-Aid right away, he told himself. Or was it, rip off the *bandage*? He couldn't remember. His head was filling up with apertures and the names of streets and squares that probably had been turned into condos and parking garages before he was born, and he was losing the words he'd grown up with. And memories. He could remember fairy path border patterns, but sometimes he forgot the Netflix logo. Or his friends' faces. Aiden Cantu had been his best friend before Mick had to start switching schools, but now Mick wasn't sure he remembered what Aiden looked like.

They take away your memories, and you try to help anyway, and then they ground you. No wonder Alison was mad.

He got mad at the Institute and the universe, glaring up at

one of the marble busts of Edward Forsyth and the other honored gentlemen. The marble made them bright white, of course, but he suspected that even in real life they'd also been—what had Miss Emmet called it, "sufficiently pale"?

While Mick was waiting for Gail, Owl entered the Great Hall's lobby from the direction of the boys' door and surprised Mick by walking over to him. "Gunner," he said.

"Owl," Mick replied.

"I hope you won't think me rude," Owl began carefully.

Mick braced himself for something rude.

"But, ah, I wonder if Miss March is quite all right?" Owl asked.

Mick stared at Owl, trying to figure out how on earth he'd already heard about the Squad's going off-sequence.

Before Mick could ask that question, Owl said, "Only I heard about the dropper who died, and it put me in mind of Miss March's... You do know, perhaps, about her brother?"

Mick nodded cautiously.

"I, ah, well, I was 'prenticing with the team that... That is, it seemed to me that the dropper might put her in mind of... and I was concerned about the distress such a thing would natural-ly..." Owl trailed off uncertainly.

Owl seemed genuinely worried, but Mick wasn't sure what Alison would want him to say.

Before Mick could figure how to respond, Owl said, "Quite right, it's no business of mine. Still, if you think it mightn't be too unwelcome, please give her my well wishes." Owl nodded abruptly and turned to walk quickly to the main staircase.

Mick was trying to figure out what to make of that when Gail and Flora entered from the direction of the girls' entrance, and Mick hustled to intercept them. He asked to speak to Gail alone and then explained what had happened and what Miss North had said, including being grounded for two weeks.

Gail sighed. "Well, she's right, Gunner. You did lack foresight. But you're a child. Children lack foresight. I wonder sometimes whether Miss North was ever a child."

"Miss Emmet says they called her 'Magnetic North' when she was a kid," Mick said. "Because she always told people which way to go."

Gail chuckled briefly. "What you did was foolish. But it wasn't cruel or dishonest, which is the main thing. So do your punishment duty. Study the Plan. Help poor Miss March learn about echo phantasms if it will solace her. Then, when you're released from the dungeon, present yourself for greeting duty."

"Thank you," Mick said, meaning it.

She turned and strode off. A few kind words had gone a long way, and he no longer wanted to murder a bunch of stone heads. He waved apologetically across the lobby at the marble busts.

He stopped, suddenly realizing something. He didn't owe them an apology after all. They were a big bunch of sufficiently pale phonies.

As he and his friends clustered at the same table in the tory common room after dinner, Mick tried to explain about the stone heads. "It's a joke," he told them. "An actual joke. By a liar."

"What are you on about, Gunner?" Leech asked.

"It's not just that Edward Forsyth wasn't an Earl's son," Mick said. "It's that he's completely made up, and so is the Earl and the … Earless—"

"Countess," Alison said absently, not looking up from *An Anatomy of Apertural Oddities*.

"Forsyth. Foresight. This is a place for people who have seen the future. And he called it the 'Foresight Institute.' It was all a big inside joke."

Leech laughed. "Do you know, I think you're right, Gunner. I've heard the foresight-Forsyth joke before, but I hadn't realized that the Viscount must have appreciated the joke as well."

"*Phony* Viscount," Mick said.

"But why is it important?" Alison asked, eyes still locked on her book.

"Because..." Mick struggled to put it into words. "We can't have servants because we have to keep our secrets. We can't take books outside the walls because we have to keep our secrets. We can't talk about our lives in the future because secrets, secrets, secrets. But *they* ... They can name our school a great big connan screaming as loud as it can, 'Hey, suckers. We're from the future!'"

"But why is it *important?*" Alison asked again.

"Because, up theirs. We tried to stop kids from dying, and this stupid place changed the wifi password to punish us." He took a deep breath. "Anyway, I don't know if it's important. It just makes me mad. And if you need help with echo phantasms or whatever, let me know."

Alison glanced up and smiled at him faintly. "Thank you, Gunner. Dolly, if you don't object, I shall read in our room until lights out. Alone."

Before Dolly could reply, Alison stood and walked toward the girls' corridor.

Dolly watched her go and then looked at Mick. She started to say something and then stopped.

"Don't be bashful," Leech told her. When she didn't speak, Leech told Mick, "She wants to know what a 'wifi' is."

The next morning, the Scriptorium was finally open again, albeit with a don sitting in a chair outside its outer door. Mr. Hartnell—not even slightly murdered by pirates—looked like he always did. Mick asked about the break-in a couple times, and Mr. Hartnell pointedly ignored him.

Tutorial with Miss North was much the same. She acted as if nothing had happened recently, not in the Scriptorium, not with the ghost women.

After lunch, Mick trudged glumly to punishment duty in the kitchens, finding Dolly and Alison already there. Leech was probably off playing footie or sleeping, the lucky jerk.

At least they didn't get dumpwaiter duty. Mrs. Robbin ordered Dolly to help the cooks and the kitchen kids ("scullions") chop vegetables for stew. Mrs. Robbin reported that Mr. Willard, the head caretaker, had asked her to assign two students to ash duty. That task fell to Mick and Alison, who had to fill a heavy, wood-wheeled barrow with coal dust from the ash bins in the cellar, wheel it up the ramp to the garden, and dump it by the gate for the parish dustman to collect. Then they had to go to the kitchens to clean out the coal dust out of the kitchener stoves. They were both sweaty, coal-smudged, and bedraggled by the time it was over and they could stagger to the stone bench beneath the London plane tree in the middle of the garden. Mick collapsed gratefully onto the cool bench, closing his eyes and savoring the breeze that flickered to life now and again.

"The next time you go off sequence, go without me," Mick said.

"I shall need to devise a plan to escape first," Alison said.

Mick laughed, but Alison didn't. He opened his eyes to find her looking at the roof. "After we spoke yesterday evening," she said, "I climbed up to the roof. I think perhaps I could climb down using one of the alley drainpipes." She pointed toward the Little Castle alley. "But I could never climb back up. And lowering the fire stairs to the ground would be far too loud."

"That's stupid," he said, more bluntly than he'd intended.

"I don't expect you to understand, but—"

"It's stupid. Even if you don't fall and get killed, Miss North will chain you to a coal bin," Mick said. "And London is dangerous at night. Especially for a kid out alone. You're the one who keeps telling me that."

"Dangerous for you, but—"

"And for you. And we've already seen everything in daylight. We won't be able to see anything helpful at night."

"The night dons have doubled patrols," Alison said. "The daytime dons are doing more patrols too. There's something happening out there."

"And the dons are patrolling it," Mick said.

"None of them can see alleys like you can. And none of them can remember like I can," Alison said.

"The dons know a lot more than us, even you," Mick said.

Alison grabbed him by the shoulders and pressed her face into his. "None of them *cares* more," she said. "I cannot watch another child fall dead out of an alley. I shan't spend another night looking out the window, not sleeping, just seeing his face there on the pavement."

His shoulders hurt, and he struggled to break free of her grip.

"I apologize," she said, dropping her hands. "It's only…"

Mick got it, mostly. It had been pretty awful running to that poor kid on Princes Street only to realize he was dead. And he hadn't watched his own brother die the same way. "You can't go. You just can't. It's dangerous. And it won't help anybody."

Alison nodded, but her gaze continued searching.

A few days passed without any real change. Mr. Hartnell acted as if everything were normal even though there was always a don sitting just outside the Scriptorium. Miss North acted as if everything were normal though even people kept interrupting Mick's tutorials with her to tell her that more and more fawkeses were appearing. Meanwhile, Mick, Dolly, and Alison mucked out dumpwaiter buckets, chopped vegetables, cleaned ashes, tugged weeds, and scrubbed floors.

Mick continued to keep an eye on Alison in case she tried to sneak out. She seemed quiet but okay, although she got surly on Sunday when she couldn't visit her friends at Orphans.

One afternoon, Mick was lying in the cool shade of an apple tree after hours of weeding, eyes closed, body heavy with sweat and exhaustion, when he felt somebody standing over him. He opened an eye. Alison.

She was holding a big book open in front of her. "This is Blake's *Disquisitions on Chronal Esoterica*." She drew in a breath to read.

"I bet it's all commas and no periods," Mick said. "Translate it for me."

She chuckled quietly. "Blake says there were a half-dozen

since 1800—the book is from 1818, so that's eighteen years. There must have been more since then."

"A half-dozen what?" Mick asked.

"People who disappeared into a stirring. Not open trances but stirrings."

"Trances?"

"It's an old word for 'alleys.' Blake uses it a good deal."

"Regular alleys or time alleys?"

"Both. Blake says that alley rats saw actual people, who were actually there in the flesh, simply disappear into stirrings for drop alleys. Not apertures, mind. Stirrings. Then she says that twelve hours later, roughly, there were fawkes drop alleys where many of the stirrings had been."

Interesting. "So," Mick said, "alley rats are investigating a stirring, and they see people disappear like they walked into a *lift* alley. Only there isn't a lift alley. And then later a fawkes *drop* alley shows up in the same place?"

"Correct."

"So you're thinking that..." Mick realized he had no idea. "What are you thinking?"

"What if we're the *cause* of the fawkeses?" she asked. "Streets and greets."

"Huh?"

"If a rat feels a stirring," she said, "the rat investigates and reports. And then more rats investigate. So there are rats walking through stirrings a great deal. Perhaps that's causing the fawkeses."

"And now everyone is patrolling more. Because of all the fawkeses." Mick laughed a little at the idea—the more they investigated why there were so many fawkeses, the more fawkeses there were to investigate.

"Correct," Alison said.

"But the book said that people disappeared, right? Nobody's disappeared."

"Perhaps they will."

"Have you told Miss North?" he asked.

Alison shook her head. "I need more evidence. From first-hand observation."

That meant leaving the Institute. "Even if we could go observe," he said, "what good would it do to walk around just seeing if anybody randomly disappears?"

Alison rolled her eyes. "Gunner…"

Oh. Right. "You mean we should go where there were stirrings earlier to see if any fawkeses open up."

She nodded.

"But how do we know where the stirrings were?"

"We street thanes meet in the evenings to discuss the day's phenomena, including stirrings."

Mick thought about it. "I know you don't want to tell Miss North…"

Alison shook her head sharply.

"But couldn't we just tell Miss Mitchell? Or one of the other dons?"

Alison shook her head again. "Even if they treated the idea seriously, they would require us to remain within the walls."

"But—"

"You're the best spotter, so you must go. And I must be there with you."

Mick sighed. If he snitched on her, she'd never forgive him. If he didn't snitch, she'd go, with or without him. "Dolly and Leech?"

Alison shook her head yet again. "Dolly would try to stop me. And Leech would blab to Dolly."

And so, in the cool, swishing shade of the trees, Alison and Mick plotted their foolishness. Alison would go to the thanes' meeting and learn where the stirrings had been. Then, that night, they'd sneak out to investigate. To avoid waking Dolly and Leech, they would stay in the common room after lights out, pretending to be doing their lessons. They weren't supposed to do that, but half the grinds did it, and the prefects never stopped them. Anybody who was still in the common room at that point wouldn't care if Alison and Mick left. Then, after searching for fawkeses, they would return to the common room and pretend they'd fallen asleep studying.

But they still needed to sneak in and out of the Institute without getting caught and hung from the Great Clock by their thumbs. Mick didn't want Alison going up to the roof and trying to use the drainpipe, so he told her there was a way out of the basement without telling her where or what it was. He didn't want her doing something dumb without him. She was going to do something dumb, of course, but Mick intended to be there for it. Idiocy loved company.

CHAPTER 18

RETURN OF THE MYSTERIOUS INTERLOPER

Shockingly, their plan worked. Mick and Alison snuck out of the common room and down the back stairs. They had to move slowly because there were more professors and dons around than usual, probably because of the attack on the Scriptorium. They had a couple near misses, and at one point, Mick caught a glimpse of Mr. Victor by the founders' busts, his cold white head as still and stern as the statues. By the time they made it to the pitch-black basement, Mick's heart was pounding like he'd just run up all the stairs at Soldier Field.

Groping in the darkness, Mick eventually led Alison into what he had decided to call the sneak vent. Partway in, Mick accidentally snuffed the candle after dripping hot wax on his hand, but they made it outside. Barely. If Alison's hair had been any thicker, she would have been too tall for the vent.

As they headed toward the first possible fawkes, Mick took stock nervously. He'd never been out in London after dark. Streets weren't allowed out of the Institute without permission, and even greets needed permission to be out after dinner. It was late enough, and they were far enough from the drunk and noisy parts of town that the streets were mostly quiet, though the occasional carriage clopped and clattered past. Enough moonlight seeped through the clouds and fog to hint at figures huddled in the shadows. Most were poor people sleeping in cold corners, and some might have been robbers lying in wait. Mick saw a few kids their age, just sitting or standing around, sometimes alone, sometimes in little huddles. Maybe they were robbers. Maybe they were just afraid to go home, if they had homes.

Alison led the way to one possible fawkes after another. They checked a dozen, finding only menacing shadows and whispers. Every block or two, Mick saw or heard something that made him tense up, half a shiver away from making a run for it.

And then a man with a dark coat and a bushy beard lunged at them out of an alley.

Alison shoved Mick forward and yelled for him to run.

He ran.

Mick cut across the empty market square, taking turns at random. Alison caught up with him and took the lead as they wove their way through the streets, avoiding the narrow, dark alleys and dodging the occasional pedestrian. Mick concentrated on keeping her in sight as she turned suddenly one way and the other. Neither of them dared to look back until they'd been running for a while along a quiet street, hearing only their own footsteps.

Seeing nothing behind him, Mick slowed to a stop. He tried to call Alison's name but was too out of breath. He succeeded on the second try.

Alison looked back at him and then the empty street. She backtracked to stand beside him as they both tried to catch their breath.

Mick's feet hurt from running in broughams, which were bricks with laces. In the moonlight, Mick's pocket watch said it wasn't long after midnight. They hadn't even been out for two hours. It felt like days. "We should go back," he whispered.

"But—"

"It's dangerous, and there's nothing out here."

"I lived for years on the streets of this city. The dangerous streets, not these," Alison said, gesturing dismissively around her.

Sure, Mick thought, but she'd told him to run as soon as the man had come at them.

He noticed something glinting in her hand that wasn't her pocket watch.

"Are you carrying a razor?" he asked.

She didn't answer, but she didn't need to. It was a razor, one of the kind that closed by folding. It disappeared up her sleeve with a flick of her wrist.

"Do you always carry—"

"Years on the dangerous streets," she said in a tone that ended that part of the conversation.

Mick took a breath. "Okay, I know you want evidence," he said. "I do too. But we need to go back to the Institute and come up with a better plan."

She was silent for a moment but then nodded.

They worked their way back to the Institute and banged their knees and elbows getting through the sneak vent.

Being back inside buoyed Mick with relief. From that point on, if they got caught, they would only be out of the tory after lights out, not out of Institute against Miss North's orders. They'd be in trouble but not In Trouble.

Still, they both froze when they spotted the gray, hooded figure a flight above them on the spiral staircase. It stood without moving, looking upward, apparently waiting for something.

The hoodie ghost.

Eventually, it started climbing the stairs. Alison was in front of Mick, and she wasn't moving. The hoodie ghost exited the stairwell. Alison started moving again, and they followed quietly, risking a look into the hallway.

The hoodie ghost had vanished.

Back in the Sixers' common room, apparently to avoid further discussion, Alison laid herself out on a bench near the fireplace and pretended to fall asleep. Mick sighed and laid down on the next bench over. He passed out and didn't wake up until the next morning, when he noticed that he was getting poked in the shoulder. He opened his eyes and found Dolly's frowning face much too close to his.

The next day, Mick was with Dolly in the kitchens, wearing a plain gray apron and chopping bottomless buckets of vegetables. After a week of much grosser chores, chopping veggies was a pleasure.

Mrs. Robbin ran the kitchens, supervising three adult cooks, women who were mostly just backs turned to Mick as they stirred pots or shoved things in ovens. There were also some scullions Mick was able to say hi to sometimes.

Mrs. Robbin was nice enough. She reminded him a little of the aunties who'd pinched his cheeks at barbecues. Of course, his aunties could remember his name. Mrs. Robbin kept calling him and the boy scullions random names. Dolly and the girl scullions were just "you girls." At least that's what it sounded like. Mrs. Robbin was sometimes hard to understand because she was missing a lot of teeth.

The scullions rotated shifts on a schedule Mick didn't understand. That day it was Christopher and Agnes. Both mumbled polite responses whenever he spoke to them, but Christopher seemed lost in some other world, and Agnes flinched whenever Mick spoke to her, watching him with nervous eyes like one of his cousin Gabriela's foster dogs. Not talking to them felt rude, but talking to them felt cruel. So he mostly just talked to Dolly.

Either Mrs. Robbin didn't care whether Mick and Dolly spoke while they were on punishment duty or her bad hearing meant she didn't notice as long as they kept their voices down. That was lucky because Dolly had a lot of talking to do. At first, Mick tried to avoid admitting what he and Alison had done the night before. But Dolly knew something had happened, so she kept at him. Also, deep down, Mick wanted to tell her. He didn't want to go out at night with Alison again, but he was afraid that she'd go out alone if he didn't go with her. So eventually he 'fessed up.

Dolly pointed out what idiots they'd been. "Still, I know you only wanted to see her safe. And she—well, her thoughts are disordered because of her brother."

"She says she can take care of herself," Mick said.

"Alison knows the roughest streets of London better than anyone here," Dolly said. "But that doesn't protect her against fully grown ruffians. She knows that. That's why she pressed so hard to have her friends saved from the streets and placed at Orphans, after all. And they're all bigger and older than she is."

Mick nodded. "I think we should tell Miss North. About the hoodie ghost."

Dolly chopped thoughtfully. "No," she said at last. "If you tell Miss North about the Interloper, you'll have to explain why you and Alison were creeping about the Institute after lights out. And then you'll be confined to the Institute for a month, and they'll likely break up the Squad. And I very much like the Squad. Besides, neither of you truly saw the Interloper, did you? Not her face, that is. If it even is a she. And the Interloper wasn't really doing anything improper. Simply going up stairs."

"At midnight? In a hood?" Mick asked. "How does she even get a hood?"

Dolly started a new carrot. "Oh, it's suspicious, certainly. But what we know isn't helpful. The professors already know the Interloper is prowling about. And there are already so many professors and dons patrolling the corridors because of whatever happened in the Scriptorium."

Mick nodded. That made sense. Plus, he liked any plan that didn't force him to have another painful conversation with Miss North. "Is all of this normal?" he asked. "The Scriptorium, the Interloper?"

"It is all most unusual," Dolly said.

"They must be connected," he said.

Dolly shrugged. "It feels that way. But we need to know, not just to feel." She started a new carrot. "I do know, however, that I would dearly love to go for a walk in Regent's Park again. And eat a half dozen spice cakes, at the least." She smiled faintly at Mick.

· · ·

Yawning after punishment duty, Mick climbed the stairs to see Miss Weathers. Leech was still insisting that Mick was in love with Miss Weathers, but Mick really did just like spending time with her because she was smart and calm. She was mostly just reading big medical books whenever he dropped by, and she didn't mind if he sat down and read too. It felt good to be quietly welcome somewhere.

Also, visiting Miss Weathers meant visiting the nursery. He missed his baby sister, and he felt a bit closer to her when he was surrounded by little kids. He especially got a kick out of tone-deaf Julia, whose face was always so serious, right up until it broke out in smiles and laughter. Emilia was like that too. She'd spend ten minutes playing with her toes with a dead serious look on her face like she was doing hard math, and then she'd look up at him and gurgle a little laugh. He missed that.

That afternoon, the toddlers were napping in sunny patches on the carpet by the window like cats in pantalettes, while Miss Weathers read about bones and Mick read about alleys. Eventually, Miss Weathers closed her book in her lap and looked up. "I do wish Mr. Gray would write his anatomy," she said. "Bichat is astute, but French is such a struggle. Still," she said, pointing to a massive book on the table beside her, "it's easier going than *Compleat Compendium of the Maladies of the Head and Skull*. Its first chapter should be 'Headaches Suffered by My Readers.'"

She set the book she'd been reading atop the *Compleat Compendium*. "Gunner, I've a question for you. Is the gossip true? *Did* you see a hooded figure in gray prowling about?"

Mick gripped the chair's arms nervously. How had she heard what he and Alison had seen last night?

"In the library?" Miss Weathers prodded.

Oh. The first time. He unclenched and nodded. "Why?"

"I saw much the same thing here last night in the small hours. I was lying in my cot"—she pointed to the window—"trying to lull myself to sleep by calling to mind the prime movers in the contraction and relaxation of the fist when I heard a faint noise. I opened my eyes to see a figure in gray, with a hood, tiptoeing across the room."

"Oh," Mick said. When he and Alison had spotted the Interloper, had the Interloper exited the stairwell on the same floor as the nursery? Probably.

"Did you see her face?" Mick asked.

Miss Weathers shook her head. "But it's interesting you think it was a she. That was my intuition too. Possibly a student?"

Mick nodded eagerly. "We've been calling her the 'Mysterious Interloper.'"

She laughed. "Give Leech my compliments on the name. I told Dr. Quinn what I saw, and she mentioned what you saw in the library. She took me to tell the Vicar what I saw, and he seemed most intrigued." She paused. "Since speaking to the Vicar, I've been reflecting. I now believe I must have seen the Interloper before, likely several times. You see, sometimes I wake halfway from slumber and feel someone is standing over me. It's inevitably a shadow or a dream, and when I realize that, I feel relieved and fall back asleep."

"Me too," Mick said.

"But now I suspect that over the past week or so, I've more than once woken and seen your Mysterious Interloper across the room. Only, I fell asleep again, thinking it simply another of my half-dreams."

. . .

During dinner, Mick wanted to tell the Squad everything Miss Weathers had told him, but too many people could have overheard. He waited until they were clustered in their corner of the tory common room.

As soon as he finished telling them, they started talking over one another, until Dolly said, "Hush."

Alison and Leech kept talking.

"Hush," Dolly repeated, slapping the table. It wasn't a loud slap, but it wasn't the sort of thing Dolly usually did. They all shut up.

Dolly's expression grew nervous, but she drew a deep breath and pressed on. "Miss Weathers' information presents an opportunity." She swallowed and then frowned, thinking.

Alison asked gently, "What opportunity?"

"To catch the Interloper," Dolly said.

"How?" Leech asked.

"According to Miss Weathers," Dolly said, "the Interloper has been in the nursery more than once recently. She may have been there quite often, or been there previously, only Miss Weathers didn't happen to wake every time." Getting no response, she added, "She may go there *every* night."

They finally got it.

"We need to keep watch on the nursery," Leech said.

"Won't the professors and the dons and everybody already be doing that?" Mick asked.

"Likely not," Dolly said. "Miss Weathers said she didn't think to mention the Interloper's other visits to the Vicar, correct?"

"Right," Mick said. He saw what she meant. The Vicar and the other adults didn't know that the Interloper kept going back to the nursery.

"But—" Alison began, then stopped.

Mick and Dolly looked at each other. "You won't be going outside the walls at night again, Alison," Dolly said.

Leech turned to Alison. "You won't be doing *what?*"

Dolly explained what Alison and Mick had done the night before.

"Unbelievable," Leech said loudly, getting shushed by several grinds.

Alison and Leech stared at one another for a while, their faces strange and shifting mixtures of anger, sadness, and concern. Eventually, Alison said, "I had to do something."

Nobody spoke.

"But it wasn't the right thing," Alison said. "Was it?"

"I should say not," Leech said. "Not at all." He'd started angrily, but by the end he just sounded worried. "And you," he said, looking at Mick, "you should—"

"I couldn't tell you," Mick said.

"You could have," Leech said. "But we're all of us eejits. Well and good, then. But let us be eejits *together*. No more secrets and sneaking."

They all nodded.

"No more secrets from each other, obviously," he added with a grin. "We'll keep secrets and keep sneaking as far as the rest of this place is concerned, else where's the fun?"

Alison giggled and took Leech's hand on the table.

"So," Leech added, "I believe Dolly was about to tell us how to trap the Mysterious Interloper."

After Dolly had explained her idea and the team had argued over improvements until agreeing on a plan, they broke apart to play their roles.

About an hour before lights out, while Alison was reading about apertural oddities and Leech and Dolly were arguing for fun, Mick headed down to the nursery. He found Miss Weathers in her rocking chair, a lit oil lamp beside her, and a big book with diagrams of veins and arteries in her lap. In the tall window behind her, her reflection rocked toward her and away from her.

The toddlers were in their bedroom, though Mick heard giggles and yelling through the half-open door indicating that they weren't yet asleep.

Miss Weathers stood and crossed to the bedroom door. "Be silent and return to your cots this instant, or I shall be very cross with you all," she said sternly. "Including you, Julia."

She returned to her chair, winked at Mick, and gestured that he sit down in the chair near hers. He did so, opening his book without saying anything. She turned up the oil lamp a bit and scooted it across the end table so it was halfway between them.

His book was a decent fantasy story about some Austrian farm brothers, but he couldn't focus. He kept looking up to see if the Interloper had somehow snuck in. When the bells at All Souls rang quarter till, Miss Weathers closed her book, saying he should let her go to bed. He nodded, put his books in his satchel with an exaggerated yawn, and left the room.

Instead of going to Tory Six, he ducked into a nearby hallway that dead-ended into some storage closets. Leech was sitting on the floor in the darkness, his face nearly invisible. They nodded at each other as Mick sat down, and they began to wait silently for the Interloper. Outside the nursery's other door, Alison and Dolly were doing the same.

Even after Mick's eyes adjusted, the hallway was a sea of dark grays. He was still amazed at how dark 1853 could be.

Future Chicago never got truly dark, not with all the street-lights, headlights, stoplights, and so on. Heck, even indoor lights seeped outdoors, so if you turned off your own lights, a hundred people's living room lights snuck in through your blinds. That didn't happen in 1853.

Every once in a while, he or Leech poked a head out to peer at the light beneath the door to check whether Miss Weathers had snuffed her oil lamp. After what seemed like a thousand checks, the line of light disappeared.

After that, it was just sitting in the shadows where they could just see the nursery door. Mick wasn't sure how long they waited. Partly, it was too dark to read his watch. Partly, he kept dozing off because he was exhausted from spending the previous night sneaking around London and then sleeping on a bench.

The bells at All Souls rang the hour. Mick counted care-fully: midnight. So he had dozed off for a half hour or so. But Leech had been awake. Probably. Mick just had to dial in now.

Suddenly, the Interloper was standing in the middle of the main corridor, a smudge of gray with a black gap where its face should be, like some sort of dark magic. How—?

He must have dozed off again. And the black gap must just be the shadow from the hood. Nothing magical.

He hoped.

He looked at Leech, whose eyes were bright and open. They both moved silently into crouches, craning their necks to keep the Interloper in sight.

The Interloper surveyed the corridor, the black hole of its face changing shape as it did. Mick tried to treat the Interloper like an alley, to calmly observe the phenomena. The Interloper did look like a student—too short and too skinny to be a professor.

A student with a hood, Mick told himself. And the slight hint of a glow from the black hole face was just from alley rat eyes. Definitely not a death demon with a hellmouth face.

Definitely not.

Probably.

The Interloper's head stopped scanning, and the Interloper started gliding down the hallway away from them.

Leech and Mick quietly followed. At a branching point, Mick went left, and Leech went right.

Looking over his shoulder, he saw Alison and Dolly plus someone bigger right behind them. Mick almost yelled a warning before he realized the bigger person was Miss Weathers. Heading down the corridor and seeing no one, he hoped Leech had been able to follow the Interloper. He was becoming painfully aware of how many places the corridor branched off as they went. The Interloper could have gone down any branch.

"Stop!" someone yelled from around a corner, up ahead. Leech.

A blur of movement appeared from that direction—the Interloper was coming straight at Mick. But not for long—the Interloper suddenly dropped a shoulder and turned.

Mick followed, turning the same corner a few seconds behind. The Interloper was nowhere to be seen. Miss Weathers appeared at his side, and they wordlessly jogged down the corridor until they reached a dark stairwell. Miss Weathers tilted her head into the stairwell, looking up and down.

Mick couldn't see the Interloper, but it was so dark he could barely see Miss Weathers two feet away from him. She pointed at herself and then up, and then pointed at Mick and then down. Mick nodded.

Not eager to fall down the dark stairway—or to run into the Interloper by himself—Mick descended cautiously, keeping one hand to the wall for guidance. He made it as far as the basement, but the stairwell door wouldn't budge.

He started to creep back up the stairs. Partway, he caught a glimpse of a motionless shadow above him. He froze, his heart racing. But the shadow wasn't wearing a hood. Mick squinted and then crept a couple silent steps upward. "Leech?" he whispered.

"Gunner?" Leech whispered back.

Mick went up the last few steps, meeting Lech on the landing. "Did you—" He stopped mid-whisper at the sound of footsteps coming down the stairs.

Leech tugged at his sleeve, pulling him into the hallway, and then into the gap between the wall and a tall pedestal for the bust of some semi-important person. Leech slipped behind the pedestal before kneeling, and Mick did the same. Holding their breath, they peered out at the corridor from opposite sides of the pedestal.

A flickering appeared, and a don stepped into view, pausing and lifting a candle lamp over her head, listening carefully. She must have heard them.

Luckily, they were hidden by stone and shadow, and the don lowered her lamp and moved on, her footsteps eventually fading into silence.

Mick's heart skipped a beat when a match flared. But it was just Leech, reading the plaque on the pedestal. "'Porter Jaynes. Master of Apertures.'" Leech raised the match a bit higher, revealing the sculpture's oversized pointy beard and massive nostrils.

Leech waved the match to snuff it. "Such a large bust for someone here in the Hall of Nobodies."

Mick had no idea why Leech was worrying about pedestals when there was an Interloper on the loose.

The two of them tiptoed back to the nursery, where they found Miss Weathers and the others sitting quietly by the window, lit by a dim oil lamp. Whispering so that they wouldn't wake the toddlers, everyone went over what they had learned, which wasn't much. The excitement was wearing off, and it all felt a little disappointing.

"Shall I report you lot to Miss North, I wonder?" Miss Weathers said. "Roaming the halls after midnight."

They all stared at her nervously.

"Of course I shan't," Miss Weathers said. "Still," she told Mick, "you could have warned me. These two didn't half frighten me to death when they came creeping into the nursery."

"We really do apologize," Alison said.

Miss Weathers waved a hand. She sat quietly for a minute, thinking. "I wonder why here? There's naught here, except noisy weans, snotty noses, and the *Compleat Compendium of the Maladies of the Head and Skull*. Yet the Interloper keeps returning."

It made no sense. The nursery wasn't even next door to anything important.

"The Mysterious Interloper grows ever more mysterious," Leech said, obviously enjoying himself.

"She'll not come back to the nursery, I wager," Miss Weathers said. "Not after being chased through the corridors."

They nodded.

"Still," Miss Weathers continued, "I shall ask Dr. Quinn for permission to start locking the doors, though she mislikes doing so. Some poor wee bairnies died here long ago in a fire because the doors were locked, you see. But under the circumstances, perhaps locking up is best."

The Squad all nodded.

"And when I do that, younglings, I shall have to explain why I'm asking, which will mean telling Dr. Quinn that the Interloper returned, though I shan't mention your involvement. And that means that Miss North and all the grandees will know soon enough."

As the Squad snuck back to the tory through the dark and creepy halls, Mick tried to make sense of what had happened. But Leech was right—the more they learned, the more mysterious it got.

CHAPTER 19

A VANISHING IN THE HALL OF NOBODIES

The next day, Mick was lucky enough to get chopping duty with Mrs. Robbin and Agnes again. Dolly and Alison were stuck cleaning skylights. The first hour of chopping was an endless pile of onions that made Mick cry so much he started to feel like something terrible had happened to him. Well, beyond getting trapped in ancient history.

Mrs. Robbin kept flipping up her apron to wipe the tears away. "It's a powerful sad pile of onions, it is," she remarked.

The third or fourth time he watched her wipe her eyes, Mick realized that he knew more about the Interloper than he'd thought.

"It's definitely a student," Mick told the Squad after dinner. They were crowded around their usual little table near the fireplace. "The Interloper's hood is an apron. From the kitchens."

He explained how watching Mrs. Robbin rub her eyes had reminded him somehow of the Interloper.

"It does make sense," Alison said. "Very well. Let's say that Gunner is right. What does that tell us?"

"That the Interloper isn't a don," Leech said. "Dons don't get sent to Mrs. Robbin for discipline."

"Or wasn't a don when she got sent, anyhow," Dolly said. "We haven't any idea how long she—"

"Or he," Leech said.

"Do you think it really might be a boy?" Alison asked him.

Leech shrugged. "It's not impossible."

Alison nodded, acknowledging the point.

Mick said, "I know the Interloper could have had the apron for years. But I bet not. Using an apron isn't a long-term solution. When Mrs. Robbin went to the gate to talk to the coster-monger's wife, I tried wearing my apron as a hood. It kinda worked, but it was hard to see out the sides, and it slid around some when I moved. I bet the Interloper realized they needed something to hide their face one day when they were on punishment duty and grabbed it because it was the best they could do."

Dolly said, "I don't think anyone had seen the Interloper before Gunner did, that first time in the library. Two months ago?" she asked Mick.

Mick did the math. "Maybe a month and a half."

"Wait, now," Leech said. "Weren't the Twos saying something about a faceless nun? Before Gunner saw the Interloper the first time? Though not too long before, I don't think."

"In any case, the Interloper was probably put on punishment duty about two months ago," Dolly said.

"I shouldn't think there were that many pupils on punishment duty then," Alison said. "We're the only ones now." She chuckled. "I do apologize."

"Plus, a lot of kids on punishment duty don't get kitchen duty," Mick said. "So they don't get aprons. If we're right, it's really not many people, is it? We just have to figure out who was on kitchen duty back then."

Dolly laughed, loudly for her.

"What?" Mick asked.

"I'm imagining asking Mrs. Robbin which students were on punishment duty so long ago."

"Oh, dear," Alison said, realizing.

"Particularly if it's a girl." Imitating Mrs. Robbin, Dolly said, "Oh, yes, at that time it was a girl. She had replaced the girl, you see. Then, there was a girl. And then came young miss girl, who was here before the other girl. A pert wee creature, young miss girl. Not at all like the other girl, who was sweet as treacle, and a great mystery it is what such a sweet girl could have done to be sent to me, I can tell you."

Alison laughed. "I suppose we shall have to ask her, even so."

Mick wondered who they'd ask when Mrs. Robbin couldn't remember. There might not be anybody. The cooks ignored students, and the scullions avoided students. And Miss North would want to know why they were asking.

Having brainstormed all they could, they turned to their lessons. Now that they were on punishment duty, the professors constantly assigned them extra work, and lessons were overflowing from their satchels like infinite frowning clowns pouring from a circus car.

Mick complained about having to memorize "famed shuttlers of the Pre-Collapse Era." "There's no point. Nobody can time-travel on purpose anymore. These days we only have—" he flipped through the book, until he found the passage he wanted. "We only have 'primary chronal journeys, arising from the whims of the alleys themselves.' There's no more, um, 'secondary chronal journeys, arising from the wit and will of the brave few who penetrated the mysteries of the alleys.'"

Leech laughed. "Gunner, they're punishment lessons, and the only lesson the professors want you to learn is to avoid punishment. The professors think that means 'Don't break the rules.' Students know it means 'Don't get caught.'"

Mick glared at an illustration of some dude named Earnest Witherstrop Putnam with a big mustache and a bigger wig who had apparently taken thirteen round trips backward in time. One of his trips had been nearly five years into the past, "the longest recorded secondary chronal journey, overshining by nigh four months even the famed journey of H.A. Braithwaite completed not long before that gentleman's vanishment from ken." The book wanted Mick to be really impressed by Putnam, but it was hard to be too impressed by somebody who had drowned while drunkenly chasing a badger into the Lea River.

The next day was full of punishment lessons and plain old punishment—more ash carting and weeding, this time on his own because Alison and Dolly were on kitchen duty.

In the common room that night, Alison and Dolly confirmed to Mick and Leech that Mrs. Robbin couldn't remember who had been on punishment duty the day before, much less months earlier.

Mick was half listening as he glared at his punishment lessons. Even Miss Emmet was ganging up on him, making him read a book about building the Institute by someone named Constance Bardon, whom Mick thought of as Constant Boredom.

"There's a whole *chapter*," he complained, "on selecting the quarry for the stone for the Institute. There's another one about the temporary stairways for building the Vault in the basement. Not the actual Vault, just the stairways. Nobody cares, Constance Bardon." Mick pushed the book away in disgust.

Alison and Dolly grinned a little. Leech looked thoughtful and picked up the book, opening it in the light of the oil lamp. He flipped pages back and forth for a while before suddenly calling out, "Eureka!"

Half the kids in the common room shushed him. "You can't silence victory," he called out, hopping to his feet and bowing in all directions.

There was some laughter and some jeering, which led to some shushing from the grinds. That led to more laughter and jeering, and a couple shoving matches broke out.

"Come with me," Leech told the Squad, grabbing the book and the lamp.

The sun was still hovering above the horizon, so the lamp wasn't necessary until they were deep into the gloomy back stairwells. Leech stopped when they reached the bust of Porter Jaynes from the night before.

"You've been unfair to Constance Bardon," Leech told Mick.

Leech handed Constance Bardon's book to Dolly and plucked a candle from a small holder, which he lit from the lamp, put back in the holder, and gave it to Dolly. "Read them the part at the bottom of page thirty-seven," he told her. "About building the Vault."

Mick tried to listen as Dolly read, but it was painfully boring. Instead, his attention followed Leech as Leech took the lamp and walked through a gap between the wall and the pedestal until he hit the far end of the niche, where slowly he raised and lowered the lantern, keeping it close to the wall. Mick started to wonder if Leech was going crazy.

When Dolly had finished, Leech said, "Read it again." He was still slowly moving the lantern over the wall.

Dolly said, "Honestly, Leech, why don't—"

"Please, Dolly," he said.

Dolly read it again. "'Owing to such difficulties and the pressing need for secrecy, the stairways crisscrossed the steel shell of the Vault and of the casings atop it, extending upward in some instances to the chamber above. Sundry supplementary stairs communicated with the crisscrossing stairs to permit access to the adjoining areas. Most of the crisscrossing stairs were destroyed upon the conclusion of construction, the rest sealed.' Shall I continue?"

Getting no answer, she repeated her question. Leech still didn't answer. She was drawing in breath to ask again when he called out, "Hah!"

"Hah?" Alison asked.

"Come see," Leech said.

Alison, Dolly, and Mick looked at one another and shrugged. Alison went through the same gap Leech had used, while Mick and Dolly used the gap on the other side.

"Have a look at what?" Dolly asked. "And why does the bust have a second face?" She pointed.

Mick looked up. So it did. Porter Jaynes had two faces, staring in opposite directions.

Alison made a little "oh" noise, but she didn't have time to explain because Leech turned and grinned at them, teeth glinting in the lamplight.

The wall behind the pedestal moved.

Mick blinked and looked again. It wasn't actually the wall—it was a door that looked like the wall.

Leech pushed it open wide enough to poke through the lamp, then his head. Then he stepped inside.

The door closed abruptly.

Worried about Leech, Mick squeezed past Dolly and pushed the door. It didn't budge. It felt just like a wall—cold stone and everything.

Right when Mick stopped pushing, the door opened just enough for Leech to stick out his head. "Now this," Leech said, "is a proper adventure. Step lively, or someone will see our secret passage."

In the feeble candlelight, Dolly, Alison, and Mick looked at one another. There were a lot of smart reasons not to go. On the other hand, there was a secret passage.

They went.

The door closed behind them with a deep thud, followed by a pair of mechanical clunks. They were clustered on a small landing. A narrow stairway led downward into darkness.

"Careful," Leech whispered, pointing down.

Mick could make out an arcing groove cut into the landing, maybe three inches wide and a little deeper.

"There's a wheel under the door," Leech whispered. "I think it helps hold up the door when it's moving. Anyhow, adventure awaits."

Leech dimmed the lamp slightly to make the oil last longer. "Though we've plenty of oil," Leech whispered. "Probably."

Dolly sighed and snuffed the candle, keeping it as a back-up.

"It's a riddle," Alison whispered, maybe to herself. "Or a jest."

"What is?" Dolly asked.

"Porter Jaynes, Master of Apertures," Alison quoted. "'Apertures' meaning openings. 'Porter' meaning guardian of doors. 'Jaynes' assuredly being an English version of Janus, the two-faced Roman god of doorways."

"Welcome to the Foresight Institute," Mick whispered. Alison snickered.

Dim lamp held before him, Leech led them down the narrow stairway. Mick was in the back, trying to stay close enough to see but not close enough to bump into Dolly too often.

The stairway seemed to be curving. It started to smell gross, maybe mildewed.

"This must be how the Interloper disappeared from the nursery," Leech whispered.

Mick realized that meant the Interloper could be waiting for them just around the bend. He could tell the others were having the same thought because everyone slowed down.

Creeping nervously along, they reached the bottom of the stairway and started along a low-ceilinged hallway no wider than the stairs. For a ways, there were no doors or windows or anything else to break up the blank walls. Or at least what looked like walls. Maybe it was actually one secret door after another.

Leech stopped where the hallway split in two directions. One was a locked door so heavy and thick that it felt like a boulder painted to look like a door.

They went the other way, which soon took them down another cramped, curving stairway. At the bottom was a small door and another arced groove in the floor. Leech pointed at the groove. Another secret door. Well, secret from the other side, anyway.

Leech turned the light down as low as it would go without losing its flame and eased the door open with a quiet creaking from the hinges. Seeing nothing alarming, he turned the light back up and squeezed through the door. The others followed, Alison ducking a bit under the low header.

Mick was the last one through. He held the lamp for Leech as Leech groped at the floor in front of the door. Leech eventually pried loose a small stone, then a larger one, before reaching into the newly made hole. "Triumph!" Leech whispered.

Leech stood and pressed the door shut. There was a heavy thud followed by two mechanical thunks, just like the ones Mick had heard after Leech had closed the first hidden door. Looking very proud of himself, Leech showed them how the locks worked. Afterward, Mick held up the lamp and stared closely at the wall. He couldn't see any trace of the door.

Mick turned to look around the musty, windowless room, which wasn't much bigger than a closet. Half of the walls were covered with shelves brimming with bric-a-brac. And dust. He fought back a sneeze.

Everyone exchanged glances and shrugged. Alison pointed across the room to a door. Leech nodded and took the lamp from Mick to inspect it.

While waiting, Mick looked at the junk on the shelves. He couldn't make out most of it in the dim light, but right in front of his face, there was a coil of rope, a watering can, and a candle stub. He pocketed the candle stub just in case.

"Odd," Alison whispered to herself. "Leech," she said, a bit louder, "some light, pray."

Leech turned and held the lamp toward Alison, who reached out and lifted a student satchel from the shelf in front of her, turning it this way and that before fussing with its buckles and pulling out a small book. "Turn up the lamp a bit," she said.

With better light, Mick knew what it was. "A journal," he said. "From the Room of Future Present."

Alison looked at the spine. "1852," she said.

The satchel held several more journals, all from 1852, including the one by Jane Yates that Mick had read. After they had looked briefly at all of them, Alison returned the books to the satchel and slung it over her shoulder. "These oughtn't be here," she said.

"Miss Emmet would have a heart attack," Mick said.

Leech held up the lamp as they looked around the little room, not finding anything else out of place among the dusty odds and ends. They moved cautiously into the next room, also small and dusty, and Mick realized they were in the sneak vent room.

Mick stopped. "I need the lamp."

Lamp in hand, Mick crossed the room to the shelves below the sneak vent.

"Oh," Alison said from behind him when she realized where they were.

Mick gave her the lamp while he clambered up the shelves to check the grille covering the vent. It was latched, but there was a thin scrap of fabric snagged in it, which he worked free. Back down from the shelves, he held it up to the lamp, but he couldn't tell what it was. He was about to ask Alison to turn up the lamp when it started to sputter because it was almost out of oil.

Dolly used the lamp to light her candle just before the lamp died. The room grew brighter but more flickering.

People's faces always looked a little creepy in candlelight.

"We ought to go back," Alison said.

Everyone nodded.

In the Great Hall, there were a few students moving about, and Mick realized they somehow still had a few minutes until lights out. Back in the tory common room just in time, they skimmed the 1852 journals and whispered about what to do next. Deep down, they knew that the professors needed to know that the journals had been so close to the sneak vent, in a room so close to a secret passage. It seemed pretty obvious that the Interloper had been cutting through the nursery to take the secret passage to the sneak vent.

Eventually, they decided that in the morning they should take the journals to Miss Emmet and tell her everything because she was less likely to yell at them than Miss North.

At condy the next morning, Mick was tired and skipped footie to sit against the wall. Miss Paisley was absent, so Owl bickered with Leech instead. After a nervous breakfast, the Squad trudged off to see Miss Emmet.

On the way, Dolly and Leech argued about what they should and shouldn't tell Miss Emmet. Mick stayed out of it. Miss Emmet or some other professor would get everything out of them in the end if they wanted.

Alison was quiet. She might have been thinking, or she might just have been exhausted. At breakfast, she'd said she'd been up until her candle ran out trying to figure out if the journals had anything in common, other than being from 1852. If they did, she couldn't see it.

Miss Emmet had been expecting Mick for tutorial but was surprised to see the others. "I presume there's an explanation?" she asked.

The Squad looked at one another. Alison set the satchel she'd found on Miss Emmet's desk. "There are seven future journals inside. Gunner says they're from the Room of Future Present."

Miss Emmet looked at Mick sharply.

"We didn't take them," he promised.

"We found them in the cellars, miss," Dolly said. "Yesterday evening."

"I see," Miss Emmet said. She took the journals out of the bag and gave them a quick inspection. "Do you often go hunting for books in the cellars?"

They shook their heads.

"And so...?" Miss Emmet asked, letting the unspoken question hang there.

The Squad looked at each other uncertainly.

Miss Emmet said, "The truth will suffice, children."

"It's all Constance Bardon's fault," Mick said.

Interrupting each other, they explained about Constance Bardon, secret doors, hidden passageways, and finding the satchel.

"And this was in a storage room?" Miss Emmet asked.

"Right next to the sn— a room with a vent in it, miss," Mick said. "I've heard, maybe, well, that some naughty children might use it to sneak out of the Institute."

"I see," Miss Emmet remarked blandly, her face thoughtful

as she flipped through the journals on the desk in front of her. "Thank you for bringing this to my attention, children. Mr. Gunn, we shall have to cancel our tutorial. I had planned to make you finish Miss Bardon's treatise for tomorrow, but now I fear that might somehow result in further inconvenient discoveries. Instead, I shall expect three hundred words summarizing closing phenomena in unframed horse kick alleys."

Mick sighed.

Chapter 20

Assault on the Vault

That afternoon, punishment was particularly punishing. Mick endured dumpwaiter duty with the Threes, who needed an extra person because Miss Paisley was, they muttered, faking illness. It was a hot spring day by London standards, and dumpwaiter duty made for an especially miserable session of sweat and stench and wishing that the Institute would hurry up and put indoor plumbing in the tories.

After that, Mick reported to Mrs. Robbin that he was done. He assumed she'd let him take a shower and lie in his cot, but she said that Mr. Willard wanted him to empty the ash bins.

After finishing the ash bins, he found his favorite bench near the big tree in the middle of the garden empty. On a warm day, depending on the wind's direction, the bench could be a little too close to the night soil cisterns. But Mick smelled worse than the cisterns, so he lay down on the cool bench and closed his eyes.

Sometimes, he would try to tune out everything and think,

"I'm Mick Nicolás Conway. My sister is Emilia Conway. My mom's name was Dorotea Chavez. My dad's name is Seth Conway. Uncle Dan only cooks with the microwave. I'm from Chicago in the twenty-first century. People have gone to the moon. You can put a library in your phone and have space left over for pictures of dogs dressed like bears and video chats with a dad on the other side of the planet who needs to come home." He would try to remember every detail of the two photographs he kept on his bedside table at Uncle Dan's: the one of his mom and dad not long after they'd met and the one of himself as a kindergartner, trying to eat the same hamburger as his dog Scootie. Once he had those pictures clear in his mind, he was always a little hopeful that he'd open his eyes and be back in the future, maybe lying near Lake Michigan with Tía Verónica asking him questions.

"You look like you've learned your lesson," said Gail's voice.

Mick sighed and opened his eyes. Still 1853. "Leech says that the main lesson is don't get caught. That's why he's playing footie, and I smell like—"

"I'm quite aware of your odor," Gail said. She was in fact keeping her distance.

"I'm going to shower," Mick said defensively.

"Do so several times," she said, with a little smile. "The dons just made a point of padlocking a grille in the cellar. I'm informed that's your doing."

"I didn't get in trouble again," Mick said. "None of us did. We just found some stuff and told Miss Emmet." He hesitated. "I *didn't* get into trouble again, did I?"

She grinned at him, flipping her hair out of her face. "I have not been so informed."

Mick sighed with relief.

"Pray keep it that way," she said. "You've the makings of a first-rate spotter. But only if you can resume patrol. So if you do something foolish to earn more punishment, I shall be forced to dunk your head in a night soil cistern."

"I've learned my lesson," he said. "Don't—"

"—get caught," she said. "Yes, yes. But do remember that it's easier not to get caught doing something foolish if you aren't *doing* something foolish. And you truly could be useful out there. Something is badly amiss with the alleys. It's become one fawkes after another.'"

Mick nodded. The kids had started calling patrol "fawkes hunting."

Gail sighed heavily. "And there were two children found dead this morning in a chemist's near the Little Cadogan epicenter. The newspapers say the peelers are calling it sinister murder, but any alley rat knows better. Another fawkes, with two more droppers dead."

Mick winced. That was terrible, of course, and it was going to make Alison miserable. At least the lock on the sneak vent would keep her inside at night.

"So do remember," she said, "that there is work to be done. Important work."

"I want to help," Mick said. "But I'm stuck in here because I tried to help, and that's against the stupid rules."

"You know better than that," she said, kindly.

Mick sighed. He guessed he did.

"Right," she told him. "Keep your nose clean, and you'll be back on the streets soon." She looked at him, sniffing unhappily. "Not just your nose. Keep everything clean, if you please."

.   .   .

About halfway through dinner, rumors started buzzing through the dining hall. Something about the Vault.

Mick was slow to pay attention because he'd showered and was really enjoying being clean. And eating his buttered baked potato, of course. Fresh-churned butter was so much better than sticks from a supermarket.

Leech, of course, was delighted by the excitement and was one of the many students flitting from table to table to gossip. Owl took advantage of Leech's absence to sit down and ask Alison what she thought was happening. Mick was considering joining Leech when a pair of booming thuds, one after the other, penetrated his thoughts.

Mr. Victor was standing with the heavy dining hall doors newly shut behind him, his gleaming blue eyes taking in every detail.

The dining hall fell quiet except for the penetrating voice of Mr. Edmondson, one of the professors, who continued complaining from the faculty table about impertinent Americans until Mr. Victor said calmly but clearly, "Mr. Edmondson, if I might."

After Mr. Edmondson fell silent, Mr. Victor stared at the students for a moment. "Return to your seats and be silent," he said. The students scrambled back to their stools.

"As some of you know," Mr. Victor announced, "there was an attempted theft from the Vault. That it was unsuccessful should not need saying. That you children should leave the matter in the hands of adults likewise should not need saying."

Mick could have sworn that Mr. Victor was looking directly at him when he said that. But it always felt like Mr. Victor was looking directly at you.

"At the end of the dinner hour, all students are to return

directly to their tories and remain there. This evening's vespertines are canceled."

Leech and Mick looked at one another. Evening tutorials
canceled and all the kids on lockdown? Interesting. They met
with Dolly and Alison leaving the dining hall, and the Squad's
excited speculation mingled with the buzz of countless similar
conversations among the students heading back to their tories.

The Sixers' common room was already packed when they
arrived, and it got even more crowded as the remaining
students trickled back from dinner. A few grinds fled to their
rooms to study in peace, but everybody else stuck around. The
common room felt like a classroom during a Halloween party.
Kids told tall tales of pirate burglars, acting out sword fights
and wrestling each other. A few kids played charades. The
prefects and two other older kids played short whist.

The Squad wandered around, catching up with the other
kids, seeing if anybody knew anything. Eventually they drifted
back together, sitting at their little table in the corner. They
decided that everyone had theories and guesses but nobody
actually knew anything.

"It was the Interloper," Leech said.

The others tried to figure out if he was joking.

"Remember Constance Bardon," he said. "The chapter that
led us—led me"—he patted himself on the chest—"to find the
secret door. That was about building the Vault, was it not?
About the special stairs and corridors needed to create the steel
shell. Remember the great heavy door, the locked one we
couldn't budge in the slightest? Perhaps that was a door to the
Vault. It must have been so heavy because it was made of steel.
Like the Vault."

"Perhaps," Dolly allowed.

"And where is the Vault?" Leech asked. "It's somewhere in the cellars, but where? Where are the doors leading to it, for that matter?"

"I think there's a stairway to the Vault in the Scriptorium," Alison said. "Behind that door behind Mr. Hartnell's desk that blends into the wall. Sometimes Mr. Hartnell has said things that hint of it." She asked Mick, "Did Constance Bardon say anything about the Vault's entrance?"

"Just that the Vault is big, steel, and somewhere in the cellars."

They speculated a little longer before the room went abruptly silent. Everybody was looking at the door to the common room, where Miss North and Mr. Victor had just appeared.

Miss North told the little boy and girl playing on the floor close to her feet to fetch any students who were in their rooms. As the little kids scurried toward the boys' and girls' hallways, Miss North and Mr. Victor surveyed the common room. Miss North's gaze rested on Mick and the Squad and she nodded faintly, more to herself than to them. Once everyone was clustered into the room, with the newly arrived students standing awkwardly near the doors to the boys' and girls' hallways, Miss North called out, "Miss Dylan and Mr. Braddock."

The prefects stood up from their card game and stepped forward.

"Is anyone absent?" she asked.

The prefects looked around the room, counting. They called out a few names, and the kids all raised their hands.

"No absent girls, miss," said Miss Dylan.

Mr. Braddock gave the room a final scan. "Two boys are

absent, miss—Mr. Becks and Mr. Austin. But they're sleeping outside the walls."

Mr. Victor stepped forward, locking eyes with each prefect in turn. "You're certain there's no one else missing?" he asked. He made it sound like he knew they were lying.

They nodded.

After Mr. Victor asked a few more questions to make sure that all the Sixers were in their common room, he said, "Miss North and I shall lock the outer door when we leave. Mr. Braddock, Miss Dylan, be certain to have your keys to hand. However, excepting a genuine emergency or instructions from an appropriate authority, do not unlock the door."

"Miss North?" Alison asked. "What's happening?"

Miss North replied, "For now, Miss March, suffice it to say that—provided that you remain within the tory—none of you will be in danger."

She and Mr. Victor left. The door closed behind them, followed shortly by the lock clicking loudly.

The room exploded into pandemonium. A few kids did Mr. Victor impersonations. Everybody started gossiping.

"It was a student who broke into the Vault," Leech said excitedly. "And now the professors are hunting the thief. Who I'll wager is the Interloper."

"Or perhaps a student got kidnapped by the Vault thieves," Dolly said, also afire with interest.

"You're both ghouls," Alison said with a faint smile. "Gunner? No theories? Perhaps cannibals?"

Mick shrugged. He was irritated that Miss North hadn't told them anything. "It doesn't matter if it's students or pirates or ghosts, does it? Not if we're locked in here."

"It matters if it's ghosts," Leech said. "Locks mean nothing to ghosts."

Mick laughed despite himself.

The oddly festive air continued after the sun faded from the common room windows and skylights. The gossiping and goofing off continued even after the lamps ran out of oil and kids had to start using their personal candles. Little kids fell asleep in the common room, some on the floor, and had to be carried to bed by the big kids.

When even the candles were burning down, Alison, Dolly, and Mick started to feel the day's punishment duty. Yawning heavily, they headed back to their rooms, though Leech stayed in the common room.

In the bathroom, Mick heard the dumpwaiter thumping against the walls of the chute, the buckles clacking way more loudly than usual. He wondered if something had broken and if there would be a mess waiting for whoever had dumpwaiter duty the next day. He really hoped it wouldn't be him.

Back in his room, he snuffed the candle and dressed for bed in the dark, wanting to leave himself at least a candle stub for emergencies. He'd learned the hard way not to use the bathroom in the dark.

He was cozily drifting toward sleep when he noticed that he hadn't closed the curtains. He sighed. If he didn't go pull the curtain rods to the middle, in the morning, sunlight would flood the room and wake him up early. But the window was way over *there*, and he was *here*, and his cot was so cozy.

Then he realized why he'd noticed that the curtains were open. There was somebody standing in front of the window.

The moonlight was bright enough to clearly make out the shape of legs, from shins to hips, though it was too dark for him to see details.

It was the Interloper. Mick was sure of it. Logically, it could have been anyone. A professor or a don looking for the Vault thief. A student secretly smoking a pipe or just staring at the stars.

But Mick was sure it was the Interloper.

Mick wondered whether he might be able to capture the Interloper. He tried to picture it. First, he'd have to get the rope ladder up to the window in place, which was hard to do even in daylight. Same with opening the window, which he'd somehow have to do silently, while hoping the Interloper didn't look down. Not to mention hoping that the Interloper was even worse at fighting than he was.

So that was a pretty terrible idea.

The bedroom door opened slowly, Leech's face flickering in candlelight.

"Ah, Gunn—"

"Shhh," Mick said. "Snuff the candle and close the door. Fast."

Leech did so.

Keeping his eye on the still figure in the moonlight, Mick whispered, "There's someone up there."

Leech came into the room far enough that he could look out the window. "The Vault thief?"

"The Interloper. Has to be."

"One and the same," Leech whispered.

The Interloper had started to move. Mick tensed up, but the Interloper didn't go far. Just pacing back and forth, barely leaving the frame of the window before returning into view.

"We should tell the prefects," Leech said, "so they can ring the night porter and let the professors know."

"Good idea," Mick said. The Interloper's pacing was picking up speed. "You go. I'll stay here."

Leech nodded. As he left, he said, "No foolishness without me, mind."

Trying to capture the Interloper would be foolishness. No doubt about that. On the other hand, what if the Interloper left? Shouldn't he follow? Not wanting to have to chase after the Interloper in bare feet and nightclothes, Mick quickly changed into his street clothes and tied his brogues.

The Interloper's pacing was erratic now—stopping and starting irregularly, disappearing longer before returning. Afraid that the Interloper might leave, Mick fumbled with the rope ladder until he got the bottom anchored.

Much like the Interloper pacing to and fro above, he went back and forth about whether to climb the ladder. If he did, the Interloper might see him. If he didn't, the Interloper might get away again.

A dozen times, Mick reached out to the ladder only to pull his hand back. Then he realized it had been a while since he'd seen the Interloper. That did it. He started climbing the ladder. After a few deep breaths, he dared to pull himself high enough to look out the window.

The Interloper was gone. Scraping some knuckles, Mick freed the latch and forced the window to swing up and out. He slid out, dropping onto the gravel with a faint crunch. He froze for a moment, listening.

He heard footsteps from across the roof. It *was* the Interloper, hood and all, maybe thirty or forty yards away. Headed for the Little Castle service alley. The Interloper was actually going to try Alison's crazytown plan of shimmying down the drainpipe.

The Interloper was soon out of sight, below the line of the roof. Since Mick didn't hear any loud thumps, the Interloper was climbing down, not falling. Now that the Interloper couldn't see him, Mick moved faster, the roof gravel crunching under his brogues as he wove through the cisterns and skylights.

When he reached the edge of the roof and looked down, the Interloper was more than halfway down the heavy drainpipe, which, Mick noted with relief, was solidly anchored to the wall. Heart racing, Mick waited until the dark smudge of the Interloper was scurrying down the alley toward the street.

Breathing deeply and not giving himself too much time to think, Mick wrapped his arms around the drainpipe. Heart thumping wildly, he half-slid, half-climbed down. Partway down, his arms started to tremble, and he felt a surge of relief when his toes reached the cobblestones.

Shaking out his arms, he ran down the alley as quietly as he could to Little Castle and looked around. He was relieved to spot the Interloper trotting west. Mick followed from the opposite side of the street, closing the gap some, but not getting too close.

The Interloper glanced backward a few times over the next few blocks but apparently didn't spot Mick.

Just before turning south onto Regent Street, the Interloper paused to remove the hood. Although Mick couldn't see a face, he could see a dark fall of long hair. So the Interloper was a girl, even though she was wearing pants. The Interloper's hood went into a bulky satchel and was replaced by a droopy boy's cap big enough to partially conceal her hair.

Moving at a brisk walk, Mick followed the Interloper down Regent Street and then Hay Market. They were both slowed by the thick crowds of people in fancy clothes, dirty street sweeps with tattered brooms clearing the way for the fancy people, and, of course, beggars pleading for ha'pennies.

Mick hadn't expected the shops and streetlights to be ablaze with light. The fancy people's silks and satins shimmered, and so did the men's freshly shined shoes. It looked magical. If he hadn't been following the Interloper, he would have gone exploring.

The Interloper went past the statue of Charles I on the horse at Charing Cross. Or was it Charles III? Mick couldn't keep all the dead kings straight. More or less where Whitehall turned into Parliament Street, Mick noticed that he wasn't the only one following the Interloper. Two teenagers had settled in about twenty yards behind her.

He checked to make sure nobody was following him.

He was wondering whether to warn the Interloper that she was being followed when she exploded into a sprint, lowering her shoulder slightly before turning sharply to cut across to King Street. The teenagers started to run after her but didn't even get to full speed before deciding to hunt easier prey.

That made sense to Mick, who had to run flat out behind the Interloper as she sped a mazy path through streets and alleys. Soon, his lungs were burning. The only good thing was that she was running too hard to look back. Of course, that meant he still hadn't managed to get a good look at her face.

On Bird Cage Walk, almost to the military chapel, the Interloper slowed to a walk, shooting a couple half-glances over her shoulder. Mick tried to blend into the crowd.

The Interloper wandered southwest to the Emmanuel Hospital and the New Bridewell prison before turning back and weaving at a trot through the crowds on Victoria Street. As she turned onto Old Pye, a shabbily dressed man inattentively thrust an empty wheelbarrow in front of her, and she danced around it nimbly.

Wait.

Miss Paisley?

Mick realized that the back of his brain had been trying to tell him this for a while. The way she dropped her shoulder before changing directions, how she sprinted, and that agile sidestep when she'd danced around the wheelbarrow—that was pure Miss Paisley. For that matter, she probably hadn't spotted Mick tailing her because she refused to learn from Miss Mitchell during concentration, so she was bad at paying attention to two things at once.

He was so startled by all this that he stopped moving for a moment and almost lost her. He was lucky to spot her turning onto a side street and then stopping at a doorway, waiting for something.

The doorway looked like a side door to the big building with its main entrance on Old Pye. He called up his mental version of the Plan. Oh, of course. The big building was where the Institute had been before moving to its present location. Now the Old Pye building was occupied by the Society for the Enlightened Advancement of Trade: the SEAT or, as English people wrote it, the Seat. Miss Emmet said it was secretly the Project's headquarters. The Seat of Power, she called it.

Mick tucked himself into a dark doorway, watching Miss Paisley as she paced back and forth near the door. On and off, her face was visible in the feeble light of a nearby streetlamp, but he was too far away to read her expression.

What on earth was she up to?

Mick didn't have his watch, so he didn't know how long he waited, but eventually the door opened and a woman's head and shoulders emerged. The woman beckoned to Miss Paisley, who hastened inside.

Mick waited a bit longer, but he realized had no idea when she might come back out, or whether she would even use the same door when she did. Trying to look casual, he crossed the street and checked the door, which was locked. He kept walking to Orchard Street and then stared back at the door Miss Paisley had used. From there, he could see at least two other doors to the Seat. Plus the main door on Old Pye and all the other doors he couldn't see.

Waiting any longer would be pointless. He couldn't watch all the doors, and Miss Paisley might be inside for hours. He started to hail a cab but realized he didn't have any money and wasn't sure anyone would be awake at the Institute to pay the cabbie.

Footsore and weary, he started the long walk back to the Institute, forcing himself to keep alert for pickpockets and cutthroats. As he walked, his mind kept replaying the face of the woman who had met Miss Paisley at the side door to the Seat. She had seemed familiar, somehow. That sense of familiarity nagged at him as he retraced his steps through the crowds of drunk rich people wandering from one brightly lit building to another, bellowing and shrieking as they went.

He had taken Regent nearly back to Oxford when he looked

left down Princes, remembering the dead boy falling out of the fawkes just up the block. That was when he realized. When he'd first seen the woman Miss Paisley had just met at the Seat, the woman had been in the fawkes alley that killed the dropper. She'd had the frizzy hair and the frizzy coat.

She was one of the echo phantasms.

CHAPTER 21

THE ESOTERICA OF ECHO PHANTASMS

From there back to the Institute, Mick had a short walk full of exploding thoughts, little fireworks that went off one after another, each fading quickly into forgetfulness as the next burst into light.

Ringing the bell at the boys' gate, he realized that, technically speaking, he had left the tory after being instructed to stay there by Miss North and Mr. Victor. And that then he'd climbed off the roof and snuck out of the Institute. At night. While he was already being punished horribly for doing something way less serious than any one of those things, much less all of them put together.

Uh oh.

But, you know what, he told himself, *this shouldn't be about being punished. This should be about getting rewarded.* He had learned some important stuff. He didn't understand it, but he'd learned it, and somebody else might understand it. People should be grateful.

He kept telling himself that while he waited. Pretty soon, he halfway believed it.

Then Mr. James opened the door with Miss Mitchell standing just over his shoulder. "Ah, Mr. Gunn," she said, dryly.

She wasn't surprised to see him, which meant everybody knew he'd left. He sighed.

"Miss North would like to see you," she said.

Mick reminded himself to act like he deserved a reward. "Very good," he said, trying to sound as 1853 as possible, "I rather think the Vicar will also wish to hear."

Miss Mitchell raised her eyebrows and smiled slightly. "Perhaps let's start with Miss North, shall we?"

Mick shrugged as if he didn't care either way.

After they'd climbed to the top floor, Miss Mitchell led Mick to the little side room attached to the solarium. When she opened the solarium door long enough to wave to Miss North, Mick could see Miss North sitting at the big table with other professors and, yes, the Vicar.

Miss Mitchell left him alone in the side room. Long minutes passed. Mick watched the minor changes in the gas lamp's low flame and fidgeted in one of the uncomfortable chairs, wondering if he should make a break for it.

As more long minutes passed, Mick made a list of all the major points in his favor. There weren't as many as he'd thought.

Eventually, Miss North entered. She closed the door and turned up the lamp, staring silently at Mick for several years.

Mick always wanted to apologize when Miss North looked at him like that, even if he wasn't sure what he'd done wrong. He resisted the urge.

"Explain yourself," she said.

Mick was glad he'd made the list of the points in his favor. "I saw someone on the roof. I thought it was the Interloper. I showed Leech, and he went to tell the prefects. I was just going to watch and wait. But then the Interloper left, and I thought I should follow. It was Miss Paisley."

Miss North started to say something but stopped herself.

Mick continued, "Miss Paisley went to the Seat, and the frizzy woman from the Princes Street fawkes let her in. I waited, but Miss Paisley didn't come out. So I came back."

It was the first time Mick had ever seen Miss North look confused.

"Leech *did* tell the prefects, didn't he?" he asked.

Miss North ignored the question as she sat down in a small chair near Mick, putting them knee to knee. "You're certain that it was Miss Paisley whom you followed?"

"Yes, miss. I saw her face in the end. In a gas lamp and everything. Also, she moved just like Miss Paisley does during course." Mick realized something. He dug into his pockets before remembering he wasn't wearing the right trousers. "The other night, when we found the vent in the cellar, near the secret door. I was checking if it was latched and found something. I forgot about it until just now, but I bet it's one of Miss Paisley's stupid hair ribbons. Miss."

"Perhaps one day, Mr. Gunn, we shall discuss how you knew to check whether that grille was latched."

Ouch.

"But for now, let us attend to the matters at hand. Are you entirely certain that the woman you saw at the Seat was the same woman you saw in the Princes Street fawkes?"

Mick shook his head. "Mostly, but not totally. The fawkes woman was a little blurry. And at the Seat, the gas lamp wasn't very bright. But the Seat woman looked a lot like the fawkes woman."

Miss North frowned, lost in thought.

"Is Miss Paisley back?" he asked. "We could ask her."

"Did she see you?"

"I don't think so," Mick said.

"I believe," Miss North said slowly, "you will need to repeat to the others what you've just told me." She tilted her head slightly toward the solarium.

"Yes, miss." Mick gulped slightly. "Am I in trouble?"

She actually smiled. Just a little, but still. "Do you know, if what you've told me is true—"

"I promise."

"Then I rather suspect that you might escape punishment. Allowing for the foolishness of youth, what you did has a certain sense. And you did send Mr. Charles for the prefects, who arrived just in time to see you disappear down that drain-pipe." She stared at him intently. "You must promise me *never* to do that again. You might easily have died. I know children never believe adults when we say such things, but this I know to be true."

Her voice sounded sad and distant when she said the last part.

"I promise, miss."

She stared into his eyes for a moment. "Good. Now, come and explain to the others. They will have questions."

Answering the grown-ups' questions wasn't fun, but it was less awful than he'd feared. He basically told them what he'd already told Miss North. Miss Emmet asked a couple gentle questions about the Seat, which calmed Mick down a bit. Even Mr. Victor's questions made him only shoulder-tighteningly nervous rather than gut-churningly terrified. Then Miss North told him that he could tell the Squad about what had happened, but only them, and they had to promise not to tell anyone else.

Mick woke the next morning in silence and sunlight. The clock said it was almost nine-thirty. For a moment, he panicked that he had missed matutinal. Then he realized that it was Saturday and remembered that, before he'd stumbled out of the previous night's interrogation, Miss North had excused him from that day's punishment duty. He didn't have anywhere to be.

Having nowhere to be was a good feeling, even though his stomach was rumbling because he'd missed breakfast. Eventually, he changed into a cleanish instisuit and headed to the common room. The Squad was sitting at their little table in the far corner, staring at him. He waved and walked over. Leech pushed out a chair, and Dolly handed him a scone and a small apple. Mick smiled at her.

"Tell us," Leech said. "Nobody else will."

Mick made them swear not to tell anyone. Then he yet again repeated the story of the night before, answering all the questions he could.

"Miss Paisley?" Leech said, incredulous.

"But why on earth would Miss Paisley..." Alison began. "And it was the woman from the Princes Street fawkes at the Seat?"

"Pretty sure," Mick answered.

"Miss Paisley," Leech repeated, still not able to wrap his head around it. "I thought all she did was complain about condy and Catholics." He shook his head. "What do you suppose she took from the Vault?"

Mick shook his head. "The way the professors were

talking about it, she didn't even get close to the Vault. You can't get in there unless you have a bunch of keys and go with a bunch of other people who also have a bunch of different keys. I think she set off an alarm. And then she freaked out and ran for it."

"How did she reach the roof?" Dolly asked. "There aren't many stairs leading up, and surely the dons and the professors were keeping watch."

Mick had been thinking about that, remembering hearing the dumpwaiter thumping and clacking in the chute. "Could she have used the dumpwaiter?"

Leech tilted his head, and Mick explained what he'd heard.

Dolly said, "There *is* a ladder in the dumpwaiter shaft, and I suppose the vent at the top might be just large enough for her to squeeze onto the roof. Though I certainly wouldn't wish to try it." She giggled.

Leech and Mick joined in. It was a funny image, the terrifying Interloper clambering up the dumpwaiter shaft.

Alison's face was scrunched with thought. "But she had something with her, did she not? Gunner, you said her satchel was full. So she took something, even if it wasn't from the Vault."

Mick nodded.

"I wonder what she took?" Leech said.

"Perhaps," Dolly said slowly, "we should ask what she *wanted* to take."

They all nodded.

"What's in the Vault?" Mick asked. "I mean, I know there are kids' journals about the future, but is there anything else?"

"Well, of course, there's—" Leech began, but then stopped himself. "Honestly, I couldn't say."

Alison nodded. "People talk as if the Vault contains dragon's gold and time machines, but it's all a bit vague, really."

Dolly nodded. "I think we can assume that she was after the journals. Alison found those 1852 journals in the cellar, after all. And of course it's clear what that suggests."

"Naturally, naturally," Leech said. "But perhaps you could explain it for Gunner's sake."

"The future," Mick said, realizing. "She's looking for information about the future."

"But how do journals from last year help?" Alison asked.

"They don't," Dolly said. "I suspect she was looking for journals from 1853. Or 1953, for that matter. But she couldn't get into the Vault—"

"So 1852 was the best she could do," Leech said.

"That's why I saw her in the Room of Future Present, the first time," Mick said, realizing. "She was looking for journals there because she couldn't get them from the Vault."

"And she must have been the one who tried to break into the Scriptorium," Alison said. "Perhaps Mr. Hartnell mentioned his stairway to the Vault to Miss Paisley as well."

Mick remembered something. The day after the Scriptorium had been locked up because somebody had tried to break in, Miss Paisley's arm had been hurt. She'd been sitting in condy with her grumpy cat face. She must have hurt herself trying to break into the Scriptorium.

"So," Leech said. "Are we saying it's 1853 she's after? Or 1953?"

"I'd wager 1853," Dolly said. "If Miss Paisley were seeking information about the far future, the journals from 1852 would do her no good. But if she were seeking information about the near future..."

"But the near future is still the future," Alison said, "and 1852 is in the past, even if it's the near past. It gives no sense."

"Maybe it isn't about making sense." Mick said. "Maybe somebody—the fawkes woman—told Miss Paisley to get journals from 1853, and she couldn't. So she grabbed some from 1852, and hoped that would be enough to keep from getting yelled at."

They nodded. They knew about doing desperate stuff to avoid a scolding.

"But why leave the satchel in the cellars?" Leech asked.

"Possibly she was planning to sneak out with it later, only we found it first," Alison said.

"To my mind," Dolly said, "the principal question is why the fawkes lady wants journals from 1853."

"Horse racing results?" Leech said. "Fashion trends? Think of all the dressmakers ready to carve up each other's guts for a glimpse of next season's furbelows and crinolines."

Dolly giggled despite herself.

"You know," Alison said, slowly, "the only thing one can rely upon finding in a future journal, any journal, is information about when and where the rat was lifted and dropped."

"And," Dolly said excitedly, "we know that the fawkes lady appeared in an alley. That she must have got into *before* its aperture began to open. Possibly whilst it was still a stirring."

"Yes," Alison said, matching Dolly's excitement. "If one of the fawkes ladies is trying to waylay alleys, she would very much want journals that told her when and where alleys will appear."

"But hasn't everything we've read about waylaying been about *drop* alleys?" Leech said. "The 1853 journals would be about *lift* alleys."

Nobody had an answer for that. They sat silently for a while.

"And why is the fawkes woman at the Seat?" Leech asked. "Is the Project involved?"

They speculated at length, but none of them really knew anything about the Project. They got nowhere until Dolly said, "Well, Miss Paisley was looking for something here. Perhaps the fawkes lady is looking for something at the Seat."

"Are there any journals left at the Seat?" Leech asked. "Surely they're all here now."

"It needn't be journals," Dolly said. "The fawkes lady could be looking for anything."

While the rest of the Squad argued, Mick tried to figure out why it suddenly felt like he was forgetting something important. He dug around in his memories but couldn't find anything.

"Should we tell Miss North?" Alison asked. "About echo phantasms?"

They all shrugged. It might help the adults figure out what was going on, and it didn't seem like it would get the Squad into trouble. They decided to find Miss North. The others chatted while Mick kept poking at his brain to figure out what he was forgetting.

CHAPTER 22

THE CRUELTY OF ALLEY PIRATES

Even though it was Saturday, Miss North was in her office and clearly wished that the Squad were not. But she let them—mostly Alison—explain what they had learned about stirrings and echo phantasms.

"Thank you, children, for coming to me with this," Miss North said when they had finished.

Mick thought she had leaned a little too hard on "children."

"Miss March," Miss North said, "I'm quite pleased that you consulted *Blake's*. I wish more grinds would read it half so attentively. As for the rest, we are already altering when and how we patrol, as you shall discover tomorrow."

"We're patrolling tomorrow?" Leech asked delightedly. "All of us?"

Miss North nodded.

"But these disgraceful urchins are still on punishment duty," Leech said.

"I am persuaded that they have learned their lesson," Miss North said. "Have you not, children?"

"Yes, miss," they said.

"And, in truth, the need is simply too great," Miss North said. "There is a great deal of ground to cover, and emptying ash bins is not a sensible use of one of our more competent street teams."

They all glowed a little bit at the compliment.

"Of course," Miss North added, "we cannot afford to have our street teams straying off sequence or clambering down drainpipes, can we?"

They all shook their heads.

"Excellent. You are dismissed, children. Sleep well tonight. You will be busy in the coming days."

Miss North hadn't been kidding. Kids started spending twice as much time on patrol, going out earlier and coming back later. Most tutorials were canceled or made into vespertines so that the streets and greets could spend more daylight hours outside. Mick still had to go to condy, but after that it was straight to breakfast and out on the streets by 8:30. Then he and the Squad would patrol together until 2:00 or so, eating lunch out of their satchels or from a street vendor. After that, the Squad would sometimes go back to the Institute and sometimes patrol a little longer, except Mick, who usually joined Gail and the Snobs.

It was good to get out of the Institute again and to have less homework, though Miss North made sure that he always had a vespertine after dinner. And he enjoyed being with the Squad. But the actual streeting was pretty uneventful. They spent most of their time looking for stirrings, which meant Leech was the star of the show. But after a few days of milking it for all he could, even Leech had to admit that stirrings were boring. A stirring might become something, and that something might turn out to be interesting. But mostly it was a faint tingling that could just have been a bug or an itch, and that was all it would ever be.

Mick did discover a new talent, or maybe a new wrinkle of an old talent. It turned out he was really good at knowing which stirrings would turn into alleys, even if they were only fawkeses. They felt a little different, maybe, and they definitely *sounded* different. With stirrings that were likely to turn into something worth noticing, he could hear the same sort of siren song that always pulled him toward an alley as it opened. With stirrings, it was faint, but once he knew to listen for it, it was there.

Greeting wasn't much more eventful than streeting, but at least he got to see new parts of London. Gail and the Snobs were covering more ground, routinely going as far north as Coleman's Doorstep and as far south as Scholar's Playground, possibly because Scholar's Playground was close to the Seat. In the first week of the new routine, they even crossed the Westminster Bridge a couple times to patrol the Spanish Cornwall cluster.

If Mick managed to forget why he was doing it, it was sort of fun. The Institute didn't really do summer vacation—it wasn't like anybody could go home for the holidays. But the new routine felt like summer camp. Less homework, lots of field trips, more time in what in London passed for the sun.

But you couldn't forget completely, not for long. There weren't any real alleys. Just fawkeses. Including another dead kid, a little toddler barely bigger than a baby that a greet team found up by the Pancras gas works. Plus there were a couple more newspaper reports about dead kids that sounded like fawkeses.

After the dead toddler in Pancras, most of the Institute kids got a little weird, Mick included. As busy as he was, he found himself stopping by the nursery to check on the toddlers, as if he could do something Miss Weathers couldn't. He went so often that Miss Weathers threatened to lock him out and Julia scolded him for making Miss Ellen cross. And anyway, the toddlers were fine. The weather was nice enough that Miss Weathers could take them out to the garden so they could dig in the mud and bicker over the hierarchy of worthy bugs. On Sundays, Mr. Phillips took the toddlers outside to play and sing, so that Miss Weathers could stay in the nursery and study in peace.

Mick worried about Alison, especially after the newspaper articles about the dead kids. But she seemed okay, at least on the surface. She said that she felt better when she was able to do something, not just sit around the Institute worrying. Finding things to do wasn't a problem, especially since she was the one who got to decide how thorough the Squad was when patrolling. So they were very thorough.

Miss Paisley was still missing. Mick and the rest of the Squad had kept quiet about her. But even the first day after Mick had followed Miss Paisley to the Seat, her absence had kids talking. It wasn't hard to connect the attempted theft in the Vault with her disappearance the next day. Soon, the kids were spreading rumors. She'd been killed by the Vault thief, who had thrown her body into the Thames. She was the Vault thief and had dodged a dozen cops while making her escape with the real crown jewels, possibly before fleeing to France or India or

America. She was still hiding in the Institute, living on food she harvested from the garden in the dead of night. That sort of nonsense.

Even a week or so after her disappearance there still was no reliable information about Miss Paisley, but that didn't stop a bunch of kids from claiming that they'd seen her. (The only people whom kids claimed to see more often were the fawkes women, and those sightings were false alarms too.) Mick started to worry about Miss Paisley. She was a jerk, but she was a kid, and it wasn't safe to be a kid out there alone.

Mick usually wrote in his future journal on Sunday mornings when some of the other kids were at church. Before and after journaling, Mick would ask Mr. Hartnell about the Vault —where it was, what the thief had tried to steal. Mr. Hartnell ignored the questions. But he would occasionally talk about the Old Pye building that now housed the Seat. The Institute had been there when he was a student, and it had still been there when he'd first become a librarian. He liked to tell stories about how everybody had thought the old building's library was haunted. Or how, when he'd been Mick's age, he'd gotten caught wandering through its cellars, trying to find the Vault. "For punishment, I spent two weeks scrubbing every hallway in those old cellars," he'd said. "And let that be a warning to you, my curious young friend."

One overcast day after streeting, Mick went back to the Institute to get an update on the location of Gail and the Snobs. The warden told him to make haste to Finsbury Circus.

"We saw the old woman from the cemetery," Gail said, as soon as Mick met her and the Snobs at the Blomfield Street entrance to Finsbury Circus. "She was walking just there," she said, pointing, "by the wrought iron fence in front of St. Mary's, turning onto East Street. She stopped and leaned on her stick for a moment as if to catch her breath, and then vanished. Stephen and I both saw it. You can feel a stirring where she was."

Squinting at the spot and turning his head, Mick could make out a green haze so indistinct he had to walk back and forth to make sure it was real. He walked over to it and stood there, the others standing around him to keep pedestrians from pushing him out of the shimmer.

Yuck. He could feel a stirring, but it wasn't right. There was the itch at the base of his skull that he sometimes felt, but it also felt like the skin there was being … stretched? Pushed? Something gross, anyway. He could hear the faint alley song that sometimes came with a stirring, but it was somehow two versions at once, one of them like little Julia, off-key and off-beat.

Shuddering, he stepped out of the shimmer, and they all walked a few dozen yards toward the Circus to get away from it.

"I thought," Gail said, "right after the old woman disappeared, I might have seen a green haze?"

Mick nodded. "It's still there, just barely. But it feels…"

"Like someone is walking over your grave," Flora said, shuddering.

That was it exactly, Mick thought. They'd seen that same old woman walking through a cemetery full of graves, after all. Maybe there really were time ghosts.

· · ·

There was a good chance the Finsbury Circus stirring would turn into an alley in a couple days. So, when the time came—at two in the morning—the Institute's carriage stopped at the Blomfield Street entrance, and Mick stepped out with Gail and Miss North. They were met by Miss Mitchell, who was wearing a shapeless gray dress to blend into the shadows. There were a couple other dons as well, keeping lookout.

After briefing everyone, Miss Mitchell and the other dons did indeed fade into the shadows, letting Mick and the others observe the alley as it started to form into a greenish glow-orb with its center at about waist height. The glow-orb was calling to Mick. He ignored the siren song as best he could, staying where he was and focusing on reciting the relevant descriptions while Gail took notes by the dim lantern Miss North held up for her.

And there was the old woman, faint and fuzzy but still brighter than she should have been in a weak streetlamp on a misty night. She looked for all the world like she was pausing to rest her weary legs. Except now that Mick knew what to look for, she obviously hadn't walked there. First, she'd appeared out of nowhere. Second, she didn't have legs below her knees. The bottom part of her cane was also missing.

"Echo phantasm," Mick said, describing it all to Gail and Miss North. He was proud of how calm he sounded.

"Miss Atkinson?" Miss North asked.

Gail squinted, taking a few steps in various directions, turning her head from side to side. "He's right, though I can scarcely see her."

As the aperture grew, so did the old woman's legs, which came into full existence when the edge of the glow-orb touched the pavement. Then she disappeared, and only the glow-orb remained.

Mick could already tell it was going to be a fawkes. Everything had indicated it would be an Eight, but it opened as a small Six, with erratic shimmers and fuzzy framing. Something was going wrong. Again.

It was still shocking, but not surprising, when a kid slumped out of the alley just before it went prematurely dark.

It was shocking, but not surprising, that the kid was dead.

Miss Mitchell reappeared to ask Miss North for instructions.

"One of your team should inform Gee Street," Miss North said. "Tell them to come for the child. The other two should remain here until then." She sighed. "There will have to be a discreet burial, with a decent service."

Miss Mitchell nodded and relayed the instructions to her team. One of them ran toward the north exit and was quickly lost in the gloom.

After the Finsbury Circus fawkes, Mick was allowed to sleep in. He woke up tired, and not just from being up late. He was tired of always being on alert. Tired of worrying. So very tired of kids dying.

He thought about maybe doing condy or studying in the common room. Instead, he dozed for a while before shrugging slowly into his street clothes and dragging himself to the warden of the day to learn where to meet Gail and the Snobs.

As instructed, he found them in Chelsea, near the Royal Military Asylum. If Gail was tired from the night before, it didn't show. They marched efficiently through the greet sheet, testing a few stirrings but otherwise not having to do much except sweet-talk constables.

Then it was a vespertine for Mick, with another new professor. He was pretty sure they just drafted any professor who had a little free time. A few times it had even been Mr. Victor, who remained terrifying. But he had taught Mick a lot about how to tell different apertural light patterns apart and what they meant. That evening's vespertine, though, was with Mr. Phillips, who was neither terrifying nor useful. Mr. Phillips knew a lot about music but not much about alleys. He hadn't ever heard alley siren song and had thought it was a myth. He looked sad to learn that there was a whole category of music he couldn't hear.

When Mick settled into his spot at the Squad's little table in the tory common room, Dolly and Leech were intently working their way through some serious-looking books. The others didn't have nearly as many vespertines as Mick, but Alison made up for it by assigning them lessons, though not as many as she assigned herself. They had started calling her the "Young Professor."

Dolly was doing nearly all of Alison's lessons. Even Leech was doing a surprising amount—and doing it surprisingly well. He was really smart underneath all the jokes.

"Where's the Young Professor?" Mick asked.

Alison answered the question by stepping through the common room door with an armload of books and a grim expression. She marched across to the table, set the books down, and began speaking without so much as nodding at any of the Squad.

"These fawkes women," she said, "are killing alley rats. They're using the stirrings to steal their way into the alleys before they open, and they're disrupting the alleys. And kids are dying."

They all nodded. It was the most popular theory among the kids. And it was more or less what the honest professors were saying, if you read between the lines.

"Of course," Dolly said, "supposedly one can't enter an alley until it opens."

They all heard the skepticism in "supposedly." The dishonest professors, or at least the impatient ones, all kept saying that it was impossible to enter an alley before it opened. Never mind that the fawkes women were pretty obviously doing it.

"We must learn *how*," Alison said. "We must stop them."

Mick looked at the books. They were thick, old books with *Reserve* stamped on their worn spines, which meant that they weren't supposed to leave the library. "Did you steal these?" Mick asked.

"Miss Emmet gave me dispensation," Alison replied.

"You cruel beast," Leech told Alison, wiping some dust off the cover of the book at the top of the pile. "Some of these had been sleeping peacefully for a century before you plucked them off the shelf and woke them." He patted the book consolingly, "There, there, poor dear."

Alison smiled faintly. "They're all from before the Collapse. Back then, more things were possible. Shuttling the alleys, of course. But other things as well. Perhaps some of those things are still possible, only we've forgotten how. I thought we might look through these books to see if there are any accounts of alley piracy."

Dolly, Leech, and Mick nodded. That was smart. They would now be bored until bedtime—maybe every bedtime until they graduated—but it was still smart. Each of them pulled a book off the pile and started thumbing through it, looking for a clue.

"Thank you," Alison said emphatically.

Over the next week or so, they put some of it together. Back before the Collapse, most time-travelers had described being able to sense the flow of things inside what they called the "alley realm." As far as Mick could tell, that was what he thought of as the "no-place," the weird plane between apertures where time and space didn't follow the regular rules. A couple of the old books used the phrases "breaching the realm" and "breaching the alley" to mean stepping into an alley before it had fully formed or opened. Apparently only a few people had known how to do it, even before the Collapse. Mick was pretty sure that none of the people who could do it had written the books about doing it. The books, on top of being written in Old Boring, often made no sense. They sounded like color-blind people who spoke only English trying to translate Hungarian descriptions of rainbows.

Still, the Squad managed to extract some basic points. If you were really good, you could "waylay" a drop alley while it was still a stirring. That let you hijack it to travel into the past (never the future). To waylay a drop alley, you had to breach the alley at just the right time—to get into the stirring long enough after it appeared that the stirring already had some form but long enough before the alley opened that you could still push yourself in.

You could also waylay a lift alley, which was sort of the opposite of waylaying a drop alley. Drop alleys were a lot easier to find because you usually got stirrings hours or days ahead of time, but they were really hard to waylay. Lift alleys were a lot harder to find because their stirrings usually appeared only a few minutes before they opened, but they were much easier to waylay once you found them. To waylay a lift alley, all you had to do was step into it before anybody else. If you got in first, the aperture would close down soon afterward, making it your alley. There were a few cases of two rats using the same alley successfully, but they both had to go in at nearly the same time.

The big difference between waylaying drop alleys and lift alleys was that you couldn't travel nearly as far by waylaying drop alleys. That could take you a year or two into the past at most, more likely months or weeks. But waylaying a lift alley would probably take you as far back as the alley would have gone anyway.

So lift alleys worked way better, but drop alleys were way easier to find. Unless...

"Unless you have an alley rat's future journal," Leech said. "Then that lift alley is easy to find."

The Squad kept coming back to this point. That had to be why the fawkes woman at the Seat wanted Miss Paisley to steal future journals. She wanted lift alleys, probably in 1853, and future journals were the only way to find them. The same was probably true for the other fawkes women.

But even if the fawkes women really wanted lift alleys, they would settle for drop alleys. And waylaying a drop alley was dangerous, both for the person doing it and for the rat who was supposed to be in the alley. Waylaying an alley could force the rat who was already in the alley to slough off in the wrong time or the wrong place. Or it could kill the rat. If the rat had a passenger, all those things could happen to the passenger too.

The fawkes women knew all that and kept doing it anyway. That made them murderers. Serial killers.

Once that sank in, the whole Squad became as grim as Alison. It had to stop.

They explained their theories to Miss North. She commended their scholarship, but they couldn't tell if she believed them. Maybe she already knew it all and was just patting them on the heads. Maybe she knew they were totally wrong.

It didn't matter. They kept going.

Mick and Gail had three late nights in a row because people spotted women disappearing into stirrings. Two were false alarms. The third, though, was real. It was the same woman Mick had seen in the fatal Princes Street alley and then again with Miss Paisley at the Seat. That breached alley turned into another fawkes, blessedly without a dead dropper. Mick was so tired that he fell asleep in the carriages to and from the fawkes.

Miss North gave him the next day off, and he mostly stayed in bed, reading fairytales and dozing. He managed to go to dinner and then study with the Squad. Or try to study. He kept nodding off, and they sent him to bed.

Mick awoke the next morning to a note from Leech saying he'd gone to St. Clare's for Mass. Mick went down to the gym, played some sleepy footie, showered, and went to the Scriptorium. Mr. Hartnell cheerfully retrieved Mick's box, and Mick took it back to one of the writing cubbies. He couldn't see out the high windows, of course, but he could just hear the toddlers singing in the garden with Mr. Phillips. The music professor's sweet, clean tone was as soothing as always, and the kids didn't sound too terrible either, although Julia was enthusiastically attacking the melody from above and below.

He'd written half a paragraph about the butterfly room at the Notebaert Museum when some poor toddler started singing the wrong song altogether. As he finished the paragraph, Mick realized that it wasn't a toddler. It wasn't even human.

Siren song.

Mick locked his journal back in the box and rushed it to Mr. Hartnell. He handed it to the archivist with an apology, telling him that there was an alley opening in the garden and rushing off before the old man could try to stop him.

When Mick burst through the garden door and looked around, he couldn't see an alley. Following the siren song, he worked his way into the garden. The song was getting louder faster than Mick was getting closer, which meant that the alley was opening quickly and was probably a lift alley.

There, he thought, spotting the first faint forest-green flickers of an alley, probably a fairy path. A little blonde girl had wandered away from Mr. Phillips and was walking determinedly toward the flicker. Julia. "Stop! Julia!" Mick called, running toward her.

Julia turned to look at him, smiling.

Mick reached her and knelt down to give her a big hug from behind, making sure she couldn't move. "Careful," he said. "It's pretty, but it's dangerous."

They were both facing the alley now, which was brighter and more active. Definitely a fairy path. "Mr. Phillips," he called out without looking backward, "there's a fairy Eight about to open. Please keep the toddlers away."

Mick heard the music professor shush the toddlers.

"You're quite certain, Mr. Gunn?" he asked. "I don't see anything."

A few yards from Mick, the shimmering was now joined by an aggressive frame pulsing in sea greens, all of it bright as a midnight bonfire. Mick hadn't been this near an alley since the one that had brought him to 1853. He'd forgotten how strong the calling was. If it hadn't been for Julia, he might have jumped right in.

Mr. Phillips appeared and picked up Julia. "Ah, yes," he said. "I do see a flicker now. Well spotted, Mr. Gunn."

"We should keep the kids away from—" Mick stopped speaking.

The costermonger's wife had left her cart at the gate and was walking briskly toward the alley. "Stop," Mick yelled. "Careful!"

The costermonger's wife didn't look over and didn't stop.

Wait. The costermonger's wife was older than this woman.

And didn't have burning bright alley rat eyes.

And didn't look like the woman from the Princes Street fawkes.

Mick was already running before his brain caught up with his feet. He hit the woman at full speed, tackling her around the waist. He tried to hold on tight, but she threw him to the ground.

He grabbed her around the ankles, pressing his shoulder against the back of her knee as she tried to kick free. She fell to the ground, but that broke his hold, and she rose nimbly in a crouch, a knife in her hand.

Mick managed to get to his feet, also in a crouch, and backed away a little.

Mr. Phillips stepped between them, his back to Mick. "Now, see here," he told the woman.

She slashed at his face, but Mr. Phillips managed to get his hand up. There was a spray of blood, and he bent over, clutching his bloody hand.

The woman turned to head back to the fairy path, but as she did, she saw the same thing that Mick saw—Julia stepping into the wildly pulsating aperture. The toddler was delightedly singing an off-key version of the siren song when she and the fairy path suddenly disappeared.

Mick's stomach lurched.

The woman rushed to where the alley had been, leaping in and out of the space as if trying to reopen the alley. When it sank in that the alley was closed, she screamed, a raw shriek of lunatic rage and despair.

The scream lasted longer than should have been possible. Then the woman went silent and staggered. She dropped to one knee, clutching the bloody knife and looking a lot like Mr. Phillips holding his hand.

Her head swiveled toward Mick. "You!" she hissed. "You..." She stood up sharply. Holding the knife in front of her, she began to stalk toward Mick.

Mr. Phillips shakily inserted himself between Mick and the fawkes woman. Mick thought about running, but he didn't want to leave Mr. Phillips or the little kids, who were standing frozen with fear. He was trying to figure out how to fight the woman when he noticed Miss Weathers moving quietly behind her. Miss Weathers' shoulders flexed and spun, and there was a loud thud. The fawkes woman dropped to one knee, then both knees, pressing the back of her head with her free hand.

Miss Weathers came another step closer, hefting a large

book in both hands, and calmly swung it again, like a kid playing tee-ball. The book slammed against the side of the woman's head, and she slumped to the ground, lying on her side with her eyes shut.

"You'll not be scaring the weans again, ye mad slag," Miss Weathers said in her real accent, giving the fawkes woman a couple hard kicks to the ribs. She paused and then judiciously kicked her twice more before digging a knee into her back.

Miss Weathers raised the book a little and grinned. In her fancy London accent, she told Mick, "Remarkably, I've at last found a use for *A Compleat Compendium of the Maladies of the Head and Skull.*"

CHAPTER 23

THE HIDDEN THREAT

Miss Weathers turned her gaze to the injured choirmaster. "Mr. Phillips, I can inspect that hand for you. Can you come to me? I'd rather not turn my back on this murderous cow."

Mr. Phillips walked over slowly and knelt unsteadily beside her, holding out his bloody hand.

"It's not dire," Miss Weathers said, "but Doctor will need to tend to it."

For a while, Mick just stared where the alley had been, stunned. *Poor Julia.*

Eventually, he realized he should be doing something useful. He herded the toddlers toward Mr. Phillips, who was gathering them a safe distance from where Miss Weathers was continuing to dig a knee into the unconscious fawkes woman's back.

"I'll go get Dr. Quinn," Mick said.

"Good lad," Miss Weathers said. "And do make sure that Miss North and the Vicar hear of this."

He ran to Dr. Quinn's office to explain everything. Partway through his tale, she rang the bell for the day porter and began packing a medical bag. Dr. Quinn sent the porter to tell Miss North and the Vicar what had happened before going to tend to Mr. Phillips.

Left alone in Dr. Quinn's office, Mick wandered to the window to look down on the garden. A group of dons had already gathered around the fawkes woman. It looked like somebody was handcuffing her.

Soon, Miss North appeared in the garden and started giving orders. Mick opened the window but couldn't make out what she was saying. The dons marched the woman inside, and Miss North followed. Then Miss Weathers lined the toddlers up, made them hold hands, and shooed them inside. Mick went to the nursery, where Miss Weathers and the toddlers appeared a few minutes later.

Except Julia.

Miss Weathers set down the heavy book she'd used as a weapon and settled into her usual chair. Mick sat beside her.

"Thank you," he said. "You saved my life."

"Don't forget the *Compleat Compendium* there." She grinned. "You're welcome. You were brave, trying to stop her. And quick. If you'd hesitated, she would have got into that alley."

"That might have been better," Mick said. "Julia would still be here."

"Perhaps," Miss Weathers said. "But she's the madwoman who killed all those droppers, isn't she?"

"I think so."

"Then she is a monster. If we hadn't stopped her, she might have gone back in time and murdered more children."

Mick nodded. And the alley had behaved normally, so probably Julia was fine. Except for being thrown way back into the past, of course. He hoped there had been a good greet team waiting for her.

Mick closed his eyes and listened to the toddlers squabbling in their room, the birds singing in the garden, and the city bustling outside the walls. It was soothing, and he must have dozed because he woke up with Miss Mitchell shaking his shoulder.

"Come with me," she said.

Mick almost asked why but realized it had to be about the fawkes woman. He looked at Miss Weathers.

"You'd best go," she told him. She sighed. "And I'd best decide how to tell the little ones they'll not be seeing Julia again."

Usually when Mick was summoned, it was to Miss North's office or the solarium. But Miss Mitchell led him to the faculty wing. They went down a quiet corridor to a door guarded by two dons who stepped aside, nodding but not speaking. Stepping through the door, he found himself in a room dominated by a large oval table. The Vicar, Miss North, Mr. Victor, Mr. Hartnell, and several other professors were sitting at the table, distributed so that they could all look at the fawkes woman, who was sitting defiantly at the middle of a long side of the table, her handcuffed hands resting on the table. A half dozen dons stood unblinking watch over her.

A few other professors were scattered in the rings of extra chairs farther from the table. Miss Mitchell pointed to Miss Emmet, who was sitting by herself two rows back from the table, staring at the fawkes woman. Mick sat down next to Miss Emmet, and Miss Mitchell sat beside him. Miss Emmet smiled slightly, putting a finger to her lips.

The fawkes woman didn't seem to notice their arrival. Her eyes were locked on the professors at the table. Those eyes were by far the brightest he'd ever seen. But they weren't her most startling feature. That was her face, which flickered ceaselessly with expressions, from laughing to crying to screaming, like an aperture shimmering right before it opened.

"Your lift alley, you say, was in 1858," Mr. Hartnell was saying, "and yet you cannot be more than forty years of age. So—"

"I was waylaid, wasn't I?" she snapped. "Sloughed off decades shy, didn't I?"

"Miss Halliwell," the Vicar said, his voice soft with sorrow, "to waylay all those children in their own alleys, to—"

"Murder them," Mr. Victor said.

"I might as well murder," she said. "I dropped three decades before I was born. That's a death sentence with no trial, just a hangman's noose at the end of thirty years' rope. And that's a heavy weight around a little girl's neck. A weight to bear until the slack runs out and I choke. If I'm to be executed like a murderer, I might as well murder."

"So you waylaid drop alleys," Miss North said calmly, "and managed to travel backward in time. Not very far back, though."

Mick nodded to himself. Alison had been right.

"Far enough at first," the woman said. "It got more difficult and shorter each time. If I hadn't become so skillful, it would have been impossible."

She was bragging, Mick realized with a shudder.

"I started a year ago by the calendar," she said, "but it's been more than three years for me. It's more than any of you have done."

"Yes," Mr. Victor said, his voice cold with rage, "you have managed to murder far more innocent children than we have."

"I needed only one lift alley," she said. "One lift alley to take me back a proper century so I could die my own death. The drop alleys simply gave me time to find it. It wasn't my aim to kill those children. I simply needed enough time to survive." She gestured around. "Even here, there's never enough time."

"And then you did find a lift alley, did you not?" the Vicar said wearily. He held up a small book. "In our very own garden." In a soft, sad tone, the Vicar read, "One moment, it was a fair June Sunday, year of our Lord 1853, and the next it was rainy winter's day, year of our Lord 1746. Even now, so many years later, the fairy path glimmers in my mind's eye, gowned in greens and twirling like a maid of May. Sometimes I remember a song, too. Mayhap it was we children singing, but I doubt we ever sounded so sweet. Poor Mr. Phillips, I do hope he wasn't badly wounded. He was kind and brave. So too Miss Ellen's friend. I lament that I cannot recall his name."

Mick gasped. Julia's journal—the Vicar was reading Julia's journal. Tiny Julia, grown up to sound like a don. And, if she was lucky, she'd kept going. Grown up all the way. Gotten old. Died with white hair and long memories of a past that stretched in both directions.

"You must have known you would fail," Mr. Hartnell said. "The girl who wrote that entry a century ago never could have written it if you had successfully waylaid her alley."

"Is that how it works?" the woman asked, mockingly. "Do we know how it works, now? Because we didn't when I was a student here. We didn't know whether time travel was sorcery or science. Whether the past is etched in stone or written in smoke. Perhaps I was just as free to succeed as to fail and merely suffered ill luck."

Mr. Victor snorted.

"Judge me all you wish, you icy Pharisee," she told him, her voice vibrating with anger and some other things Mick couldn't sort out. "But if I *was* doomed to failure, I was doomed from birth. I was born to be sent into the past as a wee gel who knew she would die young because no rat survives the birth flame. Because the universe creates us to destroy us, for sport, belike. It created that doomed, desperate me just as it created all those precious innocent children it gave me to destroy."

"I believe we are finished for now," the Vicar said quietly. "Miss North?"

"Indeed. Miss Mitchell," she called.

Miss Mitchell rose. "Yes, miss?"

"This person," Miss North said, nodding at the fawkes woman, "will be taken to Oddy's for now, in the Institute's carriage. I shall notify them directly. They are to hold her but not speak to her. You and at least three other dons must guard her. Bind her wrists. Blindfold her if you think it advisable. Gag her if you desire silence."

Miss Mitchell nodded to one of the standing dons, who set off at a trot. The other dons stepped closer, encircling the fawkes woman.

"Lord Harrowgrave and Lady Penbrook naturally must be briefed," the Vicar said. "Mr. Victor, might I trouble you to visit his lordship? And you, Miss North, her ladyship?"

Mr. Victor and Miss North nodded.

Miss Emmet poked Mick's shoulder as she rose to her feet. He followed her out of the room, and they walked silently through the Institute for a while. As they neared a side door to the library, he asked, "Is Julia really okay? Or, was she really okay?"

"As best we know," she said, unlocking the door and leading him to her office. "We hadn't time to read her journal properly. Nor to research her life."

"What about Miss Paisley? Did that woman kill her?" He remembered the knife, bloody and weaving. The fawkes woman had used that knife before.

"Miss Paisley has been found unharmed, in a cottage in Camberwell."

Mick nodded gratefully. Miss Paisley was awful, but not getting-gutted-by-a-maniac awful.

"What about the others?" he asked once they were in Miss Emmet's office with the door closed.

"Others?" she asked, while searching her desk drawers.

"The other women. The old woman at the cemetery. And the one with the wheelchair."

"Ah. All Cassandra Halliwell."

"At different ages?" Mick asked, though that didn't make sense.

"Disguised."

"But we didn't know who she was," Mick said. "Why did she need disguises?"

Miss Emmet thought for a while. "Often, the Institute isn't the only one watching. Ah, there we are." She pulled out a sheaf of papers.

"What?"

Miss Emmet looked like she might say more but decided against it. "I'm afraid I must tend to business, Mr. Gunn," she said, waving the papers. "As I'm sure you can imagine, this has set rather a lot into motion."

"But—"

"I shall escort you out," she said cheerfully, steering him first from her office and then from the library.

Back in the Sixers' common room, Mick joined Dolly and Alison at the Squad's table. He was surprised to see Alison. It was Sunday, so she should have been visiting her friends at Orphans.

They made him tell them everything. He'd gotten most of the way through it when Leech showed up, looking nauseous and shaky.

"What happened?" Dolly asked, as Leech sat down slowly.

"I was coming back from Mass, and nobody answered the door. Then that gormless Mr. James answered but wouldn't let me in. Closed the door right in my face, he did. I stood there for a quarter hour until he finally let me in. Told me there'd been 'a bit of a fire in the Great Hall,' he did, and sent me on my way. That's all he said, mind. 'Bit of a fire.' Not, 'There's been an unholy spontaneous human combustion, and there's a pack of dons circling a charred corpse like Norse raiders around a spit roast.' Which would have been bloody useful information before I filled my eyes and nose with it, I should say."

"Spontaneous what?" Alison asked.

"You don't know?" Leech asked. "They caught the fawkes woman."

"We know," Dolly said.

"Yes, well, they caught her, and then she caught fire in the Great Hall," he said, with a shudder.

"She did *what*?" Alison asked.

"Birth flame," Mick said. "Her birthday must have been today. That's why she was so furious."

"You spoke with her?" Leech asked.

Mick had to tell it all again, keeping his voice down because Owl and some other nearby kids were trying to eavesdrop and he didn't want it to turn into story hour. Fortunately, plenty of kids soon started to talk about Cassandra Halliwell's death, and the other Sixers lost interest in Mick's tale.

"Cassandra Halliwell is from 1858," Alison said slowly. "Her journal is somewhere in the Vault. She wouldn't have used her real name, but perhaps it says when and where she was born. And surely it says where she stepped into her own lift alley. If we knew that, in five years' time we could…" She trailed off.

"Wring her little neck?" Leech asked.

"Of course not," Alison said. "Merely keep her from entering her original lift alley."

"'Merely,'" Leech said ironically.

"Children died in those alleys, Leigh Charles," Alison snapped.

"Alison," Dolly said kindly, "that would break every rule. And it's not possible, anyhow. Not even the Vicar could get into the Vault, even if he wanted to."

"They can get into the Vault," Alison said. "They get the future journals out every year. They just have to decide to go in."

"I don't think it would work," Mick said. "That's what Mr. Hartnell said. The only reason we had Julia's journal is that she made it to the past. Same with Cassandra Halliwell's journal—if she wrote it, she made it to the past."

Alison fell silent, unpersuaded.

Mick was starting to understand why everybody had to keep their names and late points secret. Sure, maybe Mr. Hartnell was right. Maybe, in 1858, Cassandra Halliwell would get pulled into the past and there was nothing anybody could do to stop it, no matter how much they wanted to, no matter how much they knew about the future. On the other hand, looking at Alison's face, Mick wasn't so sure Alison could be prevented from changing the future if she knew how to find the toddler version of Cassandra Halliwell.

"Alison," Dolly said gently, "oughtn't you go visit your friends at Orphans?"

"I'll visit my friends when I please," Alison said.

"Only, you always say that the visits raise your spirits," Dolly pointed out.

"Perhaps I don't wish my spirits raised," Alison snapped.

Leech chortled.

Alison turned to glare at him but then cracked a tiny smile. "I apologize, Dolly. I shall indeed visit my friends at Orphans. But I am already with friends, and it's a lovely day, with no patrol scheduled. Perhaps first we should go to Regent's Park and visit Mayor Cakes on the way."

Dolly beamed.

They bought far too many cakes and scoffed them all before they could find a bench.

"Cassandra Halliwell's past self can't come back for vengeance, can it?" Leech asked, as they finally chose a spot to sit. "She isn't going to simply reappear tomorrow, knife in hand, is she?"

"I don't think it works that way," Dolly said. "The path of her life is the path of her life. All the past Cassandra Halliwells led to the one who died today."

Leech shuddered.

Mick remembered Cassandra Halliwell saying, *Is that how it works? Do we know how it works, now?* He said, "When people start moving around in time, nothing seems final, you know?"

"*She* thought it was final," Alison said. "She thought nothing could save her from dying in the birth flame, except doing what she did. So likely it was indeed final."

They nodded. That made as much sense as any of it. For now, it was probably better just to sit in the sun and wish they hadn't eaten that last cake or three.

The next morning, most patrols were canceled. Half the school slept in, including Mick. After lunch, Alison and Mick lugged back all the heavy library books Alison had borrowed and dropped them on Miss Emmet's desk.

Miss Emmet asked Mick to stay. After Alison left, Miss Emmet stared at him expressionlessly for a long time. Then she puffed her cheeks and breathed out slowly. "Follow me."

She stood and walked out of her office, grabbing a matchbox and the lantern hanging beside the door. They went to the back door of the library and then down a series of empty and unfamiliar stairways. They moved briskly, without speaking, slowing down only when Miss Emmet needed to select a series of large keys from a large ring to unlock a few heavy doors. Soon they were in a part of the cellars Mick didn't recognize.

Partway down a dark corridor, Miss Emmet stopped abruptly. She took a step back and handed Mick the lamp. By its light, she traced her fingers over several stones until giving a little tug at one of them. It folded out of the wall, revealing several keyholes. She inserted one key after another, turning each until a faint click came from within the wall. "It would be a grievous breach of duty to show you this door or what lies beyond, so of course I'm doing no such thing. At this very moment, we are in my office having a fascinating discussion about moving the Institute from the Old Pye building to the present building. A daunting and complex task, wouldn't you agree?"

"Yes, miss."

A door-shaped section of the wall opened inward, and Miss Emmet took the lamp back from him.

"Fortunately, there is no risk that I could breach my duty. I, as a perfectly ordinary librarian, would never be entrusted with the keys that open, for example, this door that I'm not closing behind us—do push, Mr. Gunn."

Mick helped her push until the door thunked into place and the locks clicked shut.

They continued down a short corridor. At the end was another heavy door with three obvious keyholes, plus one concealed in some ornate ironwork. Miss Emmet unlocked everything, and then they closed the door behind them.

They were standing in a small room, about the same size as the bedroom Mick shared with Leech. There was no light except Miss Emmet's lantern, which Mick really hoped had enough oil. At the moment, anyway, its light was bright enough for Mick to make out what looked like inscriptions in the stone beside the door, including something that seemed to have a bunch of eyeball emojis and maybe something about a hawk.

The inscription disappeared when Miss Emmet lowered her

lamp hand to a more comfortable position. "Feel that door if you will, Mr. Gunn."

Mick hesitated but then put his hand on the door. It was cold metal.

"Solid steel," she said. "Quite thick. Behind it is another room like this one, with an even stronger door. Beyond that are other, stronger doors with fiendishly clever locks. If one goes past this room, alarms begin to sound in various places. Which is why we're stopping here. Well, that and it's a suitably private place."

"What's on the other side of all those doors?" Mick asked.

"Do think, Mr. Gunn," she chided.

Of course. "The Vault."

Miss Emmet nodded. "Have you clever children asked yourselves about the obvious hole in Cassandra Halliwell's story?" she asked.

There had been a lot of holes. But Mick wasn't sure what was obvious anymore. "Miss?"

"You know how impossible it would be to break into the Vault, yes?" she asked, slapping the solid metal door. "And you know how miserably indeed Miss Paisley failed in her attempts to do so?"

Mick nodded.

Miss Emmet raised her eyebrows at him. "And, yet, what did our mad murderess have with her?"

Right. "Julia's journal."

Miss Emmet nodded. "Somebody gave it to her. Somebody who could access journals that are behind dozens of locks and alarms. Or that *should* be behind them."

And then Mick remembered what had been nagging at him for days. It was something Mr. Hartnell had said the first time they'd met. Something about pixies or fairies that played practical jokes at the old Institute. Crabs, and stools, and—

"Missing journals," he said. "Mr. Hartnell said there were missing journals at the old Institute. I thought he meant copies, like from the Room of Future Present. But maybe he meant originals. Did somebody steal them from the old Vault at the old building?"

"I have pondered that since I first saw Julia's journal where it had no right to be," Miss Emmet said. "I think not. Those journals are ... sacred texts of our faith. And trade secrets. And power. They would have been well guarded in the old Vault, just as they are in the new one."

"So how—"

"There was, however, a time when the journals were not in the Vault," she said.

Mick frowned. But then he got it. "When they moved them from the old one to this one."

"A future journal would not have been lost by mishap or negligence," Miss North said. "But in 1806, somebody with guile and daring might have stolen a journal. Or a dozen. And we would be none the wiser. For centuries, the Institute has kept careful records of how many journals are completed and stored for each late-point year. So, when this year's journals are tallied, we shall know if something is missing for 1853. Including Julia's. But if another journal was stolen in 1806, and it was from 1854 or 1954, we shan't know until then."

Mick thought about that. "Cassandra Halliwell couldn't have taken the journal during the move, could she? She dropped too late."

Miss Emmet nodded. "Almost two decades too late. Somebody gave her that journal, perhaps the same person who took it almost fifty years ago. Or perhaps something more ominous."

"Huh?"

"To find poor, foolish Miss Paisley, Miss North and I made discreet inquiries with people we know at the Seat. Those people work for a particular part of the Project with its own aims and goals. There are others at the Seat who work for other parts of the Project, each with its own aims and goals. The different parts of the Project are not always perfectly friendly with one another. In any large organization, there are always rivalries, personalities. But this... It may be that Cassandra Halliwell was aligned with a part of the Project hostile to the Institute, possibly even hostile to the Project itself."

"There's a part like that?"

Miss Emmet sighed. "It's all guesswork. Fretful, tiring guess-work. But someone gave that madwoman a future journal, which was forbidden. Dangerous. Grotesque, even. The Project I know can be ruthless, certainly. And its spies are everywhere. But giving Cassandra Halliwell a future journal was like starving a lioness before releasing her into a nursery. It doesn't feel like the Project."

She fell silent for a while, staring at him. "Do be careful, Mr. Gunn. You have a brave spirit, a quick mind, and an astonishing alley sight. But the ability to see alleys does not give you the ability to see perils. People and their plots do not have bright lights and telltale signs. Sometimes the most perilous ones are never seen."

She thought for a moment before adding, "Perhaps I oughtn't have told you all this. But you and your friends cannot stop asking questions. I admire that. But do remember that if you ask enough questions, you will eventually ask someone who has a few questions for *you*." She stared at him intently. "And when power is at stake, Mr. Gunn, sometimes one of those questions is, 'Why should I let you live?'"

Neither of them knew what to say next. They stared at each other for a little bit before Miss Emmet silently led him back through the long series of heavily clacking locks leading back to the stairs and then to corridors that eventually led to the surprising, airy glow of the Great Hall.

A little shaken by his conversation with Miss Emmet in the depths of the Institute, Mick visited the Squad in the common room, bathing in their friendship like sunlight.

He couldn't say why anybody else should let him live, but he knew why he was glad to be alive. For the time being, that was enough.